HER SECRET JOY

"Oh!" Honor was outraged. "You lie, sir! I have never kissed you!"

"Once?"

"Nonsense! You kissed me. *I,* if you recall, was not so lost to sanity as to kiss you back!"

"Oh, but what a struggle you had! What a joyful, desperate, aching struggle! You wanted to." Merit seemed to take pleasure in taunting her. "Tell me that I am wrong, even slightly wrong, and I will have the chaise turned about at once."

Honor shifted on her seat. She could hear the steady trot of the horses and the coachman's soft whistle upon the perch outside. She could hear the roll of the wheels upon the beaten track and her heart, hopelessly unsteady, in her chest. It seemed as if she had stopped breathing and the world had contracted to nothing but the intimate space of the chaise and its series of crimson velvet squabs.

She knew that there would be no turning back, but she lacked the courage to admit it. The longer she was silent, the more the triumph glowed from my lord's eyes.

BOOK YOUR PLACE ON OUR WEBSITE AND MAKE THE READING CONNECTION!

We've created a customized website just for our very special readers, where you can get the inside scoop on everything that's going on with Zebra, Pinnacle and Kensington books.

When you come online, you'll have the exciting opportunity to:

- View covers of upcoming books
- Read sample chapters
- Learn about our future publishing schedule (listed by publication month *and author*)
- Find out when your favorite authors will be visiting a city near you
- Search for and order backlist books from our online catalog
- Check out author bios and background information
- Send e-mail to your favorite authors
- Meet the Kensington staff online
- Join us in weekly chats with authors, readers and other guests
- Get writing guidelines
- AND MUCH MORE!

**Visit our website at
http://www.kensingtonbooks.com**

MY LADY LUCK

Hayley Ann Solomon

ZEBRA BOOKS
KENSINGTON PUBLISHING CORP.
http://www.kensingtonbooks.com

ZEBRA BOOKS are published by

Kensington Publishing Corp.
850 Third Avenue
New York, NY 10022

All Kensington titles, imprints and distributed lines are available at special quantity discounts for bulk purchases for sales
promotion, premiums, fund-raising, educational or institutional
use.

Special book excerpts or customized printings can also be created to fit specific needs. For details, write or phone the office
of the Kensington Special Sales Manager: Kensington Publishing Corp., 850 Third Avenue, New York, NY 10022. Attn.
Special Sales Department. Phone: 1-800-221-2647.

Zebra and the Z logo Reg. U.S. Pat. & TM Off.

First Printing: April 2004
10 9 8 7 6 5 4 3 2 1

Printed in the United States of America

To Clivey, Raoul, Raphael, and Rhaz,
Thank you so much for your patience
and encouragement.
I love you all.

CHAPTER 1

"Dash it, Merit, it will be splendid sport! Do say you will do it!"

"Do it yourself, if it is so very splendid!"

Lord Merit Argyll, fourth Marquis Laxton, was merely being trying. He could not mean such a thing, for it was only he who owned the bright canary-colored chaise that proclaimed him a member of the illusive, famed, and much sought-after Four Horse Club.

It was only he who could oblige his friends in this absurdly ill-conceived plan to race the carriage cross-country from Tilling to Strathmore.

Quite why this was necessary he was at pains to fathom, but he had just endured a night of unequivocal hell, first being accosted by the dowager Duchess of Straughn and then, worse, by her four simpering granddaughters. He felt he had just excuse for being a tad tetchy, and was certainly not of a mind to begin fathoming the strange machinations of his dearest, but perfectly totty-headed, companions.

These were, in no particular order, Lord Frederick Manning, Sir Peter Worthington, and the Honorable Bertram Snell. Rather than searching about for a method to soothe his nerves—and yes, they needed soothing—they began abusing him in strident tones, shocked that he could make such a foolish suggestion, even in jest.

"Don't be a fool, Merit! No one but you could do it! If

you let Freddy have the tooling of your team he would be
ditched in a moment! It is not as if there are any proper
paths cross-country, you know! No sport in that!"

Lord Merit shuddered, whether from the vision just
conjured, or from the result of last night's excesses at
Brooke's, he was not perfectly certain. All he knew was
that he wished to be left in peace, preferably with a steaming cup of hot coffee and perhaps the *Tatler* to soothe his
nerves.

He would ignore his guests—all of them perfectly capable of eating from his table and showing themselves to
the door—and forget entirely the whole matter of several
hundred guineas wagered upon his head. Really, whilst
he could not help feeling gratified that his companions
should hold him in such high esteem—why else would
they lay down such a sum on so extraordinary a notion as
a cross-country from anywhere to anywhere, let alone on
the treacherous terrain from Tilling to Strathmore?—he
was annoyed. Their confidence in him was touching, but
perforce misplaced. He had no intention whatsoever of fitting in with their schemes.

Not too far away, in a less luxurious establishment than
the marquis's extensive Mayfair residence, a *similar* conversation was taking place. Well, similar was hardly the
term, for rather than gentlemen quarreling, there were
ladies doing so, and rather than carriage-racing under discussion, the subject related to the manner in which two
thousand pounds could be raised for a season in London.
Very proper and demure, one might think, but oh, no!

The manner in which the sum was to be raised was just
as bizarre in conception as the notion of a cross-country
from Tilling to Strathmore. Only, Miss Honoria Finchley
was more persuasive than Bertram or Freddy or Sir Peter

Worthington, and a great deal more determined. She plotted and planned and firmly ignored all her sister's objections to her schemes.

Miss Faith Finchley, indeed, was looking decidedly pale, and every so often wafted some smelling salts about her nose, as if the very vapors would spare her from one of her sister's wilder schemes.

It did not, of course, for Miss Honoria, seized by an unusual spark of brilliance, simply would not give up. Faith, knowing it, both from years of experience and from the intuition that came from being such a close sister, groaned aloud and protested she had the headache.

Honoria, lost in her happy visions, took a moment to hear the complaint. When she did, she was all remorse, eyeing the circles beneath her sister's eyes with compunction. "Am I badgering you, Faith? I am a monster to do so."

"No, no, you are not. You are the dearest, sweetest, kindest sister alive, only I cannot let you sacrifice yourself so!"

"Sacrifice? What sort of dramatic talk is this? I am not going to sacrifice myself, my love, I am going to be wicked, and have a splendid time doing so!"

"You are going to put yourself beyond the pale, that is what you are going to do! And you are going to deprive yourself of a season and being presented and—"

"Tush, what nonsense is this? I was never going to have a season, Faith! It is not I who have Lord and Lady Islington as godparents! I cannot expect them to sponsor me, too, you know."

"I don't see why not. We could share gowns and it is not as if you eat all that much. . . ."

"Of all the nonsensical notions! Share gowns indeed! We would be the talk of the drawing rooms!"

"I don't care, if it means we are both to be presented . . ."

"I've already been presented, remember?"

"But that was privately, with hardly any fanfare. . . ."

"Presented nonetheless, and very tedious it was, too, for I hardly caught a glimpse of the prince regent, and the queen, though kind, droned on and on and I could hardly make head or tail of what she was saying."

"You just didn't like having to make a court curtsey and stand for hours on end."

"No, why should I, when there were some perfectly inviting chairs scattered all about? It is a nonsense, Faith, and I am not doing it again!"

Faith, noting her sister's determined attitude, wafted the smelling salts once more, and sniffed. The aromas must have given her courage, for she opened her mouth to pursue her former argument.

Miss Honoria, divining her intentions, preempted her with a smile.

"As for eating, that is the smallest expense. Lord and Lady Islington will need to procure a box for the opera and arrange seating in their carriage and a horse to be stabled for your use and a lady's maid and a walking companion and jewels for soirees, flowers, visiting cards . . . the expense is endless. I am sure they do not want any of it doubled, even if they had concerned themselves about the matter."

"But they know we are sisters!"

"Yes, and they know that I, too, have godparents. Doubtless they expect them to do the same for me."

"But they won't. Lady Sheffield is long dead and her mother, the dowager countess, is a recluse. She will have forgotten about you!"

"And very grateful I am, too, if she is such a recluse! No, Faith, I am resigned to the matter. It has seemed obvious to me since I was six, so it is not as if I were expecting a season, you see."

"Well, it still seems unfair."

"I am not pining, Faith. It is going to be my adventure. And when I have sufficient funds for your dowry . . ."

"I wish you hadn't said it was two thousand pounds. That is a prodigious sum!"

"Tush! In the circles you shall move, it will be the merest chickenfeed! You won't be beset by fortune hunters, my love, never you think it. It is well, indeed, that Lady Islington is so set on clothing you. The expense of that will far exceed any paltry marriage portion!"

"How will you secure it?'

"Oh, I already all but have! Lady Jemima and the Honorable Miss Wainright both lost their bangles to me, and though Messrs. Gilbertson and Stratford will very likely give me only half their worth, I should imagine it will be a tidy sum nonetheless."

"You really should put your incredible mind to more noble uses, Honoria."

"More noble than gaming, you mean?"

Faith nodded. Her sister looked hurt.

"You wound me! Do I not know how to converse passably in Latin and Greek, have I not an accurate grasp of the sciences and mathematics? Can I not quote Shakespeare by heart, sonnet by sonnet, and Wordsworth and Scott and even that idiot Byron? Did not even Miss Bramble proclaim me the best student of my year, despite my—what was it, now? Oh, yes, I remember! 'My deplorable lack of propriety and refinement?' "

Faith grinned. "Yes, yes, you are very clever and very naughty, Honor, but I still say your extraordinary memory should not be used to disadvantage others."

"I do not force them to gamble. It is not as if I never lose. Indeed, in *rouge-et-noir* I am forever losing!"

"That is because it is a game of luck only, like faro. In games of skill you are unequalled."

Honoria did not seem put out about this retort. Instead, she grinned an engaging smile—a smile that brought out the sunshine in her dark, vivid eyes and forced a similar, answering smile to her sister's rosy cheeks.

They were birds of a feather, Faith and Honoria, both slim, dark-haired, dark-eyed, and with perfectly piquant features marred only by slightly tip-tilted noses and a band of the faintest freckles across the bridges of each. Though separated by eleven full months, they might have been mirror images, really, except that Honoria's lips were slightly the redder and her hair was cut in the latest Grecian mode, stark and short with only the faintest curls permitted to break the severity of her style.

Faith had not been quite so daring. Her hair—her pride, it must be admitted, for she brushed it a hundred times each day and it shone like the purest silk—hung down from her shoulders and curled only at the edges, when she shook her head vigorously, or her pins had loosened. Her lips were pinker and her cheeks more often suffused with a soft blush. Frequently, her hands crept expressively to her mouth, or her eyelashes fluttered with unconscious femininity.

Honor was more inclined to look at a person directly, and her movements were fluid and confident. Now, she addressed Faith more seriously than she had done a moment ago.

"I can't think of skill as a crime, Faith. If I can change our fortunes by it, I will. I shall invest half of everything I win on 'change. The rest shall be your nest egg, invested in trust with the bankers Whiley and Whit."

But Faith wanted to hear nothing of bankers. She had a vision of Honor, like Shylock, counting up her mounting sovereigns and crowns. She discarded her smelling salts in disgust.

"No one will wed you!" This, a familiar wail.

Honor's answer afforded her no comfort whatsoever.

"Indeed, not! Why should I be schooled by a man when I can have my freedom? Do not fear for me, Faith. I will keep going until I have ample to set myself up in an establishment of my own. I do have Lady Sheffield's bequest, you know, and what was left of Mama's jewels. I shall be able to draw on those in time."

"Miss Bramble's hair would turn white if she knew of your plans."

"It already is white, for I caught a glimpse of it under her bonnet one day, when you all went to Gunter's and I was meant to be working on French conjugations."

"She was punishing you for merriment, if I recall."

"Yes, and for neglecting to curtsey to stuffy Lord Kirkby, the seminary's patron, when he called to review us all."

"No, that was another instance entirely."

"You are right, now that you mention it. You are very lucky, Faith, that you were never on the receiving end of one of her infamous switches. She procured them from that horrid man on Throgmorton Street and I never knew which was worse, the punishment or the anticipation."

"Both. How I trembled for you!"

"Silly! She did not use them so very often, which is fortunate considering the amount of mischief I managed to get up to!"

"You were a wonder! I'll never forget the leeches you introduced when she had the headache and . . . oh, Honor, do you remember her face when we discovered her curling papers upon the dais?'

"Indeed I do! Very fierce it was, especially when she cast her beady eyes in my direction!"

"She never proved you the culprit though I hardly saw her, after that, without quaking in my halfboots."

"Two years of quaking! No wonder your posture is now so . . . so . . . perfectly perfect and your manners so . . . flawlessly flawless. Miss Bramble would be proud."

Honoria ducked the ottoman cushion flung in her direction. It landed on the smelling salts and sent the delicate silver box flying to the floor. Faith did not seem so perfectly perfect at this moment! Neither sister seemed to mind the calamity of the smelling salts, for they were by now absorbed in their lively recollections.

"I know! I missed Gunter's for expressing unladylike sentiments in the reading of Byron, which I termed *drivel* and our revered headmistress preferred the term *divine*."

Both girls giggled, for the prim Miss Bramble had suffered from a severe crush on the famous poet, a source of great hilarity to the pupils of the select seminary she presided over.

When their laughter subsided, Faith, resigned to the inevitable, looked more sober.

"What will you do, Honor?" The girls had long since decided "Honoria" was too much of a mouthful and hardly ever used it, save in jest.

"I will set up a genteel gaming house, perhaps on Threadneedle Street, near the Royal Exchange. Or if not there, close by. Old Broad Street or some such. Only the very, very rich will be permitted to enter, for I shall set my stakes high."

"I pity them, then, for with your astonishing aptitude, they will walk out very poor!" At which both girls nodded in such solemn amusement that their original argument was all but forgotten.

CHAPTER 2

Lord Laxton lingered a little on the stairs, a slight frown playing curiously upon his brow. In the shadows, by the light of a yellowing gas lamp and several rather smoky candles, a card game was in progress. Not that this in itself was at all unusual, for it was no more than one came to expect of these places, but it was the manner of it that troubled him.

He moved forward, signaled for the house's best—which while not up to his connoisseur's standards was still nonetheless palatable—and ignored the private parlor that had been made available for his use. Instead, he seated himself behind the players and watched, with sharp, hooded interest, as the game progressed. A sack of gold lay strewn open upon the table. A small fortune for these parts, which was doubtless why the innkeeper was being more obsequious than usual and why a small crowd was gathered interestedly around the game.

It was impossible to glean the thoughts of either player, though clearly they were unmatched either in age or rank.

On the left was a youth, a mere stripling, garbed fashionably but by no means in the first style of elegance. His top boots gleamed in the candlelight, but were clearly not of the quality of Lobb and Lobb, the marquis's own bootmakers. His cravat, though starched stiffly and as pristine white as one could wish, was nonetheless tied in the simplest of forms, a mere boy's trick—nothing that would see him through the hallowed portals of the *haut ton* with any degree of certainty. As for the coat, why, it was too loose for fashion, but Lord Laxton conceded it must certainly win in the comfort stakes.

He almost envied the youth, for his own immaculate garb was styled to cleave to his every muscle, and though the effect was satisfying—extraordinarily so to every damsel who ever set eyes upon him—Merit, Lord Laxton, often cursed the necessity. Still, there was no grumble to be had with the boy's posture, for he held himself quite impeccably, and though his face was as smooth as a baby's, his demeanor was far more adult than his years. How else could he calmly play hand after hand, discard after discard, without revealing the faintest glimmer of triumph? The pile of coins on his side of the table was prodigious. The boy seemed either not to know or not to care. The marquis, searching the boy's features for any glimmer of expression, could not believe either to be the case.

On the opposite end of the table, a crystal glass was being refilled. Long fingernails, perfectly manicured, curled over the elegant stem. A cane, embossed in gold, proclaimed the gentleman's status as he perused his cards. The marquis thought he saw the sudden flash of rubies upon those practiced fingers. In spite of himself, his countenance hardened. He did not like to see a roue like Lord Chittlingdon fleecing anyone, never mind anyone so obviously green as the victim he had chosen. He wondered whether to intervene. He ought to, of course. But that would doubtless draw down the wrath of the gods on his head. The lad, after all, was winning.

The marquis had no doubt that this felicitous state would not last long, and that the young stripling would be sent to bed divested of every last farthing. That, after all, was the manner of Lord Chittlingdon. Cruel, remorseless, and inclined to pluck every pigeon who crossed his path, no matter how youthful or how innocent.

Merit would wait a little longer, till the pile equalized itself, then intervene. If the lad had any sense he would be relieved, but more likely he would be furious. The marquis shrugged. It really did not matter, so long as Chittlingdon was set down. There was no love lost between my lord marquis and the seventh baron. None at all.

A few words were exchanged across the cards.

Chittlingdon removed the rubies and set them squarely on the table. There was a moment's pause as the boy deliberated. Then, his eyes never wavering from the old man's face, the youth pressed his winnings over to the center and expelled a small breath. His eyes were bright—too bright, the marquis thought grimly. There was much at stake here. He suspected all of the boy's livelihood lay upon that table. Those shining, dark eyes told their own tale, no matter how prim or how well-schooled the piquant jawline.

"*Vingt-et-un*." The boy nodded. Lord Laxton watched closer than anyone might think as the cards were dealt. The child—for, yes, he was precious more than that—frowned. It was a fleeting expression, but one followed almost immediately by a serenity that surprised the marquis. If the lad was unhappy with his hand, it was virtually impossible to say.

There were murmurs and discards and faint curses from the baron. Lord Laxton was not deceived. He was too worldly wise to believe the baron would make a gift of his troubles. No, he was lulling the boy into security with his odd, carefully inserted murmurs of displeasure. It would not be long before he apologetically laid his trump hand upon the table and fleeced the boy for the greenhorn he was.

When the moment came, it was precisely as the marquis predicted. A light apology, an outstretched hand, and in a

single suave moment the winnings had disappeared into the
gilded waistcoat that would have dazzled Prinny himself.

The boy comported himself well. It was all precisely as
the marquis predicted. The baron would leave that night,
and the greenhorn would very likely blow his brains out or
trudge wearily from the tavern, too light in pocket to remain, too destitute to wait even for the morning stage. It
was horrible, all quite horrible.

But wait! A new expression had replaced the boy's shock.
It was determination and a confidence that had seemed quite
crushed a moment before. He spoke, and though his tone
was level—quiet, even—his meaning could not be ignored.

The innkeeper dropped his tallow candles and several of
the taproom occupants, including the coachman of the
Royal Mail, stopped their drinking. It was not often that a
night's entertainment came their way free of charge, but
this slip of a boy was proving positively providential.

He was speaking, now, in the clear, proud, well educated
tones that would have branded him quality, even if the cut
of his coat did not.

"I fear there has been some mistake." A slight emphasis
on the word *mistake*. The marquis, watching him, could
not help but admire his courage, even if he damned him
for a rare fool.

"Mistake?" The baron looked disdainful as he reached
out for the cards.

"Do not, I pray you, touch those."

The baron almost did, but perceiving the curious eyes of
the world and his wife upon him, chose, instead, to adopt
a loftier pose.

"And whyever not, my dear boy?" The tone was bland,
but there was a warning note that the marquis, accustomed
to the ways of Chittlingdon, did not fail to notice. He remarked the careless twist of the snuffbox as Chittlingdon

shook out a laced sleeve and drew a delicate dose from the ivory-inlaid box.

"Your cards are false. I would like, if you please, to inspect them."

The words were quiet, but the boy was on his feet, and Lord Laxton could have sworn from his stance there would be daggers drawn if need be.

The baron's eyes flashed. "Marked? You have brains in your boots, my lad! Here, innkeeper! Examine this card. Is it marked? No, of course it isn't! And this one? Humor the child, I say! Is this marked?"

The innkeeper, embarrassed—but curious, how could he not be?—inspected the proffered card. The silence in the room was audible; only the innkeeper's tabby mewed softly by the hearth, and Old Man Stone tapped out the tobacco from his ancient, whittled pipe.

"No, my lord, it is not marked."

The baron gave a trill of laughter. "But of course it isn't, my callow lad! How could it be, when the pack has not once left my hands? I am a peer of the realm, not a cheat, as must be apparent to anyone who is not as wet behind the ears as you are, young sprig."

He took the card from the innkeeper and placed them once again with the pile of discards. Then, with a benign glance at his opponent (for he could afford to be benign with a sackful of gold lining his pockets), he leaned forward and gestured for his glass to be refilled.

"I shall not call you out for such a scurrilous accusation, though none could blame me if I did. I shall set the matter down entirely to your youth, which time shall doubtless remedy. A word to the wise, however. Do not again demean yourself with behavior unfitting to a gentleman. The fates turned against you, but by God they were against me for an hour or more! Take faith in that, my little stripling, and do not test my indulgence any further by such nonsensical talk."

Lord Chittlingdon expected the matter to drop and so, in truth, did his lordship, watching from the shadows. A sad tale, but one he had seen often enough. But the matter was not dropped, and the youth, speaking in dulcet tones, now enjoyed the ears of the entire taproom.

"Sir, if my suspicions were nonsensical I would have been the first to bow and wish you well with your winnings. I never spoke of marked cards and I do not do so now."

Here, a raised brow from the baron and a titter of laughter from the blacksmith and several of the ostlers. The boy ignored them, his eyes burning with feverish concentration on the features of the baron alone.

"I staked high in full knowledge that if you drew either the ace of clubs or the two diamonds that were left, I would be at a standstill. Rather too much to stake on such uncertainties, but I am a gambler by necessity if not entirely by inclination." He hesitated. "Had you won fairly, I would have smiled and bowed and bothered you no further, I swear it!"

The speech rang strangely true upon the boy's lips, but the marquis had no time to marvel either at this fact, or at the circumstance of the child having had the courage to make it at all.

It was all too clear that the baron, slightly in his cups, was looking his menacing best. "Do you dare hold to the foolish suggestion that I am a cheat?"

The answer was given to him roundly, but politely, the boy's knuckles clenched across the table but his demeanor otherwise doing him perfect credit. He looked as calm as a sea breeze. Lord Laxton, watching him, and in the watching, meeting his eyes for a flicker of an instant, experienced a peculiar sensation. It had nothing whatsoever to do with anything rational.

His pulses quickened—more than that, he felt himself

overcome by overwhelming, masculine desire. The type of hunger that seared him more than any mistress had, the type of unadulterated . . . lust, for want of a better word . . . that left him gasping for air.

He studied the boy closer, astonished at his physical response. The boy had startled, too—he could almost swear it, for his concentration had faltered for the veriest flicker of an instant, and his hand trembled, where before it had not.

The child's lips were dry, for he moistened them slightly with his tongue. That tongue was the marquis's undoing, for it was pink, and soft, and quite beyond compare. The marquis steadied himself, damning himself for a fool. The most foolish of all fools, it seemed, for he had been taken in, and he prayed only that Lord Chittlingdon, seated facing him, had been similarly deceived.

The impossible, the extraordinary, and yes, the utterly incredible was now occurring. The boy, for all his fine features and educated airs, was dissembling. One look again at those pink, bow-shaped lips—almost red, even—those long, undulating lashes . . . good God, he must have been blind! The child was a girl—worse still, a woman, for he understood, now, the need for that ill-fitting greatcoat and for the tricorne hat that was all but out of fashion these days.

Intriguing. Highborn, too, for her manner and comportment screamed of quality. But what lady moved in such circles as this? What lady compromised herself in such an irrevocable manner? It was unthinkable! She was beyond the pale. He moved forward, wondering how much Chittlingdon had guessed, and trusted that he was too much in his cups to notice. The boy was talking, and all the eyes of the room were upon him.

"I do suggest that you cheat, sir. No, indeed, I can swear to it. That pack has been tampered with, whether by mistake or guile I cannot attest."

"Attest to my sword, you young jackanapes!" The

snuffbox was forgotten as the baron glared at the boy. By now, the hush in the taproom was palpable, and the boy looked flushed, whether from battle or from embarrassment the marquis, still watching closely, could not tell.

"I will not fight you, sir. For all my youth, you are not worthy of my steel."

Bravo! thought his lordship. At least the little fool had brains in her head. Chittlingdon would slice her in two, so frail as she was. But she was talking. He was curious to hear her.

"If a mistake has been made, I urge you to rectify it. It can be easily done. You will find that there are two pairs of hearts. The first is situated three cards from the beginning of the discard pile. The second, if I might remark, is in your winning hand."

There was an excited murmur about the room, and some rude, disbelieving laughter. Lord Laxton, more intrigued than ever, inched forward, a curious smile playing upon his lips. In a moment, he would intervene. And by all that was holy, if the chit was wrong he would wring her neck himself!

She was talking, all eyes of the taproom upon her. More—for people seemed to be creeping out of the very woodwork, from the adjoining private parlors, from the cellars, and yes, even from the servants' quarters, though it would be half a day's pay docked if the innkeeper should glance their way.

The boy—for so the marquis would think of him until he confirmed his suspicions—seemed not to notice. His burning eyes were fixed steadily upon Lord Chittlingdon, weary but intense.

"Check for yourself, my lord. If you do not, I can only assume you to be what I have called you: a cheat, and therefore unworthy of my sword."

"By God, you shall have a taste of my whip, then, never mind a sword. How dare you? You address a peer of the realm, my fine young sprig, and you shall live to regret it. Innkeeper! Fetch me my riding crop! I procured it from Swaine, Adeney, Brigg & Sons and I assure you it is one of their finest!"

The boy paled, and my lord noticed that the knuckles, still clenched, were now white.

The marquis, thinking, with some trace of alarm, that the child might well faint, stood up. It was time, he supposed, to make his presence felt, for Chittlingdon had imbibed too freely to be relied upon to show any degree of sense or propriety. The days of public whipping were long past, but the baron seemed in want of a reminder.

"My Lord Chittlingdon! How very . . . delightful to cross paths with you again!"

The marquis advanced upon the table with a jocularity that sat strangely with him. His tone belied the genial words, for it was scathing despite the civilities. Neither gentleman felt anything "delightful" at all in the encounter, my lord feeling uncustomarily inflamed and the baron decidedly put out, for the noble Marquis of Laxton spelt nothing but trouble for him.

"You!" The baron's voice scarcely concealed his loathing as he examined the fine fall of my lord's cravat. As usual, it was more perfect even than his own. Worse, whilst the pin adorning it was not so ornate, the gem it revealed was an exquisite cut-cabochon ruby, far, far more expensive than his own more meager trinkets.

The marquis bowed mockingly. "Fleecing all the greenhorns tonight, my lord baron? You really should be warned off such insalubrious activities."

"Mind your own business, Laxton!"

"Sadly I cannot, baron! My estates are in such good heart there really is nothing for me to do at all. Let me mind *your* business, rather."

The baron, who very well knew he should call the marquis out for such interference, glowered instead. The marquis was too fabled a shot at Manton's to so seriously risk one's life.

Lord Laxton appeared to know it, for his brow was raised quizzically, and his stare was odiously amused as it came to rest upon the baron's aquiline features.

"Ah, the arrival of the whip, I see. Rather inferior for so illustrious a company as Swaine, Adeney, Brigg & Sons but perhaps it is one of their earlier versions. Thank you, innkeeper." The marquis deftly took the horrid-looking instrument. It was an act that had the youth paling further—whether from fright or from relief, the marquis could not say. The baron, for his part, blustered loudly about the purloinment of his property.

"You may talk to the magistrate tomorrow, my good sir. But for now, let us resolve this tedious little issue to everyone's satisfaction. I am perfectly certain the innkeeper's wife does not want to loiter behind those draperies a second longer than is absolutely necessary."

At which remark, the innkeeper's wife, crimson, emerged from the curtains and pushed past the table, murmuring all sorts of nonsensical reasons for her prolonged presence, which brought her no good beyond a flurry of catcalls and a scowl from the innkeeper himself.

As a matter of fact, if the marquis had matters his way, he would most likely have struck the baron with the riding crop that was now tantalizingly nestled between his gloved fingers. He would then, of course, proceed to make verbal mincemeat of the child. Really, someone ought to be teaching the . . . admirable little greenhorn she could not go about staking her life on a card game, then staking all on the likes of Chittlingdon!

A tongue-lashing was just what the child needed, and by God, when he sorted this mess out it was precisely what she would get!

CHAPTER 3

Chittlingdon was not thinking of tongue-lashings. He was looking, Lord Laxton noted with amused interest, faintly sick. He made a hurried dash for the cards, as if to pack them away, but was met with the point of his own riding crop just across his jaw. It rested there, ever so lightly, but menacingly enough to force my lord baron to lift his chin in a manner the marquis considered far too undignified for his liking.

The marquis lowered the whip, just slightly, and touched the baron's ungloved hands with his own immaculate gloved ones.

"Oh, no, no! No, we don't! The lad has made an accusation. It bears investigation, does it not?"

"No, it does not!" Chittlingdon puffed himself up in annoyance, but his black eyes were beady, and rather weary of this unwelcome intercession. He could bully the boy and the innkeeper, but the marquis, with his superior rank, wit, and fashion, was another matter entirely. Chittlingdon blustered ingratiatingly.

"You are a man of the world, Laxton. You know how it is. The stupid greenhorn lost at cards and now has not the backbone to lose like a gentleman!"

"I can lose, sir, but I won't be swindled." The full force of bright eyes now scorched the marquis like a flame. He was surprised at their potency, and almost laughed out loud at the appeal in them.

By Gods, the child was expressive! Almost, he believed her.

But cheat? Chittlingdon was unscrupulous, he preyed upon the innocent, but he was not, to the marquis's knowledge, a cardsharp. The child must surely be mistaken.

He spoke sternly. "Prove your claim or be gone from here. I want to hear no more of this tiresome business, if you please!"

The youth bowed. For a fraction of a second she had nearly slipped into a curtsey, but remembered herself in time. Merit, Lord Laxton, trusted no one had noticed the error, as he had.

She pointed. "If you would, my lord? The first discard was an ace." She nodded, satisfied, as Lord Laxton revealed this to be the case. "The second, a three." She scrunched up her face, thinking. "Clubs, for the diamonds only revealed themselves toward the end game."

The marquis regarded her keenly. The devil of it, she was correct! He bowed in her direction. The baron was looking green, his eyes shifting to the door.

It was not unnatural for Lord Laxton to take a few strategic steps to bar that form of escape.

"The next card will be the pair of hearts I spoke of. See, there are two. One in the final hand, one upon the table in the discard pile."

She was right, of course. It was inevitable. For some reason the marquis released the breath he had been holding. He cast her yet another glance from those hooded eyes of his. She was pale, and trembling, but nonetheless rather sure of her claim. She managed, in fact, a quizzical cocking of her brow that very nearly matched his own. He did not know whether to laugh, to frown, or to damn her for her impudence.

In the event, he did nothing, merely announcing, in a drawl, that she was perfectly correct. Quite how she was correct he could not quite fathom, and certainly bore investigation at some other, more delicious moment. Yes, indeed, he had mapped out several delicious moments for himself, but that, of course, was for the future.

Miss Faith Finchley, comfortably seated in Lord Islington's smart barouche, was engrossed not so much with the future as with her past. It seemed that just as patches of green flashed by, and cobblestones, and turnpikes, and carefully thatched cottages, so, too, did a patchwork of memories. Happy memories they were.

Though she and Honor were never so fine as some of the young ladies of Miss Bramble's seminary, the sisters had always been popular, so that holidays had never been a hardship, and friends had never been lacking even if the frills and furbelows had been in short supply.

Oh, but it was hard without Honoria! Perhaps it would have been less so if Honor, too, were travelling to some exciting destination.

If Honor had been blessed with godparents like Lord and Lady Islington, she might even now be preparing for her season, or discussing hairstyles with some illustrious dresser. It would be fun, then, for they could compare and gossip and exchange all manner of correspondence. . . .

But no! Honor had none of these advantages and to Faith, just the teeniest bit guilt-ridden, it all seemed terribly unfair. For the hundredth time that day she wondered what Honor was up to.

Better she did not know, for it was precisely at this moment that Honor had decided to put up at the Greenstone Inn, and had procured for herself her gentlemanly array of coats, breeches, boots, shirts, and the like at such assorted hosiers, bootmakers, and hatters as Thomas Reeves, Nathan Soames, and Tipping Rigby of Ludgate Street.

Garbed in her newly purchased attire, she took tea at the Belle Sauvage Inn before connecting with the Cambridge coach.

If Faith had known, she would have trembled, for though Honoria was always surprising her with her enterprising ways, Faith had not suspected that her sister would do anything more unseemly than beating all she surveyed at cards. This, Faith knew, was unseemly enough, for to play for gain was a little . . . well, it was a little fast, but to masquerade as a boy! It did not bear thinking upon, and fortunately, since Faith remained in happy ignorance, she did not.

The progress to St. Martin's Square therefore proceeded without a hitch. This was due not only to Faith's peace of mind, but also because the change of horses at King's Crossing had been arranged several days before. There had thus been none of the usual haggling attendant on the procurement of a fresh pair. Also, though there was a stop at Malling for a light luncheon of ham, fresh bread, and a glass of milk, neither Faith nor her newly appointed maid was hungry, so the journey proceeded on far quicker than might have been expected.

The chaise was extremely well sprung, if a little outmoded, for Lady Islington preferred comfort over fashion and had no time for such fanciful fripperies as high-perched phaetons, which appeared to be all the rage.

At least Faith thought they must be, for as they converged on the wider London roads, they passed several such, and all driven by riders who were clearly of the *haut ton*. They were so fashionably dressed as to make Faith feel positively dowdy, despite her merriest gown and her brand new bonnet sprigged with snow white ostrich plumes.

Faith, her confidence fading, scolded herself for permitting her spirits to sink in so cowardly a manner.

It would not do, she thought, to be tearful, for how heartless and ungrateful would that be?

Lady Islington was the soul of kindness to sponsor her so, and Honor had seemed as merry as a grig to be escaping the rigorous strictures of society. But was she so? Or was it just her kind heart refusing to permit Faith any doubts?

Surely she could not prefer pitting her wits against the world to becoming a young lady of the first stare? Faith shook the endlessly revolving doubts from her head and smiled meekly at the maid, who had hardly said a single word on the trip. She had a sweet smile and did not seem nearly so terrifying as Miss Bramble's outspoken servants.

"Is this your first position?" she asked kindly.

The maid, released from her silence, shook her head.

"No, miss. I was scullery maid then second chambermaid to 'er ladyship afore Amelia, wot was first chambermaid, ran away to the Americas with Lord Mannerley's second footman. With child, she was." The maid's eyes sparkled with sudden animation. "Lady Islington was proper shocked, she was, an' said I could have Amelia's position an' be a proper lady's maid an' all, seeing 'as 'ow Amelia 'ad flown the coop, like."

"Gracious!" was all Faith could think of to say, for while she was very pleased the silence was broken at last, she was not so sure gossiping with the servants about matters a lady should not know of was at all the thing.

The maid subsided into silence again, so Faith fished into her reticule and drew out a stick of sugar candy that Honor had procured from Hobson's and Hobson's, the illustrious confectioner of New Haven.

"Share some?"

That rare smile again, and a shy nod, and Faith had made an ally in Millie, the exalted scullery maid, for life, though she did not quite know it yet.

"Tell me about Lady Islington's household. Does she receive a lot?"

"Oh, yes, miss! Very fashionable is Lady Islington! 'As

mornin' callers noon an' night, she 'as, an' invitations to routs an' assemblies an' all. . . ."

Faith very much wanted to ask whether so fashionable a creature was also kind, but naturally, good manners precluded her from doing so.

"Three sons she 'as, an' Master Godfrey—the second, you know—he is nobbut a trouble, like, with 'is roisterin' about an' 'is light o' loves . . . oops, beggin' yer pardon, miss."

Faith hid a smile. She did not think Millie was going to be a terribly stuffy chaperone, after all. Faith was dying to ask more about Sir Godfrey, Lady Islington's second son, but she was far too well bred to display such vulgar curiosity. Instead, she took up her sampler, long neglected upon the seat beside her, and satisfied herself with sorting the tangled threads.

"Beggin' yer pardon, miss, but that shade o' rose is darker than that there pink."

"You are right! How vexatious, for I have already used a whole length of it and I suppose it must now be unstitched. You have a good eye, Millie."

Millie beamed. "Yes, for I trim all me lady's 'ats, I do. Regular knack, she says I 'ave, an' like as not that be the very truth, for very particular is me lady!"

"I am sure. I only hope you can help me half as well."

The girl turned pink with pleasure. "Very like I can, for I already have ideas for them plumes wot's stitched to yer bonnet, like."

"What is wrong with them?" Faith sounded indignant, for indeed, she had felt very smart with those fine white feathers upon her crown.

"Nothin', miss, nothin'! All the rage they are, them plumes! Very smart, like, only they should be affixed a little higher, maybe with a 'igh poke rather than a straw."

"Why?"

" 'Ide your face, they do, which is fine for some folks wot

'as a blemish on their cheek, or a squint mayhap, or even the pox wot there is not a lot you can do for, no matter wot Old Mother Norton might say. . . ."

Faith tried hard to bite back her sudden laughter. Again, she wished Honor was with her. How she would enjoy this discussion!

"I have not the pox, it is true, but . . ."

"There you go! The prettiest little face I ought did see, an' wot do yer go an' do? 'Ide it 'neath some mighty great ticklin' feathers! Now don't you fret, miss, Millie will set yer straight. I may not be as 'igh an' mighty as some folks wot call themselves lady maids, but I am a dab 'and with a curlin' paper, I am, an' that not nobody can deny!"

"I am fortunate, then, for I confess I have never been out in fashionable circles before."

"Lordy, miss, I can tell that, all right and tight! Your 'air all braided up an' all, when it should curl softly over yer shoulders in ringlets. Nothin' that some curlin' papers and a good night's sleep can't fix!"

Faith, unused to such indulgence, merely smiled and turned the subject.

"Lord Islington? Is he in residence?"

"Oh, yes, miss, but 'e avoids the soirees like the plague, 'e does. Leaves all o' that to his sons, wot escort me lady about. Not Lord Robert, o' course, for 'e's in India, an' very like to make a fortune, they say, but Master Godfrey and Master 'Arry. Fine as ninepence is Master Godfrey, but Master 'Arry is more like 'is dad. Mad keen on 'orses an' very like not to change out o' 'is ridin' clothes afore presentin' 'imself to dinner. Fair makes me lady weep, 'e does. They say she boxed 'is ears when 'e turned up for Lady Gasset's ball wearin' nought but 'is huntin' clothes, but very like that's just a Banbury tale."

Faith, listening, quite forgot to scold Millie for such gossip. Indeed, so caught up was she in the narration that she erred in precisely the same way and prodded Millie for more.

"Is Master Harry in residence, then?"

"No, madame, for 'e gone up Oxford way."

Faith nodded. "And Lord Islington? What age is he?"

"Lordy, miss, that I cannot say! Old, but not so old as wot Lord Plethering is! Lost all 'is teeth, Lord Plethering, an' has to be served pap, 'e does, which causes a great commotion in the household, for he is forever throwin' bowls of 'is food about, bellowin' fer somethin' decent, like!"

Faith smiled. "Lord Islington is not so afflicted, then?"

"No, indeed! 'E may 'ave the odd bit o' gout, like, but otherwise all is right an' tight wiv 'im! A sportin' man, is me lord. Likes 'is 'orses. 'E 'as a very good stable, miss, what Larson can tell you of, on account of 'is being first coachman, like, an' . . ."

But Faith was never to hear the catalogue of all of Larson's duties, for her eyes were drawn to the street, where amid the pieman and the sweepers and the chandler carrying tapers neatly stacked upon long, thin trays, she caught sight of . . . well, yes. She caught sight of a puppy.

Not any old puppy, but a golden one, with tiny paws and a little black button nose. It was in imminent danger of being run over by several hackney coaches and the baker's boy, wheeling a barrow of bread.

It looked pitifully thin, and its ears, a silken gold, drooped down almost to its chin. A dog, but a doleful dog. A poor, hungry, woe-begotten scrap of a creature being kicked by a thousand booted feet as the world walked by. Or so it seemed to Faith.

Faith, who was herself timid and retiring, did not feel she could stand for such sadness. The creature stood close to a gas lamppost and whimpered. It was that small, tiny whimper, heard, miraculously, over the noise of the link boys and street-sweepers that made her act. Oh, yes, it was impulsive. Precisely the same manner of thing she was always berating Honor for doing. She did not, in point of fact, stop to think.

The lady's maid was ever after to say that if Miss Faith had not plainly seen the "wretched little varmint" whimpering on the corner of Bolton and Piccadilly, none of the ensuing havoc would have occurred.

Miss Faith would never have felt the need to leap out of Lady Islington's smart barouche, causing the handsome bay horses at the head to startle. She would never, as a *result* of their startling, have tripped over her skirts and landed in a heap of petticoats and tangling ribbons on the dusty London road.

Perhaps, if she had been standing decorously, as she had intended, the little puppy would have been more aloof with his sudden savior. As it was, sensing a kindly disposition, he abandoned his woeful stance and commenced licking poor Miss Faith to death in a plethora of delighted yelps and impossible pleas.

Miss Finchley now had not only a puppy, but a panicked maid to contend with, Millie feeling certain that alighting in such a manner outside Watier's Gentleman's Club was not conducive to Miss Faith's cherished ambition of receiving vouchers for Almack's.

As the maid tried to help her up and shake off the puppy at the same time, Miss Finchley patted the golden creature and murmured in soothing tones that he would be taken home for a good bath and dinner just as soon as he permitted her to rise.

At which remarkable words the maid panicked all the more, shrieked in distraction, and let go of Faith's hand. She turned, instead, to gather up several necessary items like a muff, the silks, and a delightful, pearl-stitched reticule that had tumbled from the chaise in the lady's haste.

"Lordy, miss, you will 'ave me dismissed without a

character, you will, paradin' hereabouts like a doxy an' me not doin' nothin' to stop you! Pray leave that nasty creature afore folks be gawpin' their 'eads off, an' you gently born an' all . . ."

She might as well have spared her breath, for the wretched little creature had now licked Miss Faith, a fact that so endeared him to her that she was prepared to withstand even dear Millie to save him from the streets. Millie eyed the doors of Watier's anxiously.

"Oh, do step back up, miss! We mustn't let nobody be seeing us, we oughtn't. Not outside Watier's, wot everyone knows is a gentleman's club and there be no denying it nohow . . . Hoy, coachman! Stop that grumblin' an' help a mite, will you?"

But Larson, intent on the horses, would only curse (but mildly, for he was right fond of the little miss, her having thanked him prettily at Malling, not to mention asking the innkeeper to fetch him down an ale and all). He muttered that he had his hands full enough with the cattle, an unwieldy pair and not well matched no matter what Sir Englefield-Hardy might say upon the subject.

This was an old grouse, and one that caused the maid to cast a caustic glance of darkest disgust in his direction.

"Nobbut trouble you are, Larson. Just 'old them 'orses, then, an' Miss will alight in a tick an' not with that there mutt wot will dirty 'er lovely coach gown not to mention 'er half-boots wot Lady Islington purchased at Madame Milford's only last week . . . Miss Faith . . ."

But her charge was not listening. She was bundling the puppy quite efficaciously into the chaise, having disentangled herself most efficiently from the footpath and the baker's cart. She appeared deaf to her maid's hopeless pleas, though in truth she did suffer a pang as to what might become of her Almack's vouchers were this particular escapade to become more widespread knowledge.

If Millie had prayed to escape unseen, her prayers were not answered. Not surprisingly (for Faith was passing pleasing to the eye even when her petticoats were not displayed to the world), several gentlemen were adjusting their quizzing glasses and gazing with varying degrees of lascivious interest in her direction.

Faith set the puppy down upon the squabs and spoke rather sternly as she peered inside and adjusted her gown. "Now. I shall take you home to Lady Islington, but only if you behave perfectly respectably."

But the puppy did not behave respectably at all. He jumped off the squabs as he caught a whiff of the baker's cart. It was filled with eel pies, so Faith was forced to descend, too.

She turned to her audience, administering the haughtiest stare she could muster (which was rather haughty, the lady having long attended the seminary for girls and perfected the technique).

"As for you, gentlemen," she said, not displaying the smallest quiver of mortification—though she rather wished the very flagstones would open and swallow her up—"I shall ask you to do the same. Behave perfectly respectably, that is. It is hardly fair sport to quiz a lady when she is at such a disadvantage. Good day to you."

She nodded, in her best imitation of the dreaded Miss Bramble. The moment was spoiled, however, for she was forced to seize the puppy, who seemed inclined to turn into a thief.

This caused an expressive, but sadly unladylike, epithet to leave Faith's pretty pink lips. The maid, stuffing all the possessions onto the interior seating, considered fainting, for really, there was no saving Miss Faith from this scrape. All the onlookers were glaring and most, she could tell, were gentlemen.

She suppressed a faint moan as she recognized Mr.

Alvaney and Lord Pickenhugh. The rest were dressed in the highest of fashion and two had collars starched so high it was a wonder they could breathe. Lords, all right, for if it were not their collars that gave them away, it was their boots. Shone with champagne, belike, for the gleam upon even these dusty London streets was better than a looking glass. Millie eyed several elegant tassels and moaned.

The prospects of the celebrated Almack's vouchers seemed to recede further into the distance with every horrible second that passed. Oh, and she had so wanted to be elevated to dresser! And to see a season through, and to pile Miss Faith's shining dark locks high upon her head with a tortoiseshell comb from Iberia itself . . . she shook herself from her mournful thoughts and regarded her mistress sternly.

"Oh, miss, leave the wretched pup. Doubtless he gets fed by the celebrated Jean-Baptiste himself, and lordy, wouldn't I like scraps from the covers of Watiers? Come, come, Miss Faith. You really must. The coaches are piling up behind poor Larson and Lord Islington will 'ave me 'ide, 'e really will, with 'is bay horses an' all. . . ."

"But I can't abandon the creature to the streets!"

"You can't take 'im up in the chaise, either, beggin' yer pardon! Lady Islington 'as just 'ad it refurbished, like . . ."

Faith looked flustered and guilty.

"Oh, dear, that would be unmannerly of me! Is it far to St. Martin's Square? Can I walk with him?"

A question that made Millie groan in the greatest of agitation, and the pup, sensing a protector, yelp pitifully.

It was that small, sad yelping that was Faith's undoing.

"No matter what you might say, the creature looks starving."

"And so am I. Famished. Absolutely famished. Which is why you find me outside Watier's at this ungodly hour of the morning. May I help you . . . eh, Miss? You appear to be blocking the entrance."

The gentleman who addressed her from without the carriage was splendidly attired in military red, with gold buttons splashed about his close-fitting greatcoat, and hessians that positively sparkled in the sunlight, so gleaming white they were. As for his breeches, well, they were the color of honey gold and they molded to his slender form far too perfectly for pretty little Faith's comfort. Faith caught a glimpse of reddish-gold curls, loosely cropped, and an endearing grin, but she did not allow herself to be cozened by the man's elegant looks, for he was insolent!

She felt the color sting at her cheeks as the puppy creased the folds of her carriage dress.

"*Miss?*" Faith seethed at the obvious hesitation in the gentleman's tone. Clearly, he was not sure whether she was a lady of quality or not. Or if he did, he was being sarcastic and implying—ever so subtly—that the matter was in doubt.

She naturally—for who would not do so?—compounded her mounting sins by announcing in lofty tones that she was Miss Faith Finchley, as if all the world should know who she was.

When the gentleman raised his brows—not haughtily, as she imagined—but in bewilderment, for the name was familiar though he could not fathom why, Faith was goaded to a response more in her sister's lively style. Instead of inclining her head timidly as she should have done, she determined to set him down, for she was quite positive he thought poorly of her.

Well, to be caught outside Watier's! It did not bear thinking upon!

She smiled regally and extended her hand as if she were the queen herself. Then, as the startled gentleman took it, wondering whether he should kiss it or merely hold it for a momentary fraction, she announced, rather airily, that she was the granddaughter of a duke.

This statement made poor Millie choke, and the gentleman in question smile a little. He bowed, however, rather civilly, kissed the hand—for after all, it was soft and warm and deliciously delicate—and announced that they certainly had something in common then, for his own father was Edmond, Lord Manning, Duke of Norwich.

By this time, a considerable crowd was clustering about the entrance. Faith felt ready to positively sink into the paving, and the only creature that seemed inclined to behave was the puppy itself.

"Miss . . . I am sorry, I did not quite catch your name?"

"Finchley." Muted, this time, for Faith had lied enough for one day.

"Miss Finchley, shall I put an end to your . . . eh . . . problems?"

Were his eyes amused, or did she only suspect them to be? She eyed him cautiously and ignored the outrageous fluttering of her heart. How tiresome to be smitten by the first pangs of devotion when one is so wholly at a disadvantage! Why could she not be gliding down a hall, surmounted with pearls, perhaps an ostrich feather or two?

"I shall take the mutt and deliver him to your door. That way, your carriage can proceed and your maid will be prevented from having a severe fit of the spasms."

Faith's eyes widened. They were the color of a dark shade of honey dew, but she was quite unaware of this fact as she answered, for whilst she might have many faults, self-absorption was not among them.

"He is not a mutt, sir, for I cannot think that such an appellation could apply to such a beautiful dog, no matter how starved . . ."

There! Those expressive eyes again! He was laughing! Faith could not help the curves of her own lips tilting, just a little. His laughter was infectious, even if the cause of his merriment was suspect.

She ignored the continued misbehavior of her tiresome heart. It must be the crowds, and the sinking feeling of imminent disgrace, for she could not think Lady Islington would be pleased.

Why, she would label her a hoyden before ever they had even reacquainted themselves! The fluttering continued, especially as he had only now released her hand, a fact that had some of the lewder spectators jeering, and several gentlemen more acquainted with Lord Freddy betting on . . . oh, several matters that would have made Faith positively sink.

"Come! Let me take the damn . . . I mean, the princely creature!" The princely creature sat, as good as gold, upon the cobblestones. He might never, for the look of him, have ever in his life been involved in any wrongdoing whatsoever.

Faith was not fooled by the gentleman's smooth correction. "Damn!" was certainly more expressive of his sentiments, but she found herself liking this unknown stranger, son of a duke or no. She caviled for politeness' sake, but really, he seemed to be offering a very tempting solution.

"It would be such an imposition—I cannot . . . gracious, you are practically royalty!"

For a moment, Faith quite forgot she was meant to have a similar rank. The gentleman grinned. It was an engaging grin, not at all toplofty, as she had feared.

"Only a third son. Not important at all. Lord Frederick Manning at your service. By the by, there is no question of imposition. You *can* hand over that specimen and you *will*."

The gentleman seemed stern—masterful, even. Lord Freddy rather liked feeling masterful, especially as Faith blushed so delightfully and seemed not to notice that his

hair was fair and curly rather than dark and sardonic, as
was all the rage. In this, of course, he was quite mistaken,
for Faith had noticed everything about him, from his high-
crowned hat with its jaunty gold buckle trim, to those
honey-colored breeches she really should not be staring at.
Almost too late, she averted her gaze, but Freddy, devising
something really masterful to utter, hardly seemed to
notice.

"I insist, Miss Finchley. There is really no denying me."
(A lie, for Freddy was always being denied, but there was
no need for this beautiful, soulful creature to know any
such thing!)

Faith smiled shyly. There was no gainsaying him, especially as the coachmen behind her were growing wild with
rage and threatening the watch, which caused Larson to hurl
his own defensive insults while maintaining the cattle.
These, of course, were now restive and relieving themselves
on the cobbles, a fact that was not making Lady Islington's
smart barouche very popular at all.

Vaguely in the background Faith heard a medley of the
different sounds of the city. The costomonger, with his cry
of "Fresh picked parsnips, pickled beet, radish oh!" The
cane seller with his pannier of fresh-cut switches. "Buy a
cane for naughty boys! Naughty boys!" Then, of course,
there were the milkmaid's bellows and the fishwife's "Fine
silver eels! Five shillings, five shillings for me basket!" A
little farther down, more sounds mingled with the passing
crowd. There were chimney sweeps and climbing boys.
"Swee . . . p, swee . . . p!" in low, base tones, the peal of the
muffin bells, the pieman with his "Penny pies, hot, hot,
hot."

All these noises seemed to fade into each other until
Faith became aware of hot, hot, hot . . . the hot licks of the
golden creature who seemed to think her gloves were for
chewing.

My lord was waiting. His fair hair gleamed in the sunshine.

Faith, already sunk that she had told such a . . . such a vulgar untruth about her parentage, could only bow her head and murmur her thanks and direction.

"Lady Islington of St. Martin's Square."

The gentleman bowed. "I know it. Here, give me the animal." Again, that lordly air that would have had his best friends chortling. Thankfully, none were present and Mr. Alvaney and Lord Pickenhugh, mindful of lunch, had now retired inside the hallowed portals of Jean-Baptiste.

Faith delivered the creature into the gentleman's hands.

Only after the carriage had moved on, far past the corner of Bolton and Piccadilly, did it occur to her that Lord Frederick might have lied. Perhaps he had no intention at all of returning the puppy. Perhaps he had just set it down on the streets once more and dined, as he had planned, at Watier's.

Her eyes flashed with indignation at the thought. Millie was still moaning into the squabs, so it was impossible to order Larson to turn around. She patted the maid kindly and sighed.

How dreadful, really, to be arriving at dear Lady Islington with her maid overset, her reputation in question, and a great big lie hanging over her head. Duke's daughter indeed! Whatever could she be thinking of? She wished the earth would swallow her up, but naturally, it didn't. Then she wished she might never see the debonair gentleman again so long as she lived.

But a tiny voice within her scolded quite horribly. There was no greater crime, after all, than self-deception. She comforted herself with the thought that it was not the gentleman she wished to see again, but the puppy. One could, after all, see handsome young men any day of the week. It was really, she told herself crossly, no tremendous affair.

She turned her thoughts to St. Martin's Square and

firmly ignored any nonsensical daydreaming. Of all the
annoying starts! She was becoming worse than an insipid
heroine off Minerva's Press.

CHAPTER 4

"What do you have to say, Chittlingdon?" Lord Laxton permitted a faint sneer to cross his features. He would gladly have run the baron through with his sword, but felt that the evening had held enough drama. Besides, he did not need further scandal to cross the path of this reprehensible, foolish, beyond-the-pale child for whom he nevertheless felt some degree of compassion—not to mention, regrettably, some small degree of unlooked-for lust.

The baron scowled, cornered, he saw, by the burly innkeeper and this annoying nemesis he had happened upon by chance. The marquis was everything he aspired to be—elegant, handsome, wealthy in his own right, and titled beyond his own wildest dreams. It was only natural, therefore, that he should loathe him, and especially so now that he had humiliated him in front of the boy, the occupants of the taproom, and the innkeeper.

This last was a matter of no small vexation, for he enjoyed the repast at the Greenstone Inn, he found the doxies to his liking, and most importantly, he ran a tab there, the likes of which no other London taverner would stand for. By the look on the innkeeper's face, that credit was now about to come to a sorry end.

"I have nothing to say, Laxton. Pray return my cards, if you please."

"By all means." The marquis's tone was smooth—

pleasant, even—but Chittlingdon was not deceived. He therefore did not reach out for the cards lying flat across the palm of the marquis's precious kid gloves, but scowled instead. Actually, it was meant to be a refined sneer, but it materialized quite definitely as a sullen scowl.

"By all means," the marquis repeated, "when you have returned the lad's winnings, together with your final wager on the last round. What was the total, boy?"

The child actually had the impudence to grin, her dark eyes illuminating for a moment with both laughter and appreciation of my lord's methods.

"It was an additional sum of one hundred guineas, my lord."

The baron winced. My lord raised his brows.

"Playing deep, my little greenhorn."

The girl had the grace to blush. "Indeed, my lord. It shall be a lesson to me."

"Let us hope. And now, sir. You owe the stripling . . . how much was it?"

"Two hundred pounds with the rubies as collateral and a shilling for the first rubber."

"There you go . . . we will trouble you for that sum and you may take your leave without a sword through your gullet."

"Oh, no, he may not!" This, a shout from the innkeeper. "He shall pay his tab before he leaves this establishment, he will! I've had me guts full of all you high an' mighty gentry folk wot can't pay an honest bill, I 'ave." The speech was slightly marred by an apologetic and thoroughly subservient bow in the direction of Laxton, who ignored him, his eyes fixed on Chittlingdon. The baron looked simply livid.

The marquis looked unmoving.

The "boy," caught in the middle, looked exhilarated. The marquis thought those dark tendrils should never have been permitted to escape. He ordered the child from the room before anyone could notice what "he" had done, in the very fraction of an instant. It would do the girl no good to be discovered in her masquerade.

The fact that it would do her reputation no good to be discovered *tête-à-tête* in his private parlor he dismissed as a lesser evil. There was little chance of such discovery, for not even an irate father, tracing her every movement, would so far forget himself as to barge in, unannounced, on the Marquis of Laxton. The very idea was an absurdity.

"Wait for me in the private parlor reserved in my name. You may order up some port and yes, two cups of hot tea, I think."

"Tea, my lord?" The innkeeper did not know which was more diverting, the argument taking place, or the notion of the marquis ordering up tea.

His lordship glanced at him, such that he rather wished he had not allowed the snigger in his tone to be so apparent. He nodded hastily, as if to avoid retribution, and snapped his fingers at once for a footman to convey the matter to the kitchens.

The girl, startled, opened her mouth to protest, but closed it when forbidding eyes locked with her own. She found she had nothing to say, for she could not object without betraying her own secret. She could hardly splutter the usual objections of propriety when she was not even meant to be a female! It was perfectly reasonable, after all, for the marquis to invite her to his private quarters when he had performed so signal a service for her. Or him. The girl sighed.

When she looked into those steely eyes of—was it green? Green flecked with something darker, she thought, but flushed a little for staring—she could almost wish he did think of her as a woman, rather than a tiresome child. But how errant were these wanton thoughts! She averted her gaze, cleverly decided not to quarrel, and remembered to bow with grace.

"Very well, sir. I rely upon you to achieve a satisfactory ending."

The marquis's eyes gleamed, for he could not help thinking of several satisfactory endings . . . but he had business at hand.

"The purse, Lord Chittlingdon."

The baron's eyes flashed, but it was as plain as a pikestaff that there would be no worming his way out of the matter. If he did not settle his debt of honor, he would be accepted in no card room in the country, never mind the assembly rooms, where he often took pleasure in dangling his title like a fish on a hook to pretty little country misses.

"If I pay, you must swear that not a breath of scandal attaches to me."

"Impossible. Already there are whispers . . ."

The baron waved his laced arm dismissively. "I am not talking of whispers, Laxton. I am talking about corroboration from your worthy self."

"And why should I not corroborate what is patently true? You are a cardsharp and a cheat!"

"And you have a predilection for pretty boys. I can also stir up hornets' nests, Laxton."

"Why, you . . ." The marquis lunged toward the baron, his fury at so scurrilous an accusation apparent on his features. Then he checked himself. The baron must in no way suspect the truth—that his predilection was for pretty girls, rather than boys. His lips curled.

"I will not dignify that with a response, Chittlingdon. And I daresay there might be several young ladies who would gainsay any such notion." My lord, being handsome, flirtatious, and eligible, was not unaware of his charms, alas to say!

"Would they? At pain of admitting to indiscreet behavior? I think not, Lord Laxton."

"I would not trouble your brain too deeply on that score, Lord Chittlingdon. However, because I am in a charming mood, and because you are going to hand over that purse to me, I shall not be a party to branding you a cheat. Doubtless someone else will perform that just service, in due course, if you persist with your activities."

Lord Chittlingdon scowled, but drew the purse from his pocket. He knew that he had scored a small victory, for if once Lord Laxton gave his word, he would not sway from its course. The scandal of being branded a cheat had, at least, been averted.

But to see all those beautiful guineas change hands! He muttered a few pithy epithets which did not bode well for Lord Laxton's future, or for his ability to produce heirs, but the marquis seemed annoyingly deaf. Instead, he counted out two hundred pounds and one shilling precisely, and handed back the purse. It was empty, save for a half sovereign, which was at once seized by the innkeeper to be offset against the tab.

My Lord Chittlingdon was not a happy man. Perhaps the marquis would have been wise if he had paid some attention to the threats flung in his direction. But no! Lord Laxton was not at all wise in this instance. He turned his back upon the table, ignored the applause of half the taproom, and took the stairs, at a serene but determined pace, to discover the location of his private parlor. It was two steps to the left and through a giant, oaken door, hinged in brass that gleamed a little by the hall tapers. He only hoped that the little fool had heeded his advice.

St. Martin's Square was an imposing address, consisting of a number of tall, stuccoed town houses, all colonnaded

and revealing large, double sets of windows with ivy creeping up many of the front walls. Gargoyles gazed down from
some of the older establishments, and Faith thought she
could catch glimpses of sunlight across several lead glass
windows.

From the street, it was impossible to see some of the
pretty—and quite extensive—gardens that attached to
these houses, but certainly it was possible to see marbled
walkways and stone steps, and, in Lady Islington's case, a
tree-lined avenue leading straight up to the front door,
where a polished knocker boldly attested to the fact that
my lady was in residence.

The carriage drove through the heavy gates and rounded
a circle, with the barouche door facing precisely as it
ought, toward the pink marbled steps cradled in shadows
from the tall trees that lined them.

Millie, still flustered, remembered herself enough to
step out first, and extend a hand to Faith. Then, before
Miss Finchley—quaking a little, inside—mounted the im-
posing-looking stairway, the maid took care to adjust her
gown, smooth out the creases, and hand the little miss her
pearl-studded reticule. The remainder of Miss Faith's
bandboxes would be unloaded by Larson, when the horses
had been watered and stabled.

"This way, miss."

Faith followed, suddenly filled with the greatest of trep-
idation. She acknowledged the butler's bow with misty
eyes and tried her very best not to be awed by the sump-
tuous luxury of the hall, which appeared to display a great
many suits of armor and other ancient battle relics. They
all gleamed with polish, very decorative, but still disconcerting for a young lady who suddenly wanted nothing
more than to turn tail and flee.

She did nothing of the kind, however, being both polite and highly conscious of the honor bestowed upon her.

Lady Islington was a patroness of the first stare, a hostess who was never overlooked in the crush of a season's invitations. She had troubled herself greatly to provide Faith with suitable town clothes, and a maid for escort. It would be a shabby thing indeed for Faith to disappoint her now.

Faith was announced in a grander manner than that to which she was accustomed, but Lady Islington herself, rising from her chair, was not so formal. She embraced Faith with every evidence of great delight, fussed over her, took in her slim figure and glossy dark hair, cooed in triumph at its length, made so many plans it made Faith's head spin, and finally, finally, bade the girl be seated.

Faith removed her gloves and smiled shyly at her godmother.

"Lady Islington . . ."

"Pooh! Do not, I pray, address me as such—it makes me feel as ancient as my old mother-in-law, bless her soul! I shall be Elizabeth to you, as I am to all of my family."

Faith nodded, though it would be strange to call this elegant stranger by such a familiar term. She compromised, therefore, and addressed her godmother as "Lady Elizabeth." This seemed to be satisfactory, for beyond a quizzical smile it drew no further comment.

"Lady Elizabeth, I cannot thank you enough for your kindness."

"Nonsense! It is sheer self-indulgence for me, for I only ever had sons, you know, and they are a sore trial. No one to have a comfortable cose with, over pattern cards and morning callers and delightful excursions to Hyde Park. They seem only ever to visit Tattersalls and Manton's and a lugubrious sort of place called Antonio's, which is very tedious for me!"

Faith laughed, her shyness vanishing.

"I shall keep you well entertained, then, because I am

longing to visit the sights and I love poring over patterns, though my needlework is not all it should be."

Lady Elizabeth smiled.

"Foolish child! That is what seamstresses are for. We shall have all the enjoyment of selection, then leave them to the tedium of achieving results. Tell me, do you like your new kid slippers? I was positively in a quake that they would not fit!"

"They do, and the gowns you sent were breathtaking."

"Trifles, my dear. But we shall get you outfitted modishly before your come-out ball, I promise you!"

"When is that to be?"

"Sunday a week, and naturally there is our court presentation before then. I have taken the liberty of choosing your gown . . . very fetching, if I may say so, in a rosebud sarcanet with an overdress of white, of course, but you shall see."

Faith smiled. Life with her godmother was going to be nothing but one treat after the next. She only hoped she did not, as Miss Bramble always feared, become too terribly spoiled.

Lord Merit Argyll, Marquis of Laxton, almost whistled as he sought out his private parlor. No thoughts of an imminent stabbing so much as entered his mind, although they possibly should have. Lord Chittlingdon, relieved of his purse, had little else to do but ponder these happy possibilities.

Fortunately for the marquis, these musings were done outside the inn, on a very cold evening, when the baron had no option but to walk the five miles to his unfashionable lodgings at number five, Upper Quilberry Street. The baron had no convenient knife upon his person, and the whip, which had held so much promise, now was just another burden for him to carry. How he hated the marquis! How he should like to kill him! But naturally, these were all very impotent thoughts and my lord the marquis remained perfectly hale and hearty as he made his way to the first-floor landing.

He did not know what to expect as he opened the door to his private parlor, but the interview before him promised of interest. He only hoped the child had heeded his advice, and not taken the opportunity to slip quietly away.

But no! There she was, perfectly composed, reading, if you please, a copy of his own *Tatler!* He wondered if it was edifying.

"Good evening to you!"

The girl stood up and made him a polite bow, though her eyes were not so prim. He could have sworn, in fact, that they were alight with laughter if he did not know any better.

The marquis drew in his breath. He had not expected, yet again, this remarkable response she seemed to draw from him. He had a compelling desire to both kiss and strangle her at one and the same moment. He ignored the sensation and closed the door firmly behind him. This was one interview he did not want witnessed!

"My lord, begging your pardon, I would prefer the door to remain open."

He raised his brows. Either her imitation of a boy was very poor indeed or she was going to admit the truth. Disappointing, for he had planned on making fair game of her.

He raised his brows.

"Open the door? Why, pray? It is chilly outside and it is not as if we have to preserve any proprieties."

"Do we not?" The girl regarded him closely. Again, he felt that strange shiver of anticipation that really had nothing at all to do with the boyish figure she presented. The reverse, in fact, for her breeches clung to her more effectively than she might have been aware, and though her coat was cut loose, he was all too conscious that there was good reason for this fact.

He answered her inquiry as coolly as he could. "No, I don't see that we do. You are not, so far as I am aware, a lady, and I am therefore not bound by society's strict prescriptions."

There was a silence as the girl digested this ambiguous answer. My lord moved toward the fire, for indeed he was cold and if it brought him any nearer to the indignant face watching him, so much the better. He wondered if she was going to confess, or hold her tongue.

"I should box your ears for that!"

Ah, spirited. But how disappointing! She was going to confess! He would delay the moment, if he could.

"You talk in puzzles. How in the world might I have offended?"

"If you had not penetrated my disguise, I would say not at all. But you have, my lord, and so you choose to insult me. I *am* a lady born. What is more, I am certain you know it."

So, she had laid her cards very plainly upon the table.

My lord regarded her consideringly.

"You do not even try to convince me of your charade?"

"No, for I knew in the taproom that I was undone. I could see it in your eyes."

"How discerning. Did you see the same in the baron's eyes perchance?"

"No, though I feared exposure like the very plague. I watched him carefully. He was far too in his cups to notice."

My lord drew off his gloves. "I don't know whether you are incredibly brave or confoundedly witless!"

The girl smiled. "I am brave, my lord, for I know very well the dangers."

"Not quite so well or you would not have consented to withdraw to my personal parlor."

"On the contrary. You are less likely to ravish me in the front parlor, within hearing distance of the kitchens, than upstairs in my own chamber."

"I don't know where your chamber is."

"You would have discovered it, my lord. Your curiosity would have overcome your qualms."

Dammit! The girl was right! He would have raised heaven and earth to find her, just because . . . well . . . he supposed it was because she intrigued him. He did not like that thought. Neither did he like her cool assessment of his character. She made him feel like a mere pawn in an exceptionally well played game of chess. It was provoking, not to mention downright annoying, for he had thought to tease her a little. How delightful it would have been to pretend he had not seen through her ruse! Interesting, too, to see what liberties she might have allowed.

"The door, my lord."

"Beg pardon?"

"You have still not opened it the requisite few inches."

"The requisite few inches are necessary only in cases where the maiden in question is above reproach."

"I think you mean virtuous, my lord."

The marquis choked. "Good God, I have never met a young lady who is as bold as you are!"

"That is very possible. I was the despair of all my governesses and very near to expelled from my seminary!"

"I should think so!" There was a moment's silence. Then Lord Laxton's curiosity overcame his resolve. Indeed, the corners of his mouth quivered unexpectedly. Laughter caught at the back of his throat, but he managed to ask, in a perfectly serious tone, the obvious question.

"Why were you *not* expelled?"

"Oh, because I was quite the best student in the classics and mathematics. Miss Bramble could not afford to lose me, so we tolerated one another."

"A sufferance for your poor teacher!"

"A sufferance for *me*, you mean! She did not, regrettably, believe in sparing the rod. Or not all that much, at any rate."

"Ah." A note of sympathetic understanding in his tone? Honor thought so, though he hid the fact with a thundering frown. He also opened the door a fraction, a fact that Honor considered no minor victory.

CHAPTER 5

The marquis of Laxton surprised himself by not advancing forward and removing the teasing greatcoat, as he had lasciviously planned. Neither did he stroke the folds of the skintight breeches procured for the grand sum of half a crown as he had been aching to do for a good part of the interesting evening.

"What are you doing, my dear, behaving like a hoyden? Your reputation—if there is anything left at all—must be perfectly smirched!"

"It is, but I do not regard it."

The marquis, rather than taking advantage of this inviting circumstance, chose to scold instead.

"You should regard it! Where, for heaven's sake, is your chaperone—or, at the very least, your maid?"

"I have neither, my lord, for it is a trifle difficult to masquerade as a boy if I have to be encumbered with a chaperone!"

"No chaperone worth her salt would permit such an outrage!"

"Precisely, which is why you find me with none in tow."

"You are a most contrary female. I should just kiss you as I fully intended to do and have done with it. You are making me feel qualms, which is insupportable under the circumstances."

"Good, for that is my intention. I could see at once that

you are honorable. Honorable men are so much easier to manage!"

"You appear to speak from experience."

My lord's tone was dry, but he felt a sudden stab of hot jealousy that was really alien to his nature. How perfectly strange! What did he care if this minx of a female managed a hundred assorted gentlemen, just so long as he was not of their number? He did not seek about for an answer, for he was uncomfortably aware that he cared more than he professed. The frown grew more thunderous than ever.

Miss Honoria Finchley turned from him and smiled. It lit up her piquant face, from the tip of her chin to the rounded forehead above her brows. My lord, examining her through a felicitously placed looking glass, could just detect freckles across the bridge of her nose. They were, to his extreme annoyance, delightful.

Miss Finchley turned her head and broke the moment's pause.

"I speak not from experience so much as common sense. An honorable man is more predictable in his actions. He will not lie, or cheat, or abuse situations of trust. Therefore, of course, he is more manageable."

"How logical you are! And how chagrined I feel! All this predictability sounds a dead bore. I am not used to thinking of myself in such terms. Moreover, I begin to suspect that it is you who are insulting me, rather than I who am insulting you! Dull, manageable, predictable . . . what other miserable terms do you have to apply to my person?"

"None that are miserable, I assure you! You have been all that is kindness."

"That has never been my intention, Miss . . . ?"

". . . Finchley. Miss Honoria Finchley, though my friends call me Honor."

"Aptly named, I hope?"

"Indeed, for I find anything less despicable."

"A curious female. I did not know that honor ranked so high among your sex."

"It does not, more's the pity. But I rank it high. That, and Faith."

"You must needs have an abundance of faith to be so foolhardy!"

"It is *because* of Faith that I am."

Honor's eyes twinkled, for there was no way in the world this stranger could understand her meaning. The Faith she spoke of was not blind trust, as the marquis imagined, but a certain Miss Faith Finchley, who even now required a dowry of two thousand pounds.

The marquis raised his brows.

"I have never met a female who so oversets my understanding. Explain, if you please!"

"I shall not, for it is not entirely my explanation to give."

"Then there is, as I divined, a mystery?"

"Possibly, but we deviate from the point."

"The only point, from my perspective, is that you need a thorough . . ."

"Do not say dressing-down. I really could not tolerate such treatment at your hands!"

"I had no intention of saying such a thing, though if you had a guardian worth his salt . . ."

"I do not need a guardian, I am quite old and perfectly entitled to do precisely as I please!"

"Including ruining yourself?"

"I should like to avert that, but naturally the chances are against me. No, do not look so sympathetic—I do not care overmuch. Almack's, from all I can discover, is overrated."

"Indeed it is. The lemonade is flat and the sandwiches too stale to feed to the sparrows. There is, however, more lost to a ruined reputation than Almack's."

The girl sighed.

"I know, but really, I can see no other way. My parents died when we . . . that is, when I was young. . . ."

My lord noticed this little slip of the tongue but let it pass. She had siblings, did she? Interesting.

Honor bit her tongue. She was revealing far too much to a stranger she had just encountered in insalubrious circumstances.

If she did not have a care, she would ruin Faith as well as herself!

"My lord, I must retire. The hour is late and you know very well I am breaching all propriety by entertaining you for a moment."

"*Entertaining* is not the word I would have chosen. *Intriguing,* perhaps."

"I do not mean to intrigue. Indeed, I rather wish I had escaped your illustrious attention. I am perfectly certain I could have managed without your intervention."

"I am wounded. Why, if I might inquire, is my attention so irksome?"

How could Honor tell him it was because he overset her? She found him altogether far too charming for her comfort and if he had been the sort to take liberties, she might possibly have disgraced both herself and her name by allowing them.

He had mentioned kissing in passing. The very notion set her to trembling, though it seemed only a matter of small moment to him. She must make her exit before anything more terrible came to pass.

"My reasons are irrelevant."

"Not necessarily to me."

"They should be! After all, you have only known me all of ten minutes—an hour, if you count watching my back at play."

"It is not your back I watched."

"The cards, then—you quibble."

"It was not the cards, either, Miss Finchley."

The gleam in my lord's eyes was so apparent that even Honor, who was unused to flirtation, had to blush. She did so now, but with such indignation that my lord had almost to laugh.

"You take liberties, sir!"

"I would not be a man if I did not. But are you not curious what precisely my gaze was fixed upon?"

"Not in the least." Honor told herself that lies, with the purpose of depressing pretensions, were perfectly acceptable.

The marquis smiled. "Very properly put. I am set down. I shall not, of course, dream of telling you what you would not wish to know."

Routed! Honor ground her teeth but smiled serenely instead. She might have batted her eyelashes, only she hardly dared. The marquis seemed to understand her thoughts too well!

"Good night, Lord . . . ?"

"Laxton. Remember that name."

She would, but there was no need to mention the fact like a silly ninnyhammer. She nodded, and made as if to withdraw.

"Wait!"

The arm upon her own was firm.

Honor startled. As she turned toward him, her heart beat faster than she knew was possible. He was going to kiss her!

But no, he was not, though her lips had opened instinctively, and she had tilted her head back—oh, shamelessly. He steered her to the table and reached into his elegant pocket.

"You forget something, Miss Finchley."

"I do?"

"Your winnings. Surely you cannot have forgotten those?"

But she had! Galloping great guns, she had! And all because Lord Laxton was too damnably attractive for his own good. Or her own good.

"It is a strange thing, my lord, but I had forgotten entirely! Do you have it all?"

"Every penny!" the marquis replied cheerfully. "Count them out."

"Definitely not! " Honor looked shocked. "I may be a hoyden but I take leave to tell you, sir, that my manners are not so shabby! Count them out, indeed, when you have gone to all the trouble to procure them for me in the first place!"

"Take care not to be too trusting."

"I do, in the general way of things."

"I may take that as a compliment, then?"

"Take it as you will, for it is the truth. My thanks to you."

"Do I not receive better thanks than that?"

Honor's eyes widened. "You cannot mean . . . ?"

"Yes?" My lord folded his arms. He was curious to learn what the lady thought he meant. Honor blushed—she really wished she could rid herself of the habit. It looked particularly ridiculous, of course, in her current awkward ensemble. She swallowed her words.

"I do not know what I meant."

"It is not honorable, Honor, to tell lies!"

"Neither is it honorable to try a person's patience. We are quits, sir."

"Such an exciting night. You cannot mean to exit on so paltry a refrain? So intolerably missish?"

Honor hated to be called "missish," as the marquis suspected she would. Nevertheless, she protested, for not to do so would have been . . . fatal.

"You cannot mean to keep me here!"

"Not against your will."

"Then I must leave, for though I might enjoy your

company—and I merely say *might*—I have broken enough of society's rules for one evening."

"Surely one or two more can be of no great moment?"

"It depends, sir, on what you have in mind!"

My lord's eyes twinkled.

"Unfair! For if I speak the truth you shall surely flee, and if I lie I am caught out by my own actions."

"Precisely. It is better, then, if I leave. Tomorrow you shall have forgotten all about me."

"I shall have sleepless nights wondering if you are repeating your adventures in every tavern in town."

"Rest easy, then. I have had my fill of taverns."

"When the money is spent?"

"I shall naturally gamble for more, but in more salubrious places."

"Such as?"

Honor was silent. "I cannot think, my lord. There is only so much I can win from young ladies and their baubles. I do not like doing it, besides, for some are my friends and I feel . . . mean."

"Do you always win, then?"

"Always, unless I choose not to. Naturally, in games of pure chance I am not so lucky. I keep away from faro and *rouge-et-noir*. Games of skill are another case entirely. I am blessed—or cursed—with my father's gift of memory."

"And your father . . . ?"

"Let us change the topic."

"How nonsensical! You must know I can make inquiries."

"Inquire away! But *you* must know it is not only my good name in jeopardy, sir. I have . . . family. I cannot bandy about my parentage, good or bad, for fear of tarring others with my own dubious brush."

"You have an extraordinary knack of stopping me in my tracks. It is disconcerting. I shall desist from inquiries."

"Thank you."

"You have chosen a lonely road."

"It is a road of my choosing!"

"Quite different from what you were born to!"

"As to that, who can say it is not better? One can tire, I suppose, of balls and routs and endless amusements."

"You do not, however, look jaded." My lord did not add that he detected wistfulness in her tone, for that, surely, would have brought a crushing denial to those sweet lips.

The girl smiled. "No, for I do not deny that if you have never been to the opera, or only once watched Mistress Siddons on stage, such delights have no time to pall! But they cannot be enduring, for once one has had a surfeit of such activities, what then?"

"What then, indeed?"

The marquis had never so much wanted to call up his carriage and demand to take a girl to the opera. In general, though he reserved for himself a balcony seat, he did not put in an appearance nearly so much as his acquaintances did. More often than not, the singing was drowned by chatter and the jewels that gleamed in the candlelight were not so much from the stage as from the lights of love in the stalls below.

"One day I shall take you to the opera. The theatre, too, and the fireworks at Vauxhall. . . ."

Honor's face lit up. The marquis thought it was worth a thousand of the gaudy fireworks of which he spoke.

"Gunter's, for I have never yet sampled one of their famed sherbets!"

"You shall have two. Gunter's then, and the Egyptian Hall . . ."

The light dimmed in a moment. The marquis saw it at once and searched about for a cause. He had not long to ponder, for Honor blurted out the reason for her sudden unease.

"Are you making improper suggestions?"

"Would you like me to be?"

"Certainly not! But we cannot do any of these things without it being . . . decidedly improper."

"You cannot fleece an aging cardsharp in knee breeches, then talk about proper!"

"So! I am beyond the pale, then."

"Yes, technically speaking, you are."

The child grew cold. He could see it from the slight shiver and the goose bumps that not even the ridiculous coat, half unbuttoned, could hide. The marquis, strangely struck, amended his statement.

"I mean to say, my precious, that if you get caught by someone other than myself, you will be."

The marquis's tone was suddenly grave. Honor, realizing the truth of what he said, wanted to remove herself from the room. Not even the term of endearment comforted her, for that in itself was a liberty. Surely he would not have used such a term, on such a short acquaintance, if her reputation was beyond reproach? She thought not. How sad that she had believed, for an instant, in the marvels the marquis tempted her with. She swallowed and made an effort to make the best of her foolish adventure.

"I can rely upon your honor, then?"

"Reluctantly, for you would make a most remarkable *chère amie!*"

"I suppose I should thank you for the compliment!"

"Strictly speaking, you should *slap* me for that compliment."

"You are right, for no lady, no matter how reprehensible her manners, should suffer such an insult. If I learnt nothing at Miss Bramble's, it was that!"

Then Honor, screwing her eyes shut—for really, she could not bring herself to look at her own handiwork, besides being just the teeniest bit cowardly—drew her palm back and almost delivered a resounding slap to my lord's cheek. Almost, because she could not quite do it and withdrew her palm within an Ames-ace of my lord's handsome features. Indeed, she could feel the warmth of my lord's countenance, so close had she been.

She could almost imagine the feel of his cheek, warm and a little grizzled, for the marquis had attended to his ablutions in the morning, and by now the evening was well advanced.

Shocked that she'd been so tempted, Honor nevertheless longed to linger over that cheek, for it was alluring, overwhelmingly so, and she had detected just a hint of sandalwood as she drew closer.

Quite extraordinary, really, for her legs were like jelly and my lord was now holding her limp hand in his. She did, she hoped, make some sort of feeble attempt at struggle.

The marquis could have reassured her on this point, only she never asked. Indeed, she was so shocked at her own indelicacy that she would have sought her vinaigrette, only she'd never held with such trinkets and so had not bothered to fill the delicate box. Besides, it was in her chamber, as she should be.

"So! Almost I have been punished. Very laudable, my dear. There can now be no doubt of your maidenly virtue."

Did she imagine it, or was he laughing? No, that light in his eye had changed from a twinkle to a determined, serious gleam.

Honor made a greater attempt to extricate herself, for her hand seemed imprisoned, and his touch, though annoying, was nonetheless perfectly, delightfully unbearable. Sinful, Miss Bramble would say.

She pushed with her shoulder, but only found herself closer to my lord's chest than she would have liked. Or perhaps this was not strictly accurate. His closeness was so delightful it made her tremble. Her brain, however, protested stubbornly, so that my lord had no option but to stem her flow of utterances by finally doing what he had fully intended from the very start. He kissed her.

Did Honor kiss him back? No, but this omission did not seem to matter to the marquis, for her tremble told its own tale. Indeed, she felt so slight in his crushing grasp that he thought she might swoon. Alarmed, he released her from his improper embrace and regarded her closely.

"I am a rogue to tease you so! You have never been kissed, Miss Finchley, and I am afraid I have frightened you."

"Not frightened, sir. Outraged."

"Naturally, for as you are at pains to tell me, you are a lady born. Dare I also hope I have pleased you?"

Honor, shocked by the sensations she was fighting on all fronts, shook her head.

"No, for it does not please me at all to be . . . manhandled by a gentleman!"

"That was not manhandling, Miss Finchley—that was wooing!"

"Nonsense, for your intentions are not honorable. Nothing in my etiquette book mentions anything about wooing in that . . . that preposterous manner!"

"It is not preposterous, it is natural! It is etiquette books that are preposterous!"

Honor, who had long agreed and had always said as much, did not think now was a good time for mentioning this. She therefore strove to control her wicked pulses and offer the most childish of retorts. "It is this conversation that is preposterous, sir! I must leave you at once."

"Craven!"

"Better craven than . . . Lord Laxton, do you have to trifle with me? I am sure there are any number of chambermaids who could oblige you!"

"But they are neither so charming nor so pure!"

Honor nearly smiled. At least he realized she was an innocent!

"If you had not discovered me gambling in a taproom, you would not be making these advances."

"True, but you would then be merely another insipid debutante. Now you are entrancing."

"A novelty. You are attracted to me because I am a novelty."

"Sage. Quite possibly true."

"I am not a novelty, Lord Laxton, I am a flesh-and-blood person."

"Do you mean to stir my senses further by such an . . . obvious reminder?"

Honor blushed. "You twist whatever I say!"

"Then say nothing!"

"No, for though I go my own road, I am, like my name, honorable. I will not succumb to your kisses."

"Kisses? I have only ever offered you one. Your argument is therefore premature, wishful, or hypothetical."

Oh, infuriating man!

"Let us say hypothetical, then, for it is certainly not wishful!"

"Liar! Even by this candlelight I see you blush!"

"I blush very easily, my lord."

"Then take care not to masquerade again, for you shall surely be discovered."

"I concede the lesson. You are an apt tutor. I shall not again be so unutterably . . . stupid. And now, sir . . . my lord . . . good night."

With this dignified response, Honor managed to extricate herself from the light clasp that seemed to be burning into her skin. If she felt a trail of regretful fingers linger down the back of her spine, she did not show it. If her lips yearned for something more than the teasing, feather-light touch they had just experienced, they remained gratifyingly silent.

So commendable was Honor, indeed, that she managed to keep her back as straight as a board—something she had learned through months of miserable deportment lessons—while moving toward the half-ajar door. Finally, and one was afraid to report, regretfully, she removed herself from the dangers of that . . . irresistible front parlor.

She did not see the long, thoughtful stare that followed her after she was gone. Neither did she hear the sigh, or the chink of crystal as my lord silently poured himself a strong draft from the decanter. Two delicate cups of China tea were doomed to go cold.

As for the illustrious bag of guineas? It lay quite forgotten upon the mantel. The ormolu clock chimed the hour as the great grandfather clock boomed from the stairwell. Neither Honor, breathless in her modest chamber, nor Merit, just as breathless in his lordly suite, heard either.

CHAPTER 6

Faith peered from the fifth-floor window. It was drizzling, the promising day of earlier fading into a grayness that made her shiver slightly. She could not help wondering whatever became of the puppy and whether Lord . . . what had he said? Manning? had released it onto those hard London streets, after all.

Though she had peeked endlessly all morning from Lady Elizabeth's Egyptian-style salon, she saw no sign of any chaise and no announcement was made of any visitor save Mr. Almamaston, for Lord Islington.

Since Lord Islington was, predictably, at Tattersalls, no more than a card reached Lady Elizabeth and no further gentlemen disturbed their peace that day. Faith had faithfully described her carriage trip, then listened with wonder as Lady Elizabeth's ready tongue washed over such topics as balls and milliners and the shocking squeeze at Rundle, Bridge, and Rundle when "dear Barty" had last procured for her a fabulous pair of sapphires.

"But where is Honoria, my love? Doubtless with her godmama? Who is it, Lady Dewhurst? Or did your mama decide upon Martha Chiswick, Lady Bolstoy? I cannot recall, which is naughty of me, really, for I do remember having had such a discussion with her. Such a dear thing, your mama—you look so very much as she did."

Unwittingly, Faith's hand fluttered to her locket, where a

portrait of both her parents lay snugly encased in the simple golden pendant. She answered Lady Elizabeth's question a little absently.

"Honor's godmother was Lady Sheffield. Sadly, she died several years back of . . .'

"Consumption. Yes, I recall reading as much. Dreadful, really dreadful. She was hardly much older than myself and I am not so very great an age!"

"No, indeed, ma'am!"

Lady Elizabeth smiled fondly upon Faith.

"Dear child for saying so, though I know to my cost how much rouge poor Lila must apply before I look respectable! However, we deviate from the point. What in the world has become of Honoria?"

"She is setting up an establishment of her own, my lady."

"What? When she is a mere twelve months older than yourself? Impossible!"

Faith shook her head. "Eleven months older, my lady, and no, it is not impossible. Nothing is impossible with Honoria!"

Lady Elizabeth thought for a moment. "Is she such an antidote, then, that she has no better alternative?"

Faith laughed. "Indeed, I hope not, ma'am, for in everything but the smallest of details, the family resemblance is quite remarkable!"

"But how fortuitous! Why, you could almost pass for twins! What could be more sensational than two identical beauties presented at court? Lady Beaufort will be green with envy, for she is always trying to seize the limelight and really, marriageable sisters as . . . as . . . yes, I will say it . . . as beautiful as you are must surely be more effective than nasty pug dogs no matter *how* many jewels they might sport upon their collars!"

Faith, unused to thinking of herself as a novelty, laughed, nonetheless, at the image Lady Elizabeth portrayed.

"I'm not sure we can compete with pugs, my lady."

"Of course you can. Terrible creatures they are, with nasty, shifty eyes and a horrible manner of always snapping at one's heels. I cannot fathom how they permit them in anything but the most common of drawing rooms!"

Which brought Faith to look out the window once more, in contemplation of a more worthy specimen that might at any moment be presented to the door.

"Lady Elizabeth, I *do* hope you do not despise all dogs?"

"Certainly not—how could I when Lord Islington is mad for the hunt? We keep dozens, you know, at our country seat."

Faith nodded, unsure whether to confess her morning's lively activities to her godmama, or to take up the thread about Honoria. She did not want Lady Elizabeth to inquire too closely into her sister's activities. On the other hand, if she were to take Honor up . . . a good part of Faith's anxieties would be over.

As if reading her thoughts, Lady Elizabeth set down her china cup and bade Faith furnish her with her sister's direction. "After all, my dear, we must needs hurry if it is two court dresses we require . . ."

"But Lady Elizabeth . . ."

"No buts about it, girl, you shall be the talk of the season. Your dowry is two thousand, is it not?"

Faith nodded a little nervously, for such a huge figure when they were penniless seemed an enormous tarradiddle. On the other hand, Honor had said the sum was as good as made. Faith tried to ignore the nasty, uncomfortable feeling she had about it all. It was just the same as when she had lied to Lord Frederick that morning. Duke's daughter indeed! No wonder he had not called to pay his respects! She was shameless. Oh, she so hated deceit and now she seemed caught up by a thicket of lies.

Lady Elizabeth, noticing Faith's wan features, ascribed

it to quite a different reason entirely. "Well, dear," she said, "to be sure, two thousand is not a lot, but take heart—it is respectable enough. Perhaps I can even cajole you to marry my reprobate son Godfrey, who is a very great headache, besides being the most unfeeling son alive! Only think! He wagered a king's ransom on a cross-country race to Strathmore!" Lady Elizabeth swung a bottle of sal volatile in front of her face. It looked very fetching, the glass being extremely delicate and more decorative than functional.

"I only came to hear of it because Lord Islington came home in a thundering rage the other day after he saw it posted, ever so impudently, in the betting books. Was there ever such a trial, I ask you, for the boy has no chance at all against the famous Lord Laxton, whom the world knows to be a nonpareil in such matters. So it is more money down that ungrateful creature's bottomless pit."

Faith did not know whether to be startled or to laugh. Then she realized Lady Elizabeth must be funning, for a proposal of marriage couched in such careless terms could not possibly be serious.

"He sounds like Honoria, who gambles shamelessly!"

Lady Elizabeth raised her brows.

"Gambles? Is she very fast, this sister of yours? I see we need to take her in hand at once! There is not a moment to be lost. But doubtless you exaggerate, my dear, and it is only a coral clasp or two. I know plenty of young ladies who indulge in such naughtiness!"

Faith swallowed, for how could she tell her godmama, indulgent though she might be, that her entire dowry was funded by her sister's predilection for play? Worse, could she expect Honor, once she had tasted her freedom, to give it all up? Honor wanted a gaming establishment of her own, not a season in London at all. Or did she?

The matter occupied her mind greatly, though she still found time to apply herself to Lady Elizabeth's comfortable

chatter and to stare out of the window when she hoped she
was not being observed. If Lady Elizabeth was puzzled by
the child's strange absorption with the frosted panes, she was
too well bred to say so.

Rather, she directed Faith to explore the residence
freely, for it was blessed with several stretches of large corridors and she suspected the child might be bored with her
company.

This was not the case, for Faith was glad of Lady Elizabeth's kindness and happy to chatter away about this and
about that, the types of things that Honor often found tiresome. Still, it would be interesting to explore the residence.
Good, moreover, to be left to her own wandering—and
often errant—thoughts.

She wondered if a certain Lord Frederick subscribed to
Almack's and whether she would ever grace its portals.
The vouchers had not yet been received, but Lady Elizabeth assured her it was only a matter of time. Faith
swallowed, uncomfortably aware that Millie believed her
chances were forever blighted. She had moaned as much
to Mason, the third footman. Faith had not meant to hear,
but life was often like that. The more one virtuously tried
not to listen, the more likely one was to hear snatches of
some forbidden conversation.

Glad, therefore, of something to occupy her time, Faith
curtseyed and began an afternoon of interested explo-
ration. She began with the suits of armor at the entrance,
then moved slowly through portrait galleries, stopping
under the stairwell to admire a Sheraton urn with tapered
legs and a shield back chair that bore the artistry, had she
but known it, of the famous Hepplewhite.

Her window-gazing had all been for naught, for the carriage she had been anticipating all day rolled up to the front
door at precisely the same moment that she discovered Lady
Elizabeth's glass armonica. It was located in a small but

prettily furnished room in the south wing. A few ballads and items of sheet music were scattered upon a brocade striped sofa, but Faith's eyes were drawn not to these, but to the beautiful painted glass that dominated the room.

The armonica was a fascinating instrument and one she had not had the privilege of viewing close up, before. The glasses, several tinged with gilt about the edges, were conveniently mounted together on a spindle. This, she could see, was operated by a foot treadle. She had heard the ethereal tones played only once, at a recital of *Handel's Water Music*. It had been a special treat for the girls, for ordinarily, not being out, they were not privy to such exhibitions of chamber music. But this had been a private function, and truly a delightful evening.

Faith could not help examining the glasses, all honed to precisely the correct thickness and size to offer the desired pitch. The bowl edges were delicately painted, beautiful to behold as well as to hear. It was a natural progression to seat herself at the instrument and gingerly strike the first tentative notes.

The sounds were light and ethereal and perfectly delightful to her unpracticed ears. Unfortunately, she had no notion of how to play, so she contented herself with a random enjoyment of the resonance and a determination to learn at once, if she possibly could.

"Miss Faith, a visitor below-stairs."

"For me?" Faith tried to keep the astonishment from her tone. Then her heart gave an enormous leap as the image, not of a puppy, but of a blond-headed gentleman with laughing eyes invaded her thoughts.

The footman nodded and bowed. He would have added, if he had not been too well trained, that more than a mere visitor awaited her below-stairs. Havoc did, too.

Faith, blissfully unaware, closed the instrument and looked about for a cheval glass. She found one, for Lady

Islington was particular about such matters. Virtually every chamber of the house had a mirror and even the corridors had strategically placed glasses at various points along the way. Faith had just the presence of mind to check that her pins were all in place and the folds of her delicate sprigged muslin not too crushed before she followed Evans, the footman, sedately below-stairs.

She had not reached the fifth stair before she realized she might possibly be in trouble. The unmistakable sound of yapping was emanating from Lady Elizabeth's receiving room. Worse, a sprinkle of exclamations and a great crash of china could intermittently be heard. Faith guiltily thought of Lady Elizabeth's Wedgwood and decorative Staffordshire dogs. She ceased worrying about her absent bonnet.

She passed the footman, who had, up until this moment, preceded her, and entered the salon with a flurry of excuses upon her pretty lips. She uttered no more than two very faint murmurs before being hurtled against the apricot-striped wall.

The golden puppy, her protégé, her acquaintance made in hell (for surely it could not be in heaven), licked her frantically and seemed to think she would be better off on the floor. Miss Faith, mindful of the broken china and worse, of the cut-glass decanter still miraculously intact, disagreed. She firmly smacked the puppy on the nose and ordered it to sit. To everyone's astonishment, it did, its ears drooping sadly, but its eyes still bright with excitement.

"Look what you have done, you bad, bad dog!"

The ears drooped further yet and the yap turned suspiciously to a yelp. Faith, feeling that it was she who should be punished rather than the puppy, forced herself to meet Lady Elizabeth's amazed stare. Then, continuing on in her own chastisement—for what in the world could possibly be worse than facing Lord Frederick in such dire disgrace?—she did precisely that. She faced Lord Frederick.

"How do you do, sir? " She hoped her dry throat did not sound as parched and as cracked as it suddenly seemed. She ignored her tears and beating heart, for tears were really for cowards and her heart had been stupidly erratic all morning.

"I do hope you have not gone to too much trouble?"

She smiled sweetly as she absentmindedly patted the cause of all this current misery.

The cause, recovering quickly from his punishment, regained sufficient of his spirit to wag his tail, offer his paw, and simultaneously cause Lord Barty Islington's jewel-encrusted snuffbox to open. Too late, Faith dived to retrieve it. The contents scattered wildly, causing both herself and the miscreant to sneeze.

Lady Islington, accustomed to her son's wilder antics, now seemed to recover her wits, signaling the hovering footman to take care of the debris. He, in agony more from the pain of stifling his laughter than from any injury to his person, bowed himself hurriedly from the room. By the time he returned with a broom and the second under-housemaid, his amusement was under firm control.

"Lord Frederick . . ."

"Why did you not tell me, child, that you have been introduced?"

"But we haven't! Well, not really! We met by chance this morning, only I feared Lord Frederick would not keep to his word."

"Confound it, Miss Finchley! Not keep to my word? Of all the rotten, scandalous things to say when I have suffered an entire afternoon with this . . . this . . . odious creature. . . ."

"Oh, dear! Was he odious?"

"Yes, when I had several pressing engagements and he must needs descend from my chaise, chase a sweep round no less than four street corners, hound my cook for tidbits . . ."

"I hope he gave him none!"

"On the contrary, the wretched creature was fed an entire quail pie."

"Well, how dreadful—you will teach him bad habits!"

"I, Miss Finchley, with all due respect, shall teach him nothing! You asked me to bring him to St. Martin's Square and by the saints, I have!"

"But you can't mean to leave him here?" Lady Elizabeth, eyeing her fragile ormolu clock, fashioned by John Brooks of Bridgewater Square, gave a faint moan.

"It is Miss Finchley to whom you should address that question, Madame!"

Faith, contrite, fluttered her lashes, a trick she was in the habit of conducting at Miss Bramble's, for it seemed to soften even the hardest of hearts. (Not Miss Bramble's, for hers was granite, but certainly some of the younger teachers.)

Truth to tell, she did not do it so much for effect as from force of habit, for almost as soon as her own heart was aflutter, her eyelashes took on a life of their own.

Freddy, mesmerized, piped down and absentmindedly stroked the creature. Lady Elizabeth turned to her goddaughter.

"Faith?"

"I am so sorry, Lady Elizabeth, I did mean to tell you but . . . well, to be honest, I thought Lord Frederick had forgotten the matter entirely."

"Forgotten? When I had promised?"

"You did not come all day! I waited endlessly, half the morning, hours into the afternoon. I could not help hoping . . ."

"Hoping? You hoped?"

Freddy suddenly forgot his annoyance and the distress of several times having to change a muddied cravat and a dirtied pair of topboots. The half-chewed book of Latin proverbs was really of no account . . . no account at all, and it would be quite easy, really, to redo the interior of his smart new phaeton. Only, it would be tremendous if she smiled. Her smile, he remembered, was perfectly angelic, and those dark locks, happily bonnetless, shone with a luster he had not seen before.

No, for Lady Kit, his sister, had mousy hair that she was forever powdering and he had not paid all that much attention to the season's beauties—Merit, Lord Laxton, had done enough of that sort of thing to last them both!

Faith, transfixed, nodded shyly. Lady Elizabeth, faintly frowning, rang her bell for tea.

"And take that wretched creature to the kitchens!"

But the "wretched creature" had other ideas, so was permitted, for the sake of the china (and Lady Elizabeth's elaborate doll house, that she trembled for), to remain at Faith's feet.

"Miss Finchley, I have . . . might I suggest a solution?"

Faith looked up.

Freddy, encouraged, tried to sound masterful. He thought of his idol and greatest good friend, Lord Laxton, and deepened the tone of his voice. Lady Elizabeth thought he had run mad, but Faith clutched at her locket and seemed more entranced than ever.

"The creature—shall we give him a name?" Frederick did his very best to sound languid.

"Oh! I should have thought of that, for after all, he cannot very long answer to nothing! Do you have any ideas, sir?"

"Rascal, perhaps?"

Lady Elizabeth snorted and Faith clapped her hands in amusement. "Yes, for I fear he has been a sore trial to you. I should not have been so impetuous. I cannot think what overcame me."

"It was kindness that overcame you, Miss Finchley, and

a rare one at that, for certainly if you had not intervened I would not have done so, either."

Faith, as Freddy hoped, blushed prettily. He was beginning to rather like his newfound ability to entrance! He cleared his throat and relented enough to pat the creature, who had shifted from Faith to his own, booted foot. Rascal did not feel starved, for Freddy's foot was going slightly numb from his weight. He did, however, have the good manners to redeem himself by looking grateful. His tail wagged. Lady Islington allowed the tea to strain and Freddy nodded his head decisively.

"Rascal it is, then. Rascal is no good company for the city, ma'am, for he needs plenty of exercise and though Lady Islington's chef might not mind his incursions into the larder—"

"Indeed Cook would!" Lady Elizabeth, though a dear soul, sounded quite firm on this point.

Lord Frederick smiled. "I thought as much, ma'am, for my own chef is threatening instant resignation . . ."

"Well then?"

"Why do we not send him on to the country, where he might chase rabbits to his heart's content and bother nobody save my brother's starched-up gamekeeper, perhaps?"

"You will send him to your brother's country seat?"

"Yes, he is the Marquis of Almsford, you know, and is perfectly at home with the creatures though none, I suspect, is quite as . . . as . . . town bred as Rascal!"

"No, for they will all be bred for the hunt."

"Rascal can doubtless learn, and if he proves a failure, why, he can be cosseted by my myriad little nieces."

"That will without doubt suit him perfectly!"

Rascal seemed to think so, for he tucked his ears into his paws and seemed perfectly content to let the conversation drift over his glossy head. Faith was relieved, for though she dearly would like to have kept Rascal, she could see that Lady Elizabeth might object to such an unruly visitor, especially one with a predilection for boots. This was apparently the case, given his lord's aggrieved account of his day's adventures.

"Very well, then, if you can bear to make another journey in his illustrious company!"

"I doubt I can, Miss Finchley, but if it is to please you, then I see that I must!"

Faith blushed at such a pretty compliment and Lady Elizabeth looked speculatively at Frederick. She had only been half in jest about Faith marrying her wayward son, and was not well pleased to see Faith and Lord Frederick on such good terms. But Lord Frederick, though blessed with superior lineage, was only a third son, after all. He would need a greater dowry than two thousand pounds to sustain his current lifestyle, so doubtless Faith was merely to be an idle flirtation.

She must warn the child, for she looked far too susceptible to his handsome smiles. Handsome was, after all, as handsome does.

CHAPTER 7

If Lady Islington were only to have known it, the damage was already done. Faith would not have looked at her son Godfrey if he were the last man on earth, for she had tumbled hopelessly, decisively, in love with Frederick.

Freddy, not used to seeing devotion in the eyes of the young ladies he conversed with—most having been warned off by prudent mamas who saw no need to waste time on mere third sons, no matter how noble—now thrived under Faith's admiring glances.

What cared he if the wretched puppy tormented him all the way to Almsford, just so long as he could have the reward of her gratitude and soft, demure smiles. And however sweetly she scolded, it was sure to be different from the shrewish screams of his sisters-in-law, or the waspish nagging of Lady Kit.

He took his bow, but not before promising to call on St. Martin's Square very shortly, and ensuring that Faith, once she had made her come-out, would be attending most of the fashionable crushes of the season. He also promised faithfully to collect Rascal on the following Thursday and convey him, as soon as he was able, to Almsford.

"Only on Thursday, sir?"

Lady Elizabeth's tone was sweet, but she was now regarding her beautiful doll house, a gift from the Czar himself, with misgiving.

Freddy made her an elegant bow. "Yes, for I have a few matters to attend to before then." Freddy hoped that *matters* sounded grand and mysterious.

They did, for Faith's heart gave another leap and Lady Elizabeth, casting him a shrewd glance, held her peace. She might not have, however, had she known what was in Freddy's mind.

It was the absurd cross-country race from Tilling to Strathmore, that she had condemned only that morning. For Lord Laxton proving annoyingly unmovable, Freddy had decided to assay the ribbons himself. Worse, he had conceived the preposterous notion that if he borrowed Merit's team for the day, he would stand in a good position to win.

It did not occur to him that Merit, discovering this impudent piece of "borrowing," might prove mildly annoyed. Neither did it bother him overmuch that the opposition was none other than Godfrey Islington, Lady Elizabeth's son. The matter would not come to her ears, for after all, such wagers were not discussed in the society of the gentler sex. He smiled, therefore, quite sweetly and bade the ladies goodbye without so much as a frown to trouble his conscience.

Rascal, the only creature to suspect mischief, objected with a few sharp barks. Freddy followed the butler out of the salon and down the winding front stairs with relief. Though he could endure much—he thought—for the sake of Miss Finchley, he did not think he could stand another minute in the company of that fiendish hound.

Dawn crept softly into Honor's room. She awoke with a feeling of unease, for she was more used to her tiny attic chamber at Miss Bramble's than this strange, high-ceilinged, camphor-smelling room of the inn. Light peeked softly through the blinds and it was a moment before Honor woke with a start, remembering all that had happened the night before.

Almost without thinking, her fingers crept to her lips, for the kiss had burned deeper than she thought and seemed to still be with her, though she knew perfectly well she was being fanciful.

She accomplished her ablutions quickly and with the cold water of the night before. After some thought, she dressed in a morning gown of sunrise pink with a pretty overdress of slighter deeper tones. Around her waist she bound a sash of crisp blue satin that exactly matched the trim of her neat, slightly understated bonnet.

As a matter of fact, it was the only gown in her valise, for she had not thought to wear one, her breeches, shirts, and neck cloths taking a much higher priority than the feminine articles she had forsaken.

Her thoughts, then, had not been so much on which gown to wear as on whether to wear one at all. It would look odd, indeed, if the youth who had hired the room suddenly became an unaccompanied maiden!

On the other hand, she did not want to risk Lord Chittlingdon seeking her out in the bright light of day, when he might be more sober than the night before. If Lord Laxton (she tried to prevent her heart missing a beat as she thought of him) had penetrated her disguise, it was simply not as good as she had supposed. Stupid to risk public exposure by a mean-spirited and aging cardsharp. In her demure morning dress of feminine pink, she would hardly merit a backward glance.

Stupid, stupid reasoning, of course, for Honor underestimated her beauty and the fresh simplicity of her attire. She seemed born to stir heads, but was surprisingly unaware of the fact. Chittlingdon, if he saw her, would undoubtedly have noticed her appealing freshness though he might not have suspected the switch.

Fortunately for her, this eventuality was hardly likely to arise, for Chittlingdon had left hours and hours ago and was even now tucked up in an uncomfortable bed at number five, Upper Quilberry Street.

Honor dreamed up a series of tortuous excuses why it was she, not the youth, who was to settle the bill with the innkeeper. Some of these were perfectly nonsensical and she had to revise them several times. Her brother had been called away on urgent business and had charged her to settle the account. Why did she not have a maid? Oh, she was travel sick but would be journeying with them from the next way station . . . No . . . no! Her brother had been struck with whooping cough in the night and the doctor had sent her . . . no! Perhaps merely a regal tap on the counter with a gloved hand, eschewing curiosity with a haughty stare. Honor sighed. It was no use! She was in a pickle and her wits were wandering.

Worse, she was beginning to realize that her winnings were not safely tucked in her greatcoat pocket, as she had thought. She must, then, have left them in Lord Laxton's private parlor.

Oh, how dreadful—how perfectly, perfectly awkward! Wild horses would not drag Miss Finchley to seek him out and request it back. She put the temptation from her wayward mind at once. The marquis would doubtless find the episode perfectly amusing and point out, once again, that she was not cut out for a harsh world of independence, let alone the establishment of gaming houses!

A small voice told her that he would also think her mercenary for caring so much about the winnings. How much more noble to be able to shrug them off as of no consequence! Besides, he might construe her seeking him out as a common, trumped-up reason to pursue the acquaintance! A strumpet's trick!

Honor's cheeks burned even as she thought such a

dreadful thing. But she was wise enough to know that her thoughts were not entirely nonsensical. She knew many a young lady who would employ such a ruse and she did not want to be thought to number among them. For some unaccountable reason, Lord Laxton's good opinion was worth more than her little bag of coins.

So! Her decision, after all, was not so very taxing. There was only one viable option open to her. She would march out of her room, pay her shot (no silly excuses, what could she have been thinking of?!).

She would ignore her stomach's ravenous protests and order simply what she could afford: a hot pot of chocolate and perhaps a slice of bread and butter. She would not mope or feel a nasty bout of the dismals, for such mawkish behavior was to be despised.

She told herself this as sternly as she could and reminded herself that matters could be worse. She could be a drudge at Miss Bramble's Seminary for Young Ladies—perish the thought!

No, she would take the mail to Dartford or Malling and consider her options as she went. She needed to recoup some of her losses, for pawning her pearl droplets was unpalatable and hardly a long-term solution, though she would do it if she had to.

Setting aside Faith's two thousand pounds, there was precious little in hand for her own expenses. She had been so certain she could gamble her way to a fortune! But Lord Laxton now held not only her winnings, but her hard-earned initial stake. Oh, if only she had not been so shaken by his stupid kiss! Honor berated herself as she gathered up the last remnants of her stay: a book, a bag of oatmeal muffins, and some toothpowder. These she untidily prodded into her valise before checking the room for anything she might have left behind. There was nothing, only the remains of the wax candle she had brought with her to read by. It was down almost to the wick and she had done no reading. She tied her valise firmly shut and softly closed the door.

In the suite of rooms below-stairs, my lord had long since made his ablutions. He had spent a tiresome night admonishing himself not to meddle, but for all his good intentions had decided to anyway. Gracious, there was an innocent young woman, unchaperoned, ready to throw away her reputation and character for a few paltry bags of gold.

He should be disgusted by her mercenary intent. He would be, if he believed in it, but frankly, he did not. He had never known a light of love not to greedily check her earnings when given the chance. Honor had been given that chance and scorned it. He had never known a gamer, no matter how inebriated after a particularly triumphant hand, ever to negligently forget his winnings. Miss Finchley had not been inebriated but she had been negligent.

Interesting. She seemed driven to destroy her reputation despite both breeding (for despite the sketchiest of knowledge of her origins he could tell she had that) and beauty. She had practically told him there was someone she wished to protect from the shadow her own reputation was falling under. A brother, perhaps, or a sister. He had her name, the rest must not be so difficult.

My lord resolved for the twentieth time that morning to bide his time and ignore the nonsensical notion that he had conceived in the early hours of the morning. Doubtless, when the moon shone bright upon one's counterpane, when one heard the hoot of a barn owl and the gentle clip-clopping of distant hooves, one's brain could not be considered one's own. It seemed to leap into a contrary life and wander down paths that one would never, in one's waking moments, dare dream of traversing. Last night had been such a night, and Lord Laxton's mind had led him a merry dance, so twisted and enchanted had been its paths.

Perhaps Merit, Lord Laxton, should not have been thinking so much of gaming. If he had not been thinking of wagers he might not have conceived his outrageous scheme. But alas! There was Freddy and his stupid Tilling cross-country race challenge on his mind. There was also Honor, not stupid, gaming for her livelihood. It seemed but a mild skip to the conception of his own plan, when ordinarily it would have been a giant leap over a precipice.

A leap he would not have conceived, much less contemplated, if the moon had not hung so low, or the owl had not hooted so eerily. My lord smiled. He could think of nothing but Honor, with her direct gaze and her prosaic, artless hold upon his heart. How such a thing had come to pass he could not conceive, for his heart was as hard as ebony. He had been told as much countless times.

He believed it, for he was unmoved by tears and pleas and all the usual feminine ploys so disconcerting to his friends. He could give the cut direct with impunity and never anguish over the matter. He had wounded his man without a moment's hesitation on the occasion of a duel some four years before, and he had never, never, bent when applied to for funds from any of his nephews. They had railed at him and called him hard-hearted and as cold as granite, but the words were like rain on the feathers of a snow goose. They rolled off harmlessly and left him untouched.

He had, on the odd occasion, cause to administer a whipping. These had been to bullies and tormentors and once, after several warnings, a recurring thief. He had not, then, been softened by any excuses or whimpers. He had been deaf to belated pleas for clemency. Indeed, there were a fair few who remarked that his lash was calculatedly steady and cut deep.

This was not to say that my lord's scrupulously cold assessment of himself as hard-hearted was necessarily accurate. Dozens of people could have told Honor stories of his kindness and largesse, and pensions to the wives of soldiers wounded or killed in the war, of schoolrooms conceived and funded by himself. Dozens more could have told her of hot eel pies delivered to the alms houses and sweep boys rescued from miserable masters. All had been assured gainful employment upon his estate, or if not on his, then on Freddy's, or Peter's or the Honorable Bertram Snell's.

He could not have so hard a heart as he thought, for he never saw one of those cheery, plump little faces waving to him without feeling fiercely glad.

Now, he wondered whether to wait—for doubtless she would shyly come to collect her winnings—or to go down to breakfast. It did not occur to him in his wildest imaginings that the little fool would forsake her masquerade and assay the mail.

Oh, true, he'd admonished her a good part of the night for her pitiful disguise, but he did not think she would shed it on the main Cambridge interchange without first procuring a traveling companion or maid.

But she had! My lord, still torn between breakfast or luring Miss Finchley into his lair, stepped onto his terraced porch and stared at the bustling scene below him. The mail coach had arrived. It was clearly the mail and not a private chaise, for it was enameled in the traditional maroon and black and bore the four orders of the knighthood. The wheels were red (lest there be any further doubt, which in my lord's case there was not), and the ostlers were hustling about their business, providing oats, checking the team, hurrying the paid passengers to the right, where a door stood ready and ajar.

There were four occupants seated inside, which meant there was room only for three more passengers on the roof. Two seats were quickly occupied by a burly man clutching a basket full of live quail, and a thin, sickly woman, dressed in mourning. The mail, thus nearly full, seemed set to leave, but the coachman was drinking tea inside. This was laced with brandy, but what the eye did not see, the lips could not complain of—and my lord could hear the tinkle of a bell calling the third and final outside passenger.

Imagine his surprise when a young lady, fresh as a country meadow, set down her valise and stared dubiously at the third seat. It was obvious she was a novice in such matters, for she was looking about for a means to ascend the chaise and did not seem to realize that her baggage ought to be stowed in the foreboot under the coachman's feet.

My lord's surprise dawned, at first, from interest. Force of habit made him interested in any tender young thing who looked as pretty as a picture and in need of some male assistance.

Miss Finchley, with her pert poke bonnet and her pretty blue sash, looked utterly delectable as she waited, half shy, half bold, with her unremarkable valise and her half-boots already soaked, a little, in mud.

As she swept a tendril out of her eyes, she stared nervously at the upper window, as if aware that she was being watched. My lord permitted himself a mocking salute, then choked on his own smile. Those eyes were unmistakable! And that blush, as her hand faltered close to her lips, then dropped helplessly, foolishly, to her side, was memorable. He may have last seen her in garb very different from this delectable spectacle, but my lord knew perfectly well that the transformation had been made.

Miss Finchley, for some reason, was leaving the Greenstone Inn. Not only was she leaving it, the ungrateful wretch was departing before breakfast and without so much as an adieu to him. Worse, she had forsaken her masquerade, she had not a sign of a maid and, most incomprehensible of all, she had not one penny's worth from her handsome bag of coins.

CHAPTER 8

My lord, bereft of all speech, waved away his attendant and threw on the breeches and fine lawn silk that awaited his attention. He did not bother with his cravat (a matter that would have rendered his valet speechless had he but known), and he barely made time for his clocked stockings and his topboots.

All the while, he knew he was being ridiculous. There was no way he could get himself below-stairs and pull Miss Finchley off the mail before its horn blew a final time. There! He was right! It pealed, now, and he could hear carriage wheels crunching on the flagstones.

Of Miss Finchley and her small valise, there was no sign.

The strangest of emotions swept tumultuously across the marquis's features as he caught a glimpse of the carriage dust on the Eastern road. He would be hard-pressed to explain them, for he had not believed himself to be obsessed with the child, merely solicitous.

Now he knew he was fooling himself. He never wanted anyone so much in his life and he could—should—no longer think of her as a child. For all her youth, she was a woman born, for else his heart-strings could not be tugged at so, nor his desires—hardly in check—so passionately aroused.

But this was no time for introspection! If he made haste, he could easily catch up with the mail, for that was taken at regular stages and his own team was fresh, besides bearing a lesser burden in the form of his airy, light, and well sprung chaise.

Merit scribbled a hasty note to Lord Aston, the reason he was in so remote a place in the first place. Lord Aston was to have shown him some bloodstock and a country estate he was mindful of selling. The marquis, half inclined to increase his own stock, had agreed to look the place over.

Now such matters flew from his mind, but Merit was neither so rude nor so behindhand as to leave without an explanation. He therefore penned a polite apology, left it with the landlord (who was now the happy beneficiary of a gold sovereign), and departed in haste.

His coachman, a burly man with a deceptively light whip hand, did not fail him. He had the coach brought around in a twinkling and Merit, not having the foggiest idea of his end destination, ordered him to follow in the path of the mail coach, but to "make all haste!" Ah, joy to the ears of Master Tom, who loved nothing more than to be permitted a breakneck speed along rough-hewn roads. For once, my lord did not demur, or complain that his carriage springs were not up to Tom's lively pace. Indeed, he was tempted, when the chaise slowed around a corner, to take the driver's seat himself. But, wise at all times, he held his peace.

Miss Finchley, unaware of all these maneuverings on her behalf, wished she'd had the presence of mind to throw upon her shoulders not a simple wrap, but a warm pelisse, buttoned to the chin. It was a mixed blessing, then, that she was sandwiched on the side of the burly gentleman, for whilst his bulk occupied rather more than his fair share of the seating, his proximity provided warmth and a little respite from the chill winds. The thin lady, dressed in black, sat behind and seemed to mutter incessantly about the quail. These, though relatively well behaved, nevertheless seemed to know nothing about coach etiquette and tried several times to escape from the confines of their wicker prison.

The burly man—for so Honor thought of him—would squash the lid down upon their heads every so often and ignore the consequent chirrups of indignation. The thin lady would continue with her muttering and Honor, inclined to agree with her, could feel the onset of a headache.

Well, a headache was better than a heartache and no more than she deserved, she told herself sternly. It was impossible to make plans on an empty stomach (the bread had been thinly sliced and very meagerly buttered, which was why my lord had erroneously presumed she had not breakfasted).

Honor decided, therefore, to assist with the quail—which was very much better than trying to ignore or fight them— and thus permitted the basket to be placed upon her lap. The burly man grinned and doffed his cap at her, but the thin woman scowled behind Honor and increased her muttering, which was a shame, had not the wind caught at her words and sent them scattering, unheard.

My lord, traveling fast behind, could from time to time make out the familiar colors of the Royal Mail as it rounded bends he had not quite reached. He could not see Honor, only a dark vision in a poke bonnet that sat high upon her head, delicate ribbons modestly streaming from behind. He hoped fervently he was chasing the correct mail coach and again cursed that the ribbons were not in his hands.

At length, however, he was satisfied, for the mail slowed to cross a particularly rugged bit of terrain, where the road had been partially washed away. My lord, with a more able team and a higher sprung coach, was able to overtake. But Tom, intent upon the chase, rather overreached himself by chasing farther than he needed to.

Now my lord was in front, but not before he saw what he needed to see: a bright pink gown, a blue sash, and a bonnet made of straw. He could not see the piquant face he had hoped to glimpse, for it was obscured by a flurry of quail. Lord Laxton grinned as he tried to make contact with his coachman. It was a perfectly useless task, so he settled back into his squabs.

Tom, perfectly happy, jostled past another two carriages at breakneck speed and slowed only for the toll. My lord, in good humor, scolded him not at all.

"Faith, dear, I do think you look peaky. Perhaps the fresh air will revive you. Godfrey, do escort Faith about town today, will you?"

Lady Elizabeth, deciding that Faith was sweet-natured, adorable, and a general steadying influence, had made up her mind that she should marry her son Godfrey. She had suffered not a few pangs to see the debonair Lord Frederick Manning stroll into her salon, but the qualms had eased when she reflected that Freddy, though handsome, was not nearly so worldly wise as her Godfrey, nor so partially inclined toward the gentler sex.

Freddy was good-natured, but lacked town bronze. Young ladies from the country—especially romantic young ladies like Faith—were more inclined to view them as brothers than lovers. Godfrey, now—*Sir* Godfrey, by the grace of His Majesty—in his high starched collar and multitude of gold fobs, was far more of a prospect. Too bad none of the fobs was paid for, and a number of his tailor bills were squashed hurriedly in Lady Elizabeth's writing desk!

Lord Islington was far too harsh with him. His pin money, poor darling, was really quite insufficient for a young man of breeding. She would settle the bills quietly and think it a good investment if the elegant attire attracted Faith's sweet attention.

Oh, how she yearned for a grandchild to dandle on her knee! But her eldest son showed no signs of obliging her.

He was too caught up in politics, and besides, had long since stopped listening to her little scolds. No, it would have to be Godfrey. If she did not take pains to see him wed it would not be a nursery she visited but very likely a debtor's prison! Her son needed settling and Faith was just the one to do it.

Faith, smiling sweetly, set down her copy of Miss Austen's *Pride and Prejudice*—an interesting read—and inquired whether such a ride would not be too much trouble.

The subject of all this musing bowed in her direction, took a delicate pinch of snuff, and rather caustically agreed that it would be too much—far too much—trouble.

"Well, actually, it is, now that you mention it. I have a very pressing engagement this morning. . . ."

"Nonsense, Godfrey! If you are talking about one of your horrid cockfights, then I am very pleased you shall miss it! Come, don't be so churlish—this is Faith's first day in London!"

"Oh, but I should hate to be a trouble!" said Faith.

"You are no trouble at all! It is Godfrey who is troublesome! You shall go fetch your pelisse at once while I ring for the horses to be brought around."

"Mama, I am not riding today—I am taking my phaeton."

"Ah, all the better, for those high perches are all the rage and Faith shall look well seated beside you. I am very glad, Faith, that I had your carriage dresses so well made up before your arrival. The plum velvet will do nicely, my dear, for it will match Godfrey's carriage coat. Oh, you will look so well together!"

"Mama!"

But Lady Islington would not take no for an answer, rather regally holding up her hand and advising her son to make haste, for it would not do for the glorious weather to turn to showers and that was what always happened if one dawdled too long in pointless argumentation.

"Do be a dear, Godfrey, and go over the rest of those bills. I shall settle them for you before Papa is dunned for them. He will be very angry, you know."

Godfrey did know, and also that he was being black-mailed in the sweetest possible way. There was nothing for it; he would have to take the chit for a whirl around the park at the very least. Maybe even for one of those over-sweet marchpanes at Gildewhite's confectioners on Marylebone Street. But he would have to hurry! He withdrew the bills that had been haunting him in the few sober moments of his day and handed them over to Lady Islington.

Lady Elizabeth glanced at them, raised her brows, but said nothing to embarrass her son in front of Miss Finchley, who was looking rather flustered.

"Shall I change? I shall only be a few moments—"

"Yes, dear!"

"No!" This, from Sir Godfrey, who looked close to an apoplexy.

Lady Elizabeth frowned and tapped absently at the bills.

Foiled, Godfrey consulted his fob and the mantel clock. Both, not surprisingly, stated the same gloomy fact: he had but an hour to escort Faith about before he was due to set out for the five-mile journey to Tilling. He drew in a deep breath and summoned up some of the charm he fancied he possessed in such abundance.

"Miss Finchley, you already look utterly captivating. No new array could possibly alter the perfection of your features. Let us leave at once!"

Lady Elizabeth, satisfied that Faith's glorious looks had not somehow escaped her son's seasoned tastes, almost purred with satisfaction. She therefore did not insist on the plum velvet, but rather bade Millie, who had just entered the room with a small curtsey, to make haste at once.

"There is no place for the maid in the phaeton!"

Godfrey sounded exasperated as the minutes ticked loud in his head.

"Oh, very well then, I suppose since you are practically her cousin . . ."

Godfrey was no such thing but he saw no point in arguing. "Indeed, so there is no need for any formality between us."

"No, indeed!" Lady Elizabeth smiled warmly. "Go on then, Faith darling, have a good time."

Miss Finchley looked troubled, as did Millie, who thought it her duty to stand between Miss Faith and "a gennelman wot knows no better than to fumble a poor maid when she is not awares!" This she later muttered to the upper housemaid, for she dared not say such a thing to Master Godfrey's face.

In the meanwhile, however, she contented herself with a disrespectful glare and an imploring look at Lady Elizabeth.

She might as well not have bothered, for Lady Elizabeth seemed unaware of her concerns. Sir Godfrey, however, was in no mood for Millie, whom he uncomfortably regarded as a sly puss, if a rather well endowed one. He was just about to say as much, though in more genteel terms, when Faith annoyed him by taking up the argument.

"Perhaps I *should* take Millie. Miss Bramble always said a maid was as indispensable to a young lady as her reticule."

"Did she? How very amusing! If you would feel happier with her . . ."

"Mama, I should look a quiz in a phaeton with a maid between us!"

"Then take the barouche, Godfrey. I can never understand why your phaetons and curricles are all such a rage. They hardly keep the wet out, they are monstrously high . . ."

". . . not to mention dangerous and uncomfortable . . . yes, Mama, I have heard you say all this before! But I am determined to take my phaeton. Masters has already brought it around. Perhaps we should save this . . . eh . . . splendid excursion for a more promising day?"

"Nonsense, what day could possibly be more perfect than this?"

"Mama . . ."

"Don't scowl, Godfrey, it is not becoming. I am certain you would not wish Miss Faith to see you at such a disadvantage!"

Godfrey, who did not care how Miss Finchley saw him, grimaced and bowed. It was useless talking to his parent when she was in such a mood, so he dismissed the maid with a snap of his fingers, resigned himself to the inevitable, and hustled Faith from the room.

What he did not see, however, was the hound. Yes, the same one that had sat meekly at Faith's feet all morning. He did not see it, for he had rudely pushed past Faith and taken the stairs rather faster than he should have. He did not hear his mama's last remarks to him, nor would he have cared to. He was working out quickly that he'd still have a quarter hour to spare if he took the ribbons, trotted around the park at breakneck speed, and delivered Faith to St. Martin's Square in half the time his mama had intended.

It could be done, which would give him just sufficient time to arrive at Tilling breathless, but not undone. And oh! What joy it would be to have his pockets well lined again, when that ridiculous Freddy Manning lost to him, fair and bloody well square.

Not for the first time, Godfrey thanked the lucky star that shined upon him. It could, of course, have been Merit, Lord Laxton, himself who had taken up the impetuously made wager. If that had been the case, he would have been utterly sunk in gloom, for the odds would most certainly have been set against him. Why, even his own father had railed at him for unutterable stupidity! As it was, he had more than a long shot, for though Freddy's horses were always impeccable, they were bred for reliability rather than speed.

Sir Godfrey's horses, on the other hand, had cost him a rare packet (not to mention a less rare scolding). Lord Islington did not approve of his high steppers any more than he did of his opera dancers. Nor, indeed, did he approve of any of the other indispensable accessories to Godfrey's status as a gentleman, save the blood stock he himself had procured for the hunt.

All this aside, with a light curricle and a well matched team of bays, Godfrey felt he could accomplish anything. He was almost mellow as he handed Miss Finchley up and mildly adjusted her skirts. He made no protest when Rascal made a flying leap onto the perch and avoided injuring himself on the wheel spokes by nothing short of a minor miracle.

He said nothing, for he did not notice.

Doubtless, if his sharp eyes had alighted on this circumstance, his equally sharp tongue would have had something to say.

But Godfrey, intent on winning at all—positively all—costs, simply did not notice the hound, who had alighted on his far side. This could not be said for Rascal, whose hackles rose every time Sir Godfrey drew near.

Faith *did* notice, of course—how could she not when the wretched beast was crushing her morning dress of saffron muslin?—but she made no demur. Doubtless he would enjoy the morning sunshine and if Sir Godfrey did not quibble, why, after all, should she?

This happy state did not last long, for Godfrey set a cracking pace, despite the carriage traffic. This naturally had the effect of sending both Faith and Rascal hurtling forward, the one to grip at the high phaeton perch, the other to growl throatily as it cleaved its paws into the floorboards.

"What in hellish tarnation is that fiend doing up upon my phaeton? Miss Finchley . . ."

"Actually, it's Miss Faith. Miss Finchley, strictly speaking, refers to Miss Honoria Finchley, my sister."

Faith tried not to tremble at Sir Godfrey's tone, for it was far too fierce for her timid spirit. Also, she wanted to laugh, for Rascal looked as outraged as Godfrey and possibly more menacing. She neither trembled nor laughed, but chose, instead, to stand upon the finer points of Sir Godfrey's form of address.

Sir Godfrey looked at her as if she had run entirely mad. "What in the saints do you think I care? Miss Finchley, Miss Frencham, Miss Faith . . . it is all the same to me and if you think I am all set to marry you, think again, for I am in no way so inclined—good gracious, if that dog does not leave off yapping he will startle the horses!"

At which sage words the horses did, indeed, startle. Rascal found his way onto Faith's lap while Lady Islington's son had his hands full with the reins and his mouth full with sundry curses. Faith could not quite discern all the mutterings, but she was perfectly certain it was the type of unedifying cant she had always been warned about.

She did not complain, however, and nodded approvingly when Godfrey turned the team around in a perfect semicircle. It was a magnificent feat, considering the hedgerows he'd had to avoid and the two pedestrians he only narrowly missed.

"I am taking you back to St. Martin's Square immediately. I should never have let Mama talk me into such madness!"

"Is it such madness to take a young lady driving in the park? I had not thought so."

"It is not madness if the gentleman in question has no other pursuits planned for the morning!"

"Do you?"

"My dear young lady, I have a vital . . . a most pressing—nay, an absolutely critical—appointment!"

"A duel?" Faith's eyes lit up with shy excitement.

"No, something far more important, and, I must say, it is pretty shabby of you to try to hold me up with that dog trick of yours!"

Now Faith looked indignant. "It is not a trick, Sir Godfrey, and why you should think I harbor the remotest interest in keeping you from your business I really cannot fathom! I had no notion Rascal was going to come bounding up! It is your fault, for I remember specifically Lady Islington asking you to tether him, or to hand him over to one of the gardeners."

"Oh, now it is my fault, is it?" Sir Godfrey could hardly contain his sarcasm as he swiped at the creature that was causing him so much annoyance. Unfortunately, the reins were in the hand he chose to use and worse, Rascal took affront at such ill usage. It therefore could be no real surprise to learn that Rascal bit Sir Godfrey at the precise moment that the horses bolted off the path.

CHAPTER 9

Lord Laxton's chaise was traveling so swiftly that the first posting house flashed by before Merit could signal to Tom, or Tom could slow the cattle.

By the next posting house, however, some communication between driver and coachman had been restored and Lord Laxton was able to nimbly alight from his chaise, smile indulgently at all the attendants who had been sent scurrying out to serve him, and inquire of the innkeeper the timetable of the Cambridge chaise.

"Oh, pleasin' yer lordship, that be another hour away but if ye be lookin' fer a fresh change of 'orses, like, I'd be glad to obleege ye—them stages are troublesome things, not at all in the style wot yer lordship is accustomed to, if I may make a small remark, beggin' yer parding. . . ."

Merit, who was tempted to inquire how the man knew what style he was accustomed to, held his pace. The man was merely being helpful and did not deserve one of his cutting set-downs. So he smiled, removed his gloves, and murmured that he had no wish to travel by stage, only an interest in the time of its arrival. Since it did not arrive for an hour or more, he would make use of the inn's private parlor and possibly a *Gazette,* if there was one available.

"Only the *Tatler,* pleasin' yer lordship, but we do a good lunch with boiled pork an' pease pudding. . . ."

My lord suppressed a shudder. "A coffee will do nicely, thanks."

"Ah, a coffee . . . Jenkins, see to a coffee. But me lord—"

"Yes?" Merit took a step forward on the gravel path and watched as Tom brought the carriage around to a halt and muttered something to the ostlers.

"Me lord, might I recommend our famous beer of Cadding Hall?"

"Beer of what?" Merit sighed, realizing he was not going to be able to shake off the innkeeper without slighting his feelings terribly.

"Cadding Hall, me lord. Famous aroun' these 'ere parts. Not a smidgen less than four egg yolks—fresh, mind— sugar, water, orange juice, spices, an' wot not. Me Betty whisks the whites till they are frothy, then heats a quart o' the inn's finest, adds it to the glass, then stirs in the whites. Oh, it is a fine drink, me lord, a fine 'un!"

"It sounds so. I will have a coffee, nonetheless."

The innkeeper, fearing that this smart lord was nothing but a nipfarthing after all, brightened considerably when his fears were proven to be unfounded. My lord pressed a handsome coin into his hand and begged him, besides, to send a Cadding Hall special up to Tom the coachman.

Then Merit checked his fob, adjusted the fall of his greatcoat (elegant, but just a tad travel-weary), and awaited the arrival of both his coffee and a young maiden clad all over in a pretty shade of pastel pink.

Precisely on the hour, the marquis folded his newspaper and strode across the cobbled courtyard to watch the arrival of the mail. Not his customary activity, but one which he now found particularly intriguing, especially as the slender woman he'd glimpsed earlier was swatting the quail with her parasol (a hideous ochre color) and the birds, in turn, were flapping their wings in the basket and squawking enough to deafen the coachman, were he not making an even louder commotion on his old tin horn.

Only the burly man seated next to the lady in pink seemed at all complacent, for he was eating a sandwich and taking great care not to get crumbs upon "me lady, bless 'er purty little heart's" morning gown. He did not succeed, naturally, but Honoria was thinking less about her gown than the possibility of escape from this unexpected Bedlam. Possibly, she could rest a while at this stop and pick up the following mail to Malling. But what then?

It, too, may be overcrowded, Honor realized. Worse, it may not have seats at all and then she would be stranded at this unknown watering hole, perhaps for days. Besides, she was not sure if her ticket would allow for such adjustments. Her thoughts came to a more decisive turn when the parasol hit not the errant quail this time, but her bonnet. It drooped gently at the corner. Honor could feel it, though she had no glass to assess the damage precisely. She was not vain, but she felt the loss of her only bonnet keenly.

"Madame, I must implore you . . ."

The woman said, "Sorry, ducks, it was that there chicken I was after—just you wait till I lay me hands on 'im—I'll wring 'is sorry li'l neck, I will . . ."

The burly man intervened in the type of deep, aggrieved tone that forced Honor to sit back on her seat and close her eyes with a sigh. If only she could as easily close her ears! The man leaned over her knees to speak, unsettling the basket.

"Chicken? Chicken?" he boomed at the female passenger in outraged accents. "It is not a chicken, you madwoman, but a quail! And if you've damaged so much as one feather on my little birdie's body . . . 'im wot'll fetch a fair fortune at Knightley market, you see if 'e don't. . . ."

The small matter of Honor's bonnet, which was adorned with no feathers at all, seemed to recede into insignificance.

The woman resumed her mournful diatribe and the gentleman took the basket back onto his lap. His sandwich, it seemed, was finished, save for what lay in the folds of Honoria's pleasant morning gown.

The inside passengers disembarked; then the burly man stood up, basket and all, and doffed his hat affably in Honor's direction. His tone, with her, was really quite pleasant.

"Fifteen minutes, love, then we'll all be back atop. Best stretch them legs of yourn an' take a wee draught."

Honor nodded. He was being kind, in his own way, only she felt forlorn and a little silly as she clambered down the carriage steps and looked about her.

The other woman, who at first had elected to stay on her perch, now changed her mind. Honor moved out of the way to avoid having her pinched, black boots wreak further destruction upon the remains of her bonnet.

"Miss Finchley!"

No, it could not be true! Honor's heart missed a beat. She was hearing words on the wind; she was daydreaming; she was being a stupid, silly, green girl, wishing for the moon. The thin woman grumbled and pushed past her. Honor hardly noticed.

"Miss Finchley!" There it was again, and more insistent this time. She turned her head, hardly daring to believe her ears.

But how silly! He was there, in the flesh, grinning triumphantly and holding out one elegant, gloved hand. He drew her apart from the carriage where a few desultory eyes were suddenly fixed upon her.

"My lord! How could you . . . this is impossible! How in the world . . ."

"No time for questions, Miss Finchley. I am officially taking you under my wing."

Honor took a deep breath. The tears stung suddenly and

her throat seemed a little drier than it should, given the chocolate she had drunk earlier. Half of her wanted to throw herself onto his immaculate shirtsleeves and beg to be held there forever more. The other half wanted to slap his face or, at the very least, present him with a haughtily turned back. Neither half had its way, for she stood stock still and silent.

Lord Laxton drew closer, so the space between them was much too close and she could almost feel his breath upon her cheeks. Honor looked up, but did not increase the distance between them, though she felt herself trembling.

"My lord, you know very well that though I might be irregular, and my exploits, to date, are not perfectly proper . . ."

Merit raised his brow. It was a very distinguished brow, one that seemed to harbor the weight of authority and justice. Honor felt rather like a child caught out in an untruth. She corrected herself crossly.

"Oh, very well, then! My exploits have been positively wicked! I might yearn for all sorts of unsuitable things but I am not that sort of . . . why, that sort of . . . of . . . flibbertigibbert! Gracious, if you have chased over half the countryside merely to be told *that* again, I am very sorry for you indeed!"

"Miss Finchley, you wound me! What a disreputable character you must think I possess and how interesting a portrait you paint of yourself! Yearning for unsuitable things? My poor girl, I must investigate that statement thoroughly!"

Honoria flushed angrily.

"You deliberately misunderstand me, sir. I speak plainly only so you may know my resolve."

"Very laudable, but I am afraid it only confirms me in *my* resolve."

"You are . . . you are . . . gracious, you are a villain."

Honor's tone was incredulous, for though she regarded the marquis as highhanded and dangerous and altogether too tempting for her comfort, she had at no time viewed him as villainous.

The marquis looked affronted, though his eyes twinkled.

"And I took such pains, last night, to convince you otherwise!"

"Is that why you kissed me?"

"Not precisely. But we shall discuss my rationale later, in a more amenable environment."

"This is amenable enough, my lord, for the mail leaves in precisely five minutes!"

"Ten, and you are wrong, for I have bribed the innkeeper to hold up the mail."

"Impossible—one sets one's watch by the mail. It will leave on time."

"Would you wager your bag of coins on it?"

"Sir, I no longer have that bag to wager."

Honor spoke rather stiffly, for she'd had a tiresome morning and it was really the outside of enough to have to deal with a basket of quail, a carte blanche (mortifying but horribly tempting), and a squashed bonnet all at once. Worse, she was aware that her ravishing morning dress was creased and her overdress of soft satin was adorned with the quail man's crumbs.

"If I give you that bag?"

"You are bribing me? Take care, my lord, for I really *will* slap you! My patience runs dangerously thin."

"Honor, Honor, where is your humor? It is as crushed as your pretty dress! Come, let us not cross swords, my pretty, but rather partake of a handsome repast and determine what is to be done!"

"I know what is to be done! I am to resume my journey and you are to forget all about me at once!"

"But that is impossible, for once having feasted on your brave loveliness, I cannot again partake of a humbler morsel."

In spite of herself, Honor grinned.

"Very fine, my lord, all this talk of food, but you are mixing your metaphors horribly."

"There you go! Would I offer carte blanche to a shrew who has the temerity to correct my wit? I think not, my love!"

"Then stop addressing me as your love!"

They walked a few paces away from the carriage, for the horses were being changed and they were in the way of the ostlers.

There was a silence between them as they stepped upon the stony path. It was cold beneath Honor's slippered feet, but she hardly seemed to notice as she tried to think furiously, while all the while my lord destroyed any chance of that by supporting her with his arm.

How in the world could she be expected to think while the warmth of his person crept into her very being and she longed—oh, she longed—to be caught up in an embrace that would be as unseemly as it was flighty? Why did she keep thinking of my lord's kiss when she should be thinking sensible thoughts like how she could recover her stake and who she would find to challenge her at her journey's end?

My lord murmured something, but his voice was low and hopelessly intimate, so Honor could make no sense of his meaning at all.

"Oh, do be quiet, I cannot think!"

My lord smiled as his eyes raked her face. It was adorably expressive and he might just have succumbed to his own temptations had he not known that so much was at stake. He turned her back, toward the Royal Mail.

"Very well, I shall hold my impetuous tongue, Miss Finchley, if only you would have the goodness to remove your valise from the foreboot of that wretched chaise!"

"I am tempted, my lord, but you must see that I cannot!

Even if, as you say, your motives are pure, who would believe it?"

But this interesting conversation was not permitted to
continue, for the burly man pushed past the scrawny
woman and endeavored to seat himself at the back, quail
and all. The woman, outraged, clambered aboard and muttered a great deal about "gennelman wot knows nought of
respect fer grievin' widows, like" and the coachman, on
the dot of the quarter hour, arrived smartly to take up his
position.

Two of the inner passengers had alighted, but a clergyman
had taken up one of the places and the fourth gentleman,
rather slowly ascending the stairs, looked about him for the
remaining passenger.

The coachman, a pungent ring of the innkeeper's finest
about his lips, looked about for Honor. My lord cursed.

"Foiled! That driver drank the beer even faster than Tom
coachman! It was a long draught meant, I assure you, for
a further ten minutes at the least."

"If I had had my guineas I would have won."

"So right. A chastening thought." My lord grinned.

The coachman, spying Honor, motioned her to climb
aloft at once.

"I must go. You must see I must. The coachman is
waiting."

"I, too, am waiting. I have a plan, really I do."

"More than just making me one of your . . . your . . .
flirts?"

My lord grinned. Too handsome, really. The tin horn
blew in Honor's ears.

"So circumspect, my little Honor! Do not allow delicacy
to hold you back, I pray you! Though I indeed intend to
make you one of my flirts, I do not intend to induct you
as a light-skirt, if that is what you mean."

Miss Finchley could not have blushed pinker if she

tried. She hardly heard the annoyance of the coachman as she walked firmly toward the mail coach, the marquis's steps precisely matching her own.

The driver, already settled upon his perch, had no wish to descend again from the steps.

"Hop aboard, missie. There is space inside and you can settle the difference at the next stage."

Honor hardly heard him, for the marquis had taken her hand and was staring into her eyes and she really thought he might very well kiss her despite the interested eyes of all about her. Not the least of these was the scrawny widow, who was now tut-tutting about sharing her seat with "ladies wot know no better than wot they ought to." She was silenced by the burly man with the quail, who had a tender heart and could see that more was at stake than the timely departure of the chaise.

On the stroke of the last gong from the grandfather clock at the inn's open door, the coachman, losing patience, signaled to his team and the carriage began its slow rumble east.

Honor had to step back to avoid having her hems caught in the wheel.

"Wait!"

But it was useless trying to stop the Royal Mail, and her heart was in such a flutter she was not perfectly certain she wanted to.

"My valise is stowed in there!"

"A paltry thing. I can buy you another."

"My lord, I am not accepting one penny farthing from you!"

"Very well, then allow me to return your property so that you can once again resume your . . . interesting independence."

Honor hesitated, but she realized at once how foolish—

not to mention churlish—it would be to refuse what was, after all, rightfully her own.

"Thank you, my lord, I am very much obliged."

The marquis smiled. He withdrew the little pouch from his greatcoat and pressed it into Honor's hand. His smile lit up the corners of his eyes and removed every light crease his handsome countenance might have possessed.

Of a sudden, Honoria felt lighthearted, too, for though she was behaving scandalously, and felt dangerously close to an unsuitable attachment, wasn't this what she had always dreamed of? Doing something deliciously unacceptable, flinging niceties to the wind, behaving wickedly—oh, wickedly! Miss Bramble would turn in her grave. Spin, more like. Honor laughed, her eyes bright.

The marquis, more relieved than he could fathom, laughed, too.

"Shall we walk? That gown, though decidedly prettier than last night's attire, is rather thin. You look cold."

Cold? Honor wasn't cold, she was warm. As my lord penetrated her with a glance of sheer satisfaction, she felt warmer yet. Also, a little alarmed.

"Sir . . . my lord . . ."

"Merit will do."

"Merit? Good gracious, what a pair we are . . . Honor and Merit!"

"Indeed, a graceless pair for such presumptuous virtues! I always wanted to throttle my mama for saddling me with a name like Merit!"

"I, too, for such stalwart names as Honor and F . . ." Honoria stopped herself before she mentioned Faith's name. It was one thing to positively throw herself beyond the pale, another to draw Faith into her misdeeds.

Merit noticed the pause and wondered. He had suspected there was a sibling; now he drew the conclusion yet again. He wondered what the name might be? Whimsical, he was sure. Fortune? Felicity? Fidelity? Felix, maybe, if it was a male. His ruminations ran on for so long—it is remarkable how many virtuous names there are beginning with "F"— that they rounded the dovecote and the pig pen at the back of the inn. He still was no closer to an answer—and some of his imaginings now bordered on the absurd—but it mattered not. When he needed to know Miss Finchley's immediate ancestry, he would doubtless do so. For now, Miss Honor could have her secrets.

"You were saying?"

The marquis prompted Honor, for her words had trailed off and the silence between them was growing so large that either he would have to, indeed, kiss her, or else restore the flow. Since the back of a pig pen did not seem an auspicious place to commence any amorous activities, he chose the latter, signaling to Tom as they rounded the bend and found themselves back on the front path. They had now done virtually a complete circle of the inn and were standing close to the carriage house and the ostlers. Tom grinned and had the infernal cheek to wave. Honor noticed him at once.

"Do you know that man?"

"He is Tom, my coachman, and an impudent young jackanapes!"

"He must be very swift to have overtaken the mail as he did. I thought you were still sleeping when I left."

"When you sneaked off, you mean. A churlish thing to do, Honoria! Churlish and cowardly! We have unfinished business, you and I."

"And what might that be? I have said I will not be your light of love."

"Thank goodness! A very bad light of love you would make, my sweet!"

This caustic sentence, designed to reassure, did nothing of the sort. Honor began wondering precisely why she would not make a good light of love and realized, with some sorrow, that she was not pretty enough, not beguiling enough, and altogether too ignorant to be anything of the kind.

So if my lord was truly not interested in such a thing, what in heaven's name did he want with her? A momentary dalliance? But surely he would not have chased the mail for that? And without a cravat, too!

My lord, conscious of her eyes, and endeavoring to read every thought in her pretty little head, now realized the self-same deficit.

"Gracious, I am practically undressed! My valet, when he sees me, will have spasms. I wonder if I can procure a neckerchief from the innkeeper before we leave?"

Honor, now examining my lord more closely, blushed, for his lack of neck dress revealed some tantalizingly soft curls peeking from his sheer lawn shirt. Not even the high shirt points (though not *too* high like some of the dandies she had seen) hid the shadows of those silken strands. For an instant, she longed to stare.

As a matter of fact, she *did* stare, until my lord said rather roughly that she had better wait with Tom while he attended to the matter at once.

By this time, however, Tom had the chaise skillfully brought around. The team, well watered and magnificently matched, stood perfectly still as if awaiting further instructions.

"I cannot . . ."

"My girl, you can and you will."

My lord, thinking he had borne more than enough for one morning, especially since Honor's lips were so disobliging as to exactly complement the soft pink of her gown and were damnably inviting besides, brooked no argument.

"If I have to abduct you, I shall, for I would rather have you safe in my carriage than chasing after some villain's chaise which I shall undoubtedly have to do if you persist in your nonsense."

"What nonsense?"

"The nonsense of shedding a perfectly good masquerade and rushing into the countryside, pretty as a picture, with no maid, no valise, and no suitable guardian to fight off the dragons!"

Honor, pink with pleasure that he had called her pretty, was nevertheless not lost to the fact that he was also being imperious, bossy, and precisely the sort of thing she hated—fusty.

"If I choose to have no maid, that is my business. As for dragons . . . I know little of such things but I should say, my lord, that you are more likely to be one than not!"

"Bravo, my discerning little maiden, but I am a very pleasant dragon, you will find, while others are rather less so! Now hop into my lair, will you, and I shall be back just as soon as I am respectable."

Honoria, aware that Tom was watching her with a very cheeky grin, clutched at her bag of coins and realized that if she had thought her reputation was in shreds last night, she was now practically an abandoned woman!

To willingly enter a man's chaise, unchaperoned and clutching a fistful of coins, was really about the worst and wickedest one could get. She colored. No, it could be wickeder yet, and the worst of it was that truthfully she would not mind.

Impossible! Oh, the whole matter was simply impossible! Why could she not simply turn her nose in the air and walk away?

There was no stopping her, for she had her winnings—she could catch a stage to London. She could employ a maid, for heaven's sake! She could establish her gaming house with a bit of calculated good fortune. Oh, why was she standing like a fool, staring at this devastatingly attractive man as if she had not a thought in her head?

The devastatingly handsome man, searching her face, abandoned his idea of the cravat. Something told him he had better not leave this little minx to her own devices for one second. He stepped forward, pulled open the carriage door, and gestured more firmly than Honor would have liked for her to enter.

CHAPTER 10

It was almost precisely at this moment that Rascal, tooling about in the park, decided to bite Sir Godfrey. He would naturally have liked to sink his teeth in deeply and perhaps take a little flesh as a memento, but this, sadly, was not to be. He only managed a quick nip through Sir Godfrey's riding gloves and these, disappointingly, were thick.

But oh, what a fuss! The ensuing havoc was one greatly distressing to Faith, whose kindly heart felt great pangs of anxiety both for Godfrey (who deserved to be bitten), and for Rascal, who would undoubtedly be punished. But Rascal was looking as docile as a lamb and the horses, once again feeling their master in control, slowed to a sedate trot, albeit off the beaten path.

"We could have overturned the curricle!"

"Indeed, but we didn't, thanks to your skill with the reins." (Miss Bramble was always saying there was no harm at all in flattery.)

"Are you badly hurt?" Faith, who trembled a little at the sight of blood, nevertheless determined to see the worst of the injury. Sir Godfrey, scowling, removed his glove and examined the evidence. Rascal, relatively satisfied with his morning's endeavor, reclined across the floor boards and contented himself with sniffing at Miss Faith's delicate half-boots of pastel kid.

"It is naught but a scratch, but that animal is a menace!"

"Indeed, it is a very good thing Lord Frederick is collecting him on Thursday. He will do much better, I think, out in the country."

"I assume you refer to Lord Frederick Manning?"

"Of course! I have not been about society long enough to be acquainted with more than one Frederick at a time! Are you sure that that hand does not need binding?"

"It pains like the very devil, but I shall survive, miss, which is more than I can say for that hound when I get my hands on it!"

Rascal did not seem to know his fate was under discussion, for he opened an eye sweetly and proffered a golden paw to Faith. Her gown was now horribly dirtied, and she was feeling somewhat queasy, both from the carriage ride and from the sight of the nasty scratch across Godfrey's palm.

"You wicked dog! It will be nothing but bones and the smallest bowl of milk for you tonight."

Rascal blinked.

"Bones and a bowl of milk . . . are you mad? The wretched creature must be abandoned now, I tell you. Once a stray, always a stray. He should be glad I have no time to administer a decent whipping!"

"Oh! You are a monster, Sir Godfrey! You cannot mean such a thing!"

"But I do! Indeed, I really do!"

"You are perfectly heartless! If you set Rascal down, you shall set me down, too!"

"Gladly, Madame, for I tell you, it was never my idea to take you up in the first instance!"

"Oh!" Faith's slender bosom heaved in indignation. She had never felt so ill-used or so annoyed in all of her life.

"Very well, then, I shall alight and walk home with Rascal, who I am sure is every bit as good a companion as you are, sir!"

She gathered up her skirts in a great flurry of outrage, though the tears were not very far from her bright eyes. They had driven far in a very short time, for Godfrey had been determined to do the whole thing at a really impossible speed. She had never been in these parts before and knew perfectly well that the walk back to St. Martin's Square could take hours, even if she did not get horribly lost, which was a real possibility.

Oh, how tiresome to her dignity that the curricle's perch was too high for her to alight without assistance! She did try, but truly she was far too short to avoid the very high wheel spokes. She thought of jumping, but if she twisted her ankle it would not only be undignified, it would be a disaster.

"Sir Godfrey, I require assistance." How the words stuck in her throat! But she uttered them, for she had no other choice and to remain in his loathsome company a moment longer was now out of the question.

But Godfrey, eyeing both her and the dog and his expensive silver fob rather speculatively, caustically muttered that he was now completely out of time and she would just have to come along, too.

Yes, sad to say, Sir Godfrey had, in but a few moments' reverie, formulated a cunning scheme. He would foist both the girl and the mutt on Lord Frederick, who could be relied upon at all times to be chivalrous. Too bad gallantry did not equate to wisdom!

With two horrible hindrances and a far heavier curricle than he had bargained for, Freddy Manning could kiss his stake good-bye. That meant that he, wise Sir Godfrey, could dine out at Boodles for a sennight. More, his bed could be warm with opera dancers, for he knew a very good shop on Milsom Street that sold precisely the trinkets they liked. Paste, of course. Godfrey would not waste his blunt on jewels when trickery was so very much more affordable. He whipped the horses up and was suddenly deaf to all Miss Faith's protests.

Miss Faith, clutching on to Rascal and praying she would not be sick, closed her eyes and dreamed, not of revenge, but of deliverance.

Honor, leagues and leagues away from her sister, was dreaming not of deliverance, but of the strength of will to decline the very thing she yearned for. My lord was offering her an open door to the type of heady, wicked life she had always wanted.

So, foolish girl! What must she do? She must needs, at this late hour, decide that she was not so very wicked after all! She, who tossed her head at niceties, now balked at climbing into a carriage, unattended, with the man of her very dreams.

No, not quite, for no one could have the imagination to dream of such a one as Merit. The forbidding turn of his head, the slight frown in his eyes, the alarming allure of his arms, only inches from her own—these were not things one dreamed of.

One dreamed of summer days and golden locks. . . . Honor knew what she dreamed of, but the picture, always so bright in her mind, now seemed blurry, and everything seemed to jumble only to reappear, infuriatingly, as Merit, the precise man she wished to expunge.

Why did those eyes light so beguilingly, as if he read her very thoughts? He could not do so; no one could! Honor dared not seek his face, for she knew she would see that familiar mocking glance that dared her to deny him. He held the door open firmly and Tom, up on the perch, muttered something almost inaudible, but not inaudible enough. My lord threatened to whip him, at which he only grinned but refrained from further comment.

"Come, my dear, we must leave." The words were a strange combination of patience, tenderness, and inner tension.

Honor, too horrified at her own inclination, shook her head dumbly. There were tears in her eyes, but she could not make that simple step to what she believed was complete and utter wantonness. She was just formulating some acceptable method of explanation when she felt strong arms encircling her waist. She gasped, for the sensation was as unexpected as it was supremely heavenly. He was going to kiss her good-bye—she was sure of it!

Tremulously, she closed her eyes, for surely it would be a cruel and grudging world that denied her this one last solace?

But no kiss ensued.

Instead, she felt those muscled arms, rather stronger about her now, and more purposeful. Then his scent, almost intoxicating, and the brush of his cheek against her own. Then her slippered feet were no longer on the floor, but flying. Flying? No, indeed, she was simply being carried, then thrown rather roughly against the squabs.

Before she could protest, she felt his warmth against her—far, far too close—and the slam of the carriage door and the crunch of wheels upon the path and the jerk of the frame and the squeak of the springs and the jolt of the horses—a hundred, it seemed, but she was simply being fanciful.

"What are you doing?"

The question was only a whisper, for as she saw the inn receding in the window, she knew perfectly well what he was doing.

My lord removed the errant thigh that brushed so tantalizingly against her own, increased the space between them to a more acceptable level, and grinned.

It was not a fiendish grin, as one might expect in such

circumstances, but rueful and charming and pleasantly self-satisfied.

"My dear Honoria, it should be perfectly obvious. I am abducting you in full daylight. I am a man of my word and I think I promised you as much a moment ago.

"Come, don't look so outraged! No one at this godforsaken outpost can possibly know who you are, so your precious reputation is quite intact."

"My reputation, as you know, is not so precious as my virtue."

My lord smiled. "Now here we have a little conundrum, for though I would dearly love to strip you—tenderly, I might add—of all that virtue, I am reminded at all times of my name."

Honor raised her brows. Almost, she smiled. My lord could see the dimple just peeking through her cheeks. "Merit?"

"Indeed. Being 'Merit' is a tedious business, but I endeavor at all times to live up to the expectations of my parents, bless their souls."

"But you don't succeed if abducting maidens against their will is your usual type of enterprise."

"I cavil at the 'against their will' aspect of your speech, my dear."

Honor blushed, for he had scored a palpable hit and he knew it.

"I said I was not coming!"

"Wicked lips, for your eyes said otherwise."

"One does not speak with one's eyes, my lord."

"You do."

Oh, confound the man! He always had an answer, for he seemed to read her like the pages of a book. How mortifying to be so hopelessly transparent! But truthfulness forbade her to contradict him. She *had* wanted to take that leap. She had wanted her adventure and now it was staring her in the face in the precise manner Miss Bramble had taken such care to warn her about.

"I shall have to guard my expressions, sir!"

"Can you not call me Merit? And how hideous to have to assume deception when honesty is so much plainer and purer."

"Honesty can sometimes be troublesome."

"Indeed, but is it not more troublesome to be caught out in a lie?"

"I may not be caught out."

The marquis smiled. "You will, my dear Honor, I am confident of that!"

"Smug, you mean!"

"Precisely! Now answer my question. Why must you hide those fleeting expressions that dance across your face? They are your most delightful asset."

"They are nothing but a nuisance and might prove embarrassing."

"It is not embarrassing to feel attraction, Honor."

"You speak plainly, my lord!"

"Why should I not? Your mind is as acute as my own. Why in the world should I play society's games?"

"Because they are safer?"

"You do not want to be safe, Honor! I know it, I feel it, I have seen it in the way you slay a man at cards and I have felt it—"

Honor, breathless but somehow transfixed, interrupted as he hesitated.

"How have you felt it, my lord?"

"I have felt it in the way you kiss, Honor."

"Oh!" Honor was outraged. "You lie, sir! I have never kissed you!"

"Once?"

"Nonsense! You kissed me. *I*, if you recall, was not so lost to sanity as to kiss you back!"

"Oh, but what a struggle you had! What a joyful, desperate, aching struggle! You wanted to. You wanted to so desperately it was like a living pain. Tell me that I am wrong, even slightly wrong, and I will have the chaise turned about at once."

Honor shifted on her seat. She could hear the steady trot of the horses and Tom's soft whistle upon the perch outside. She could hear the roll of the wheels upon the beaten track and her heart, hopelessly unsteady, in her chest. It seemed as if she had stopped breathing and the world had contracted to nothing but the intimate space of the chaise and its series of crimson velvet squabs.

She knew that there would be no turning back, but she lacked the courage to admit it. Every turn of the carriage wheel now spoke volumes, for she had only to lie and be released from this strange journey.

The longer she was silent, the more the triumph glowed from my lord's eyes.

Honor was bound by her name. She could not, in honor, deny the truth of my lord's claim. She had trembled in his arms and trembled at his kiss, so exquisite was it, and freely, fiercely given. She would not deny such a wondrous thing, for to do so would be to deny her very self. They would not deal in lies, she and Merit, though she knew not what they would deal in, or how.

"Say it, Honor."

"Say what, my lord?"

"Say that you tremble for me and dream of me and most wickedly, sinfully, woefully, want to be in this chaise with me!"

Honor took a deep breath, mindful of the hand that now clasped her own, and of her extraordinary response to this man, whom she had known but a few hours in a very long— or so it seemed to her—lifetime.

"Lord help me, Merit, but I long for you, I *did* dream of you, and I most *willfully* wish to be in this chaise with you!"

"You changed *woefully* to *willfully*. Do not think I am not honored by such a generous truth. Even the best of women would have lied, or prevaricated a little."

"You said no games."

"I said none of society's games. Between us, my dear, there will be games aplenty."

"Where are you taking me?"

"Don't you mean, where is my lair?"

"Yes, if you must speak so plainly!"

My lord's eyes gleamed. "I am taking you, my dear Honor, to the lair of the greatest dragon of all."

"Not you?"

"Tcha! Next to Great Aunt Petunia, I am hardly a dragon at all! The veriest puff of smoke, I am afraid!"

"You are taking me to your Great Aunt Petunia?"

"But naturally! Having established that we are both far too attracted to one another for our own good, having established that you do not want to take up my kindly made offer of . . . what did you call it? A carte blanche? Did I actually *make* that offer, by the by, or was it a whisper, again, of wishful thinking . . . no! Do not pull your hands away—it is really very churlish!"

"*You* are churlish, sir, to tease me so!"

"Indeed, but I do so love to tease, for it brings all the color to your cheeks and a martial gleam to your pretty brown eyes! Are those freckles natural, or do you pencil them in?"

"I pencil them in, sir, diligently every morning!"

"Ah, I thought so. Such perfection in profusion could not possibly be nature only."

"You are laughing at me!"

"Only because you are so perfectly delicious to tease."

"You are changing the subject by making my heart rage

painfully in my insides. It is not a comfortable feeling. Stop doing it!"

"My dear girl, a hammering heart is the very least I can offer you, with all due respect. If you value your current chastity, be satisfied. I should not hold myself in any esteem at all if your nerves were not tingling at my every utterance."

"It is all very uncomfortable, especially when you lower your voice in that . . . that . . . oh, that horribly deliberate manner!"

Merit laughed.

"One day I will be far more horribly deliberate than that! Oh, don't glare at me so! I shall foil my own lascivious plans for you by delivering you to the gorgon's door."

"Great Aunt Petunia?"

"The very one! She is a positive fire-breather but beneath her flames is a heart of the purest gold. You will like her, I think."

"Why have you gone to all this trouble to abduct me if you are going to simply deliver me to a querulous chaperone?"

"Did I say querulous? Great Aunt Petunia is not querulous, she is bossy."

"Bossy, then."

"I have my reasons, my sweet."

"And I have mine! I am not traveling all the way to goodness-knows-where simply to have my plans overset! You don't understand—I need to win a fortune!"

"Need?"

"Yes, for I am penniless, save for this paltry bag of coins and two thousand pounds which I have already promised away. . . ."

"That is a lot of money to promise away! I fear you are going to prove expensive!"

"It is not for me, it is . . . oh! You are a beast! You are teasing again!"

"Indeed, though I confess a certain curiosity as to the beneficiary of your largesse."

"A secret, sir."

"From me?"

"Yes, for it is not my secret to share."

"Very well, then. I shall allow you your secrets, for something tells me they are more noble than most."

"Not noble, my lord, but I daresay honorable."

"Honor, honor! I should have guessed. Your parents had a lot to answer for, blessing you with such a name! Listen, my little miss, understand that I am a very wealthy man. One does not become a gentleman of my rank without possessing a certain degree of largesse."

"Nonsense! Look at Prinny himself! His Highness is the highest-ranking man in the kingdom, save the king, and he has squandered almost *all* of his fortune!"

"*Touché!* I begin to learn the more sobering aspects of conversing with a bluestocking."

"I am not a bluestocking!"

"No, very likely a pink garter, if I dared to look, which I shall not, for fear of your wrath!"

Honor grinned. "White, laced in pearl, if you must know. And don't think you can cozen me into changing the subject!"

"I don't think to cozen you at all, though to kiss might not go amiss."

"Leave such appalling rhymes for the poets, my dear sir, or you will have me in convulsions!"

The marquis's eyes twinkled.

"Very well, for when I have you in convulsions I'd be mortified if it was merely over an ode."

Honor smiled, but her heart still beat faster than she could have wished, and though my lord took no more liberties, she did not feel the degree of relief she ought to have done.

CHAPTER 11

The road to Tilling was hilly and well worn. Sir God-frey's horses seemed to slow, but he pushed them on, refusing to forfeit the wager simply on time. He knew very well that if he didn't show, Frederick would have the right to claim a victory. It was a pity to tire the horses before the race, but it had to be done. After—well . . . after, he would have so much of an advantage that he was bound to win.

"Can you stop that dog yapping?"

"No, I cannot! You are driving far too fast and will cause an accident!"

This, from a furious Faith whose usual timidity had flown to the winds with every unnecessary crack of Sir Godfrey's riding whip.

"You are a worse encumbrance than I thought! I can't think why Mama has taken you up—you are hardly even pretty, though I daresay if you could cover those freck-les . . ."

Instinctively, Faith's hand flew to her nose. She prided herself on being able to hide those wretched imperfections with a conserve of red roses and apple, mixed in equal quantities in a fold of thin cambric. This she diligently applied to the bridge of her delightful nose every morning—to the hilarious chortles of Honor, who was not mindful of such things—and consequently was perfectly certain that the blemishes had dimmed beyond notice.

To have them brought to her attention, thus! She was mortified. Sir Godfrey was wholly lacking in any finer sentiment. Her annoyance made her inclined to pat Rascal, who was now enjoying himself thoroughly by barking at every turn of the curricle wheel.

Lord Frederick Manning, in the meanwhile, blissfully unaware of the fate that was imminently to befall him, was tooling along Billing Hill toward Tilling with hardly a flutter in his heart. He was perfectly certain he had the measure of that sorry-faced prig Sir Godfrey Islington, so he bent his mind to the more interesting prospect of the delightful Miss Faith Finchley, and precisely how many days it was before he was likely to see her again.

Oh, but she was adorable! Freddy, suffering from all the pangs of first love (for he had more or less loathed females as a species up until this time) now eminently made up for his fault by imbuing Miss Faith with all the qualities of a goddess.

Such ravishing looks, such perfection of face. That long, lustrous hair—he fancied he'd glimpsed a curl or two—all perfectly natural, no artifice at all . . . and her nature! Lovelier yet, with her limpet tones and sweet, sweet smile. Now *she* was a lady of whom his mama would approve! And Merit, too, though he had such a damnable eye for the ladies Freddy shouldn't wonder if Merit might steal her himself.

But no! Those were unworthy thoughts. Merit was the best—the very best—of friends. If Freddy made his intentions perfectly plain to the marquis from the outset, Faith would undoubtedly be safe.

Oh, it was a marvelous day! What was more, he had the pleasure of driving Dapple and Dimple, two of Lord Laxton's finest grays. He *did* feel a slight guilty qualm, but he was doing this for Merit, who would appear to be shocked refusing a wager from a knucklehead like Islington.

Lord Manning, trotting along at a cracking pace, fancied he made a splendid substitute. He stopped feeling guilty. Merit would thank him in the end, for being so diligent a friend. It was not as if he *needed* his grays or his Four Horse Club Chaise—they were sitting in his stables doing nothing at all. Besides, it did not do to feel wracked with guilt before a race. Freddy determined, therefore, not to dwell on the matter any further.

It was a simply perfect day, not a whisper of a wind or showers. If he did not beat Godfrey he would eat his socks. Besides, in a cross-country he was at an advantage: he knew the downs like the back of his hand. Sir Peter Worthington and the Honorable Bertram Snell had been over the grounds the night before and had marked the route out for him perfectly clearly on a hastily drawn map. They had implored him not to do it, of course, but they were the greatest of good friends and had capitulated readily in the face of his stubbornness.

They had decided to map out the course, saying, with a sigh, that if Merit's team was going to be so abused they had best ensure that Freddy did not stumble down a ravine or into the series of nasty thorn bushes that lay over the first copse. Freddy, armed with this knowledge, smiled. He knew all the shortcuts and he was counting on the fact that Sir Godfrey did not.

Sir Godfrey, thinking precisely the same thing, arrived at Tilling, out of breath and short of temper, within a minute of the appointed time. Frederick and his supporters had already arrived and hailed him cheerfully from the canary-colored chaise embossed with the insignia of the Four Horse Club.

"I say, you can't drive that thing! It does not belong to you!"

Godfrey pulled his horses to a stop with very little caution. He would have jumped down, but he did not trust Faith with his reins and was mindful how necessary his team was for success. So he drew up alongside Lord Frederick and scowled.

Frederick only grinned. "Good day to you, sir, too! I am perfectly entitled, you know, to ride this rig, for I am acting for Lord Laxton."

Godfrey wanted to argue the point, but Lord Manning had just noticed the two occupants of his chaise. His companions did, too, for they raised their brows and muttered how irregular it was to bring a female to such an event.

"Miss . . . Miss Finchley! I did not expect to see you here today! Are you supporting Sir Godfrey?"

Lord Manning looked green, all of a sudden, and his companions regarded him with alarm. Faith, shocked—but a little thrilled—to see Lord Frederick, of all people, shook her head vehemently.

"No, the horrid man has used me dreadfully and I would rather tame a rattlesnake than spend one moment longer in his company! If this is a race, I am hoping for you, Lord Frederick, be certain of that!"

There was a cheer from the Honorable Bertram and the freckle-faced Sir Peter, who now looked at Faith with renewed interest.

"You must be Miss Faith Finchley, of whom Freddy has ceaselessly filled our ears!"

"Hush!" Frederick nudged his companions and Faith blushed in shy delight.

Rascal, who had, up until now, been rather well behaved, decided it was the perfect moment to resume his attempt at taking a morsel from Sir Godfrey—this time his derriere.

Unfortunately for him, Sir Godfrey was not so well

muscled as he would like to be. As a consequence, he regularly engaged his tailor to add a layer or two of padding to breeches that would otherwise be sadly lackluster.

Rascal's teeth therefore did not hurt, but he managed to profoundly annoy Sir Godfrey. This was especially so as the cheeky Rascal refused to let go of the hand-stitched kid that had cost his victim a small fortune at Rigby's.

"What? Oh, confound that hound! I will shoot it!"

Lord Frederick (who disliked Sir Godfrey) and Sir Peter (who loathed him) could not help but laugh, but Faith looked distressed and begged to be helped from the chaise, for she could not stand a moment longer with the unfeeling fiend.

Three pairs of hands rushed to help her as Merit's grays calmly chewed the grass and seemed not at all put out that they were driverless.

With some unusual modicum of tact, Bertram stepped back so that it was Frederick who had the honors. Faith's fingers melted in his own and he half forgot the hound in his pleasure at her presence.

But Rascal was not one to be forgotten! Recognizing Frederick as his savior, he let go of Godfrey's breeches (nasty things) and bounded over Faith's gown and down onto the heath without a moment's hesitation. Then, wagging his tail and dancing circles around Freddy while at the same time eyeing the Honorable Bertram and Sir Peter with interest, he permitted Miss Finchley to be helped down from Islington's high perch.

"Where is your maid, Miss Finchley?"

"Oh, it is a long story, but I have none!"

"But this is highly irregular! I must get you home at once!"

"But you would forfeit the race!" This, in an outraged chorus from Bertram and Sir Peter.

Sir Godfrey, high above them, nodded in ill-concealed pleasure. "Too bad, old chap. But she *would* come!"

"You . . . you . . . you scoundrel! I did *not* ask to come and you very well know it! This is all just a ploy to make his lordship lose!"

Sir Godfrey, holding the ribbons lightly with one hand, made a small, self-satisfied bow.

"Indeed, but note how very cunning I am, how skillfully contrived my ingenuity . . . how . . ."

"Oh, stop it! You appall me!" cried Faith.

"My dear girl, I might return the compliment, but do I do it? No, I do not, for I am filled with all the finer feelings."

"Finer feelings? You wouldn't recognize finer feelings if they stared you in the face! How your delightful mama can have produced such a sorry disappointment I am at a loss to fathom."

Faith, once started, found herself perfectly able to ignore Sir Godfrey's darkening features. She drew another breath and expounded further on her theme.

"What is more, I should tell you that the only certain thing you are filled with is not finer feelings but a load of unadulterated codswallop!"

Faith, usually so timid, was now goaded beyond all endurance. For such an utterance she would normally have earned herself a stern lecture on the comportment of young ladies. This would naturally have been followed by a punishment of sorts, but she was no longer at Miss Bramble's select seminary, and she was no longer in the company of stodgy old spinsters with a mind to etiquette.

As a matter of fact, she had fallen in with a very shimble-shamble lot, and consequently earned herself a hearty hail of approval for her unmaidenly protest.

Both the Honorable Bertram and Sir Peter Snell found themselves liking her exceedingly, and Freddy, of course . . . Well, Freddy was positively besotted in love.

He grinned meltingly so that Faith, already overexcited,

thought her heart could not possibly tolerate much further strain.

"Bravo! An excellent speech, Miss Finchley!" Frederick smiled. "But come! I must take you home at once, before it grows too much later."

"No!" Again, the dismayed chorus from his supporters. Freddy frowned meaningfully, but Faith took up their cause.

"Your lordship, I do not want you to forfeit the race! Can I not remain behind with your friends?"

"Certainly not! A ramshackle pair, Miss Faith, and so I tell you!" But there was laughter in Freddy' s eyes and maybe a little regret, too.

"Slander, Miss Finchley! It is Freddy who is the most ramshackle amongst us. *W*e are the very souls of discretion and propriety! However . . ."

Sir Bertram hushed Faith as she tried to interrupt.

". . . However, much as we would like to keep you with us—an excellent piece of good thinking—we can't. Frederick has the only carriage. We, you see, arrived by horse."

Indeed, Faith did see, for two handsome stallions dallied by the creek. She had not noticed them in the excitement of the preceding moments. Her face fell, for she could not bear Frederick to lose because of her or Sir Godfrey to win for the same reason. He was perfectly shameless, utilizing such a trick!

"Lord Frederick, let me race with you! That way if you lose, it won't be for want of trying!"

"I cannot, Miss Faith! I would be a monster to put you through such a thing! It is cross-country, you know, not at all the type of journey a young lady is accustomed to."

"I am not so frail as I look, and I assure you I could tolerate anything to have you win the race! A few jolts and rattles and even bruises, sir, are perfectly acceptable to me! Oh, do please take me up! I can be your eyes and your

ears! Whilst you are concentrating on the cattle, I can concentrate on the terrain, for it looks full of pitfalls!"

Frederick, tempted (for he loathed the idea of handing
over a vast fortune to a swine like Godfrey), looked to his
friends.

To Faith's surprise, they did not immediately reject the
matter out of hand, but discussed it as if it had a great deal
of merit. Faith cast pleading eyes in their direction and if
she had remembered to bat her eyelashes (as she had been
taught) she would have done so.

Instead, she waited rather impatiently and stroked Rascal, who might otherwise have been inclined to investigate
the countryside.

Finally—it seemed like an age, but it was actually only
a few whispered moments—Lord Frederick addressed her
once more.

"Very well, Miss Finchley, I shall take you up. The
hound, too, I suppose, though he is more likely to lose me
the race than not."

"Nonsense! Rascal shall be perfectly well behaved now
he is in the company of a gentleman."

This last, said with emphasis as she looked haughtily up
at Sir Godfrey. He did not feel obligated to reply to this
jab, but just muttered shortly that he hoped Lord Manning
had the ready, for he would make Tilling by tea time at the
very latest.

To which Freddy replied cheerfully that he should never
count chickens before they hatched, and might the best
man win.

Then the Honorable Bertram took out his pocket watch
and went over the rules a final time. This did not take very
long, for there were no rules to speak of, really, save to
keep off the carriage roads and arrive, one way or another,
at the handsome marble colonnades signifying Strathmore

Park. He and Sir Peter would take the more conventional route and thus doubtless precede them all on horseback.

After muttering something about fairness and having no supporters of his own, Godfrey nodded shortly to the gentleman. He wanted the race to begin before his advantage was lost.

Sooner or later someone would realize that though they might reach Tilling by tea, they would definitely not reach St. Martin's Square by dark.

One of the gentlemen might offer to escort Faith home by sidesaddle rather than risk the disaster of compromising her. He did not know where Sir Bertram resided—it might be quite close to fetch another horse, chaise, or saddle. He did not want this to happen, as the extra weight in Freddy's chaise was a desirable advantage. So he set aside his scruples and nodded in a grudging kind of way.

Bertram and Peter lost no time in helping Faith and Rascal up, in warning Freddy several times—several times—about Merit's excellent paintwork, and the cost of the axles and the exorbitant replacement value of the handmade springs and leather straps used in the undercarriage until Freddy looked green and Faith had to point out severely that they were not helping their case at all.

So after that, there was less chatter and more attention as the two competing carriages lined up carefully on the grass.

Sir Peter drew a makeshift start line across a bit of mud where there was a natural break in the long, thick grass. He used the branch of a willow tree to do this but it snapped halfway across in his hand, so the carriages had to draw closer to make use of the smaller length of line already drawn. Faith could have sworn that Sir Godfrey deliberately splattered the canary-colored chaise with mud as he pulled up, wheel for wheel beside them, but Freddy, generous spirited, said it might have happened to anyone.

Still, Merit's chaise did not look nearly so cheerful, or so smart, as it usually did. Worse, that nasty knot of guilt was in danger of resurfacing horribly. Almost, Freddy wished he had not had the inspired notion of taking Merit's chaise. His own would have done perfectly well. Well, if not *perfectly* well, then tolerably so.

But the starter's flag was raised (a carriage blanket, striped in tartan) and there was no time for such regrets. Freddy kept his eyes on the blanket and when it dropped, he expertly maneuvered Merit's chaise across the patch of mud and over the dip in the long grass.

It was a good start, but not so good as Sir Godfrey's, who did not have a tail-wagging hound to deal with, nor the extra weight of a passenger, nor the bother of wondering whether she might fall out with the speed.

Freddy need not have wondered, for Faith proved herself quite remarkably by holding on for all she was worth, digging her heels into the floorboards, and soothing Rascal with outrageous promises of chef's best cutlets if he behaved. Remarkably, the hound seemed to believe her, or else her tone was pleasantly satisfactory, for despite the interesting speed and the excitement of the wind in his fur and the scent of fox and goose and squirrel in his nose, he comported himself very well. As a matter of fact, probably for one of the first times in his canine life, his conduct was exemplary.

CHAPTER 12

Exemplary conduct was almost the undoing of Merit, Lord Laxton. He found he did not like exemplary conduct at all, for it forced one to grind one's teeth into one's tongue or to avert one's gaze from certain interesting curves.

These curves had a delicious habit of presenting themselves at unforeseen moments, like when Miss Finchley wished for air and moved halfway across his muscled form to adjust the crested lead glass window on his far side.

"It doesn't open." Shocking, really, that her closeness should affect him so. "I can stop the chaise if you need air."

"No, no, I am perfectly all right." How regrettable that she had to withdraw her hand and sink back into the far corner as if wishing that the very velvet would swallow her up. Especially regrettable as the shadows danced across her demure bodice and suggested all manner of possibilities. Possibilities my lord should really not be thinking of. Well, not if he wanted to merit his name Merit, which to be honest was not something that was uppermost in his mind at present.

Ah, she was resting a little more forward now, straight-backed but flushed. He could no longer see those delightful curves. Yes, she was perfectly modest, only pink with consciousness and her eyes sparkled brightly. If he knew no better, he would think those eyes a positive invitation to lasciviousness, for they fluttered up at him artlessly, then remained captive in his gaze when he held them.

Oh, she looked away just as soon as she was able, but her breathing was rather shallow and my lord could swear he saw a pulse moving swiftly at the base of her bare, unadorned neck.

Yes, he was right—far too swift was that revealing pulse! Her hands—yes, her hands, too, spoke of consciousness, for they trembled through her lavender gloves with their soft, pink rosette trim. She should hold them still, for those involuntary movements were almost his undoing. The desire to seize them roughly was really becoming overwhelming.

How pretty that sash looked, tied beneath her waist, but oh, how artful! It accentuated her curves while the soft color of her overdress matched the flush in her cheeks. She placed her hands in her lap which drew his attention (as if it needed any more drawing) to the slim waist and that wretched, wretched, high-stitched bodice again! The laces were not tight, but they might just as well have been, for where only subtle shadows drew the shape of Honor's girlish proportions, my lord's imagination was quite capable of rather accurately penciling in the rest.

He should not stare so, but really, she was like a siren, and her sheer lack of artifice captivated him more than he was inclined.

She was talking—he could see the sweet softness of her lips and the earnest consideration of her features as she answered some of his questions. Between them, there was something more than her words; they both knew that, but he bound himself to listen.

". . . That is why, my dear sir, I rather think I should have been born a boy!"

"Do you really believe that?"

"Yes, for boys have so much freedom, so much courage . . . so much possibility set before them! I have never felt so alive as those precious moments when I transformed myself into a youth!"

Honor forgot that those were the very moments she had stumbled across Merit. She forgot that even in boy clothes she had not felt very much like a youth—not, that was, since she had dispatched Lord Chittlingdon so comprehensively at cards.

"Do you not think it is possible to feel so alive as a lady?"

"No."

"You lie!"

"How can you know what I feel?"

"I can guess, Honor. I guess that the untruth you have just uttered was not a lie yesterday. Today, however, it is a nonsense. Today you feel more alive as a lady than ever you have ever felt before as a girl, or as a green youth in masquerade. Tell me it is so, or I shall stop this chaise at once!"

Honor was silent.

"Well?"

"You force me to reflect on matters I would rather retreat from, sir!"

"Yes."

"You do not apologize?"

"No."

"Then you are arrogant and unchivalrous!"

"I am arrogant but not unchivalrous, Honor! If I were unchivalrous, I would have used the knowledge I have!"

"What knowledge?"

"The knowledge that you are aware of my every movement as much as I am of yours. That you long to throw yourself against me just as much—every bit as much—as I wish to crush you to my side. That you are safe from your desires only because I wish you to be. Is that not true, my most honorable of all Honors?"

"What if it is?"

"No shame, if that is what you are implying! And you

will note, my lovely girl, that contrary to both my desire and yours, I have not touched so much as a curly strand of your silken locks."

"Not so curly."

"Here and there a curl. I have examined you closely!"

"Then you are blind, for my hair is cropped too short for curls. To what end have you examined me, pray?"

"Ah, a good question, my lady! Do you not think we can appease ourselves, a little, by one kiss?"

"Tom coachman is nearby!"

"What of it, oh modest one? Tom is driving and has seen far worse!"

"Oh!"

My lord sustained a rather nasty kick to his shins. He laughed.

"Vixen! But you cannot be surprised when you are constantly throwing my *chère amies* and light-skirts in my face!"

"I am not surprised." Honor's tone was stiff. She played with what was left of her bonnet, which did nothing at all to enhance that ill-fated creation.

"I do believe you are jealous!"

Honor was nearly goaded into a denial, for my lord looked far too pleased with himself for his own good. Yes, a delighted gleam had entered those compelling eyes and a smile hovered fleetingly—almost triumphantly—at the corners of that entrancing mouth.

Honor found it perfectly maddening for she was certain he was laughing at her.

Undoubtedly, he felt some of the heat of feeling she was currently lashed with, but it could not be of the same strength for him to be so calm and annoying about it.

She did not deny the jealousy charge, for it was true. How humiliating for that to be so, but she burned with anger for those unknown young ladies who had savored of my lord's lips and strong arms and heaven only knew what else, when she simply longed to be in their place. But that was not strictly true. She did not want to be merely one of many such. To be one of many was worse than being nothing at all!

Which was why she now sat up primly, folded her arms, and swore she would no longer succumb to any of the little lures he was so skillfully casting in her way.

But Merit, wary of these signs, would have none of it. He sought to sway her by leaning forward and whispering softly in her ear. His very breath tickled and if he came any closer she could swear his tongue would have touched her lobe. Honor sat as still as she could to prevent such a catastrophic event.

"Don't fight it, Honor!"

"I must."

"Why must you, dammit?"

"Because I like you too much, Merit."

"The strangest reason I have ever heard."

But the danger had passed, for my lord sat back more appropriately on his squab and regarded Honor quizzically.

"You really are an extraordinary woman!"

"Why?"

"For one thing, you know nothing about lures—gracious, you have passed by every opportunity—yet you are the most alluring female I have ever encountered. You are a passing marvelous male, too, with the most—positively the most—extraordinary memory I have come across to date. Were you born with the talent or was it acquired?"

Honor, relieved to have the subject on firmer ground, laughed.

"Both, I think. I had an unusual aptitude even when I was in swaddling clothes! But I was taught by my father never to take it for granted, always to stretch the limits a little further, and so I do."

"Cards only?"

"Heavens, no! Cards are merely expedient! If I can think of a better way to use my memory and earn myself a fortune I shall be positively delighted!'

"You don't enjoy playing?"

"I do when I am well matched, but mostly I feel like a rather mean cardsharp. I am not cheating, but my memory makes matches unequal. There is little joy in the winning."

"I see that. But you hold to your guns."

"Mostly, for I am perfectly serious about needing to make a fortune. I have no scruples against the likes of the baron, but with my friends it goes against the grain."

"Which is why you are venturing so far afield?"

"Yes. That, and I can't afford to develop a reputation for winning. I have a far better chance of being accepted for a hand if I look green."

"Rather than the seasoned veteran that you are?"

"Yes! Do not laugh, Merit, I have been playing since I was three!"

"I am duly cautioned. You don't mind me saying it seems an odd sort of life?"

"Certainly not! It is!"

"I am a rich man, Honor . . ."

"So you keep telling me, my lord, but to what end I cannot fathom."

"So blessedly bright and so wickedly dim! A creature of many moods. Honor, Honor, I am rich. You need not waste your talents on fleecing poor individuals taking the waters at Bath, or Tumbridge Wells, wherever is your next destination of choice. I shall settle some large amount upon you and we shall live happily ever after."

"We?"

"Indeed, for you shall never have to shuffle a card again and I, in turn, shall have obliged my father."

"In what way?"

"By spending my inheritance wisely."

"Squandering your inheritance foolishly, you mean! I am not even tempted to take your money, Merit. It would be unconscionable to do so."

"Not even if you marry me?"

There was a sharp intake of breath. Then Honor expelled it slowly. "To marry for money is certainly in vogue, but I have always been an unfashionable creature."

"Contrary, too! You shall change your mind."

"I am very stubborn and perfectly decided. I have always been determined not to hang on a man's coat sleeves and I won't begin now!"

The tremble in Honor's voice was poignant, so my lord hid his immediate disappointment—or was it relief? He was not perfectly certain, for he seldom acted impulsively and proposing marriage when no such thought had entered his head a few hours before seemed more irrational than was his custom.

Honor, for her own part, could not help but feel a certain exultation. It was mingled with regret, of course, but no less sweet for the mixture. Oh, she was more than an opera dancer to him! A gentleman did not propose marriage to every lady he happened to tumble in a swift-moving chaise.

As a matter of fact, he hadn't tumbled her at all, but she refused to dwell on such technicalities. He had wanted to— he still did; that was the marvelous, astonishing point, for she knew perfectly well that while she was not an antidote, her beauty would pale considerably next to any of the season's diamonds. Amelia de Santa Carlo, for example, had cheeks that were almost translucent in their paleness. Lady Camilla Hargreaves was positively renowned for her excellent cleavage, a fact that could not be lost on the marquis, who attended the highest *ton* parties and was bound to come face-to-face with her perfections on a fairly regular basis. No, she would not think about this, for it caused her to feel desolate and hopeless rather than deliciously comforted.

Her thoughts flitted across her face in such a mixture of delight and agony and pride and yes, a tiny smidgen of temptation, that my lord forgot his own ruminations to study her. So expressive, yet so headstrong! She had a will of steel and he liked her the better for it. Not many could withstand the temptation he knew he offered her.

She did, and though he felt a little chagrined, slightly ill-used—and disappointed, dammit!—he did not admire her any the less. Far from it. She had rescued him from himself and smiled whilst doing so. Yes, there was no denying he had gone further than he'd thought to this morning. He had been saved from parson's mousetrap by the bait itself. Now there was a rare thought!

But my lord, strangely, was not amused. He was rather out of sorts, in fact. Like a churlish schoolboy denied of a treat. He had not thought of marriage as a treat! He always considered it an unenviable duty that would one day befall him.

But oh, if it could befall with such a one as Honor! How different that would be! He nearly pressed her in his sudden wisdom, but true to his nature followed constraint instead. He sat back in his seat.

"Wine? Wine is usually considered *de rigueur* in awkward moments like these." My lord touched an interesting device on the paneled wall and revealed a tray, a decanter, and several crystal glasses fitting snugly into a chestnut box wrought for the purpose. He drew out two glasses and flicked them lightly with an ungloved finger. The notes were pure. His smile, though, was slightly wry as he raised his brow inquiringly at Honor. She longed to close the space between them and tell him to forget all about the wine. Instead, she nodded civilly and watched closely as he poured.

The canary-colored chaise was so fast and well sprung that Frederick forgot all his qualms about driving Merit's rig without explicit permission. He felt so cheerful, in fact, that even when they hit some particularly rocky terrain, he refrained from uttering any unsuitable oaths and grinned instead.

"All right?"

"Perfectly." This was not strictly true, for Faith was rather more frail than her sister and unused to anything but sedate journeys. She would not, she told herself sternly, disgrace herself by being sick, but rather turn her mind to doing something helpful.

"Lord Manning, there is a rabbit hole to your right."

"Bless me, so there is!" said Freddy, missing the danger by a hair's breadth as he swerved expertly to the left.

It was all Faith could do to cling on to the side of the perch, but the excitement was perfectly satisfactory to Rascal, who was cheering the winning team on with a series of barks that would have frightened any squirrel from its tree. Fortunately, no such calamity occurred, for there was nothing Rascal liked more than a good squirrel to chase.

"You drive to an inch." Faith's eyes glowed as she shyly regarded her hero on the right. Frederick, more used to being told he drove like a jackass, was roused to further heights by such obvious admiration. By the time a quarter of an hour had passed, he was positively puffed up in his own conceit and enjoying the ride tremendously.

Godfrey Islington was, rather like the hare in the tortoise race, taking his time at a more leisurely pace. It was not that he had suddenly lost his heart for the race—far from it!—it was just that he was counting on Lord Frederick's natural exuberance to do his work for him.

Sooner or later, Lord Manning would fly over a precipice at breakneck speed and the race would be his.

To be fair to Godfrey, he did not, in all his happy ruminations, anticipate Lord Manning's actual demise. He merely reflected on the opening of his purse strings as a mangled chaise lay sadly shattered at the side of a deep ravine.

The little curricle, however, had splendid spirit. It positively soared over streams and grass and little ridges of grazing terrace. Though its wheels were covered in mud and Faith's teeth chattered from the force, there was no stopping or hesitating or even slowing. Once, Freddy drew out a hastily scrawled map, but his hands never left the reins and though the team might have slowed a fraction, Faith hardly noticed at all.

"What are you doing?"

"I am checking my landmarks. It would not do, you see, to get lost."

"No, indeed!" Faith wondered at this sublime understatement and smiled. She was in such good, safe hands. Lord Manning was so capable, so completely master of all he surveyed. . . .

"My lord!"

Freddy was tempted to drop those reins at the pretty smile that caused her face to illuminate.

"Yes?"

"Do you not think . . . that it is . . . you do know there is a field of barley growing in the next valley? I saw it at the last bend we took."

"Why, of course I do, my sweet, it is on the map! But it is not barley, I think, but wheat. We are going to cut across the unharvested fields. I'll wager anything Sir Godfrey will not have thought of traversing private land! He will go around and we will have found ourselves a desirable route."

"Will the farmer not mind?"

Faith looked doubtful, for the horses were already negotiating the descent into the valley and apart from feeling rather precarious on her perch, it seemed a very long way down indeed.

Frederick laughed. "He will mind, all right, until he is

compensated for his loss. I daresay he will be pleased not to have to harvest the path that we take."

"Right through the wheat?"

"Right through it." Freddy was firm. He eyed Faith worriedly for a second, wondering whether she was going to suddenly turn into a watering pot, or worse, a shrieking little termagant. He was familiar with these qualities in females—which was why he generally loathed them and left the womanizing to Merit—but thus far had seen no such ominous sign in Faith's countenance.

He was not disappointed, for Faith was nodding composedly, just as if he had been suggesting a mild picnic excursion through Highbury Park.

"Are you ready? As soon as we are at the bottom I am going to set the team to a canter."

"Carriage horses?"

"Lord Laxton's team—this is his, you know—are chosen for their speed and spirit."

"Then we will win!"

"Oh, I think there is a passing good chance of it!"

Freddy laughed as Faith's countenance brightened adorably. At the same moment, her bonnet sailed away as the breeze became stronger and her pins were no longer up to the task of anchoring the confection down. It sailed away in a delightful stream of rose ribbons and soft, rather downy peacock feathers.

"Oh, stop! That was absolutely my best bonnet!"

"I shall stop, but Sir Godfrey is hard on our heels."

"Is he? Then go on, only I have no idea what Lady Elizabeth will say when I return home in such a ragtag fashion."

"You are the very height of elegance! You should always wear your hair down, tumbling over your shoulders. Very beautiful. Now get ready—this is going to be quite a race!"

They had reached the bottom of the sloping valley with a decided bump, the high wheels jolting too quickly for any

springs Merit had taken pains to install. Faith gasped and
Rascal nearly fell from the sides, but otherwise all went
precisely as Freddy planned. The horses, responsive to his
touch, broke into a very pretty canter and the brave, canary-
colored chaise—now rather muddy—responded perfectly.
Through the barley they chased, carving a path through the
long, golden strands of wheat and coughing as great gusts
of corn brushed against their faces.

"Wait!" But Faith's words were lost on the wind as
Freddy drove onward, exhilarated, certain beyond all certainty that the race was his. But as with all such certainties,
disaster was imminent. It was Faith who first heard the
creak of the carriage axle, cracking, then splitting, then
shattering, sadly, beyond all repair. Behind them to the east
was a long, unbroken track of crushed grain. In front of
them, to the west, was a forest. A golden forest, it was of
long, unharvested wheat. The horses fretted. Rascal whimpered on his perch. Frederick, eyeing the ruins, very much
wanted to do the same.

CHAPTER 13

Great Aunt Petunia's house was not so much a house as a castle. It was so huge that even Honor, used to such things (or more so than Faith), gasped. It seemed to have a hundred minarets and turrets. There were old battlements and carelessly creeping ivy—everything, in short, that one might expect to see in a Gothic castle.

Merit watched Honor's unspoken amazement in satisfaction.

"Hideous, is it not? I told you this is the dragon's lair!"

"I still do not see why you have brought me here."

"You will."

"Cryptic, if not forthcoming!"

"Your punishment for refusing to entertain the notion of marrying me. You could have spared me a great deal of trouble, but no, you are as stubborn as you are beautiful, so Aunt Petunia it shall have to be. No, don't look at me like that! You, my dear, are going to be respectable whether you like it or not! Aunt Petunia might be a dragon, but no one can deny she is a formidable chaperone!"

Since my lord's tone was relatively cheerful, Honor felt more curiosity than qualm, but she *did* panic for a moment when she realized she had arrived without so much as a change of gown, never mind a valise. She murmured her concern to Lord Laxton.

"I doubt Great Aunt will notice. She never emerges from her chamber."

"You are a beast, Merit. You are trying to give me the shivers!"

"My dear girl, if I wanted to give you shivers I have far better methods than introducing you to my maiden aunt!"

Honor smiled, for really she believed it was true.

The carriage wheels were crunching on the flagstones. In a moment it would have drawn to a halt and Honor was surprised that she felt such a sudden and strong sense of loss.

"My lord, is this the start or the end of our great adventure?"

Merit grinned. "Shall we say both? A suitable beginning and a suitable ending would be to take you in my arms, stop up your pretty little mouth—for it has been far too full of spurious objections—and give you the kiss I have been promising you this age."

"You've promised nothing."

"Then why is your heart beating like one of Trevithick's new steam locomotives? Come, you are a very bad liar. You know perfectly well my intentions have been clear from the outset. But I shall tease you a little longer, my sweet, and allow Tom to help us down instead."

Honor wanted to mutter that he really *was* a beast, for there was no denying the disappointment she felt at such an unexpected reprieve. But Tom was opening the carriage door and bowing—though with a very knowing grin. Honor felt flushed again, this time from embarrassment.

"Go wash your face, Tom—your lurid imaginings are really far off the mark, I am afraid."

This from the marquis in colder tones than he normally applied to his staff. In truth, whilst he did not mind teasing Honor himself, he was positively furious that his coachman was drawing the wrong inferences. Honor was more

to him than a common strumpet and she needed courtesy
to be afforded at once.

Tom, chastened, doffed his cap and murmured that he
would attend to the horses first.

"Good. There is a pump around the back—see that you
use it."

Tom nodded forlornly. He was unused to such uncompromising tones from his master.

"After that, you may present yourself to the housekeeper
for a large dose of her partridge-and-game pie."

Merit's sternness vanished and the light returned to his
eyes. "Wheedle her for a draught of home-brewed apple
cider. It is, if I recollect, rather good."

The coachman, not down in the dismals for long,
beamed his thanks. He also bowed to Miss Finchley, a sign
that he'd learned rather smartly from his mistake. Lord
Laxton nodded.

Poor Tom! He could be forgiven the error. After all, Miss
Finchley was an extremely beautiful young lady. He'd trav-
eled with such before and to far different effect! Merit knew
the coachman would not make the same mistake twice.

Neither would Frederick, Lord Manning, stuck in a
wheat field several miles away and miserably surveying all
about him. He would not make the same mistake twice because Merit, Lord Laxton, would throttle him first. It was
all perfectly simple.

Oh, *why* had he not taken his own chaise? He had a ser-
viceable barouche sitting in his stables. True, it did not
bear the insignia of the Four Horse Club, or have the delicate paint work of cheerful canary yellow, but neither of
these factors any longer seemed compelling.

Why had he not listened to the cautious pleadings of the
Honorable Bertram? Or the youthful wisdom of Sir Peter?

Frederick, regarding the sad ruins of Lord Laxton's chaise, forgot for a moment that he was in the very throes of bliss. He forgot that only moments before he had considered himself the luckiest—the very luckiest—man alive. This happy conclusion had come about because Faith appeared to regard him in a marvelously heroic light. When he was with her he felt like St. George, slaying dragons, or Sir Lancelot, bound by a code of knightly chivalry. He, ordinary Frederick—had never dreamed this was possible.

Of course, there were always ladies on the catch for a duke's son, but he'd never felt the slightest predilection for them and had oftentimes blessed the fact that he was born third rather than first.

His brother had been positively *hounded* before securing the lineage by marrying Lady Aurelia Lifton and thus ending the dreams of half London's debutantes. But Faith, oh Faith was a different matter entirely! He just wished he was not in such a pickle now, for apart from feeling decidedly foolish, he felt the weight of responsibility besides.

It was all very well to destroy a chaise, but a maidenly reputation was another thing entirely. Unless they were rescued rather quickly, Miss Finchley could say good-bye to being returned to St. Martin's Square at any respectable hour.

Freddy no longer considered himself so terribly fortunate. Besides, he could not help noticing that Dapple and Dimple were restive, the carriage useless, the race a nightmare, and that a man with a pitchfork was now advancing toward them.

From the angle of the fork and the scowl upon his face, Freddy did not think this was a welcome sight. He could not hear what the man was bellowing—he was still too far away—but his approach was ominously imminent. Stunned, Freddy climbed down from the wreckage and decided that the day could not be much worse.

He was wrong, of course, for in the distance above them the steady roll of carriage wheels and the gentle clip-clopping of a team of chestnuts could be heard. Lord Manning's eyes rested fleetingly on Faith's countenance. She looked pale and unutterably stricken.

He followed her gaze to the point above them where a conveyance, hardly even slowing, progressed steadily around the ridge.

It might not have been so bad had Sir Godfrey—for naturally, the carriage belonged to him—not stopped to doff his beaver in their direction. Faith wanted to slap his smug, smirking countenance. Unfortunately, he was too far away, so she was not permitted this satisfaction. He cracked his whip and the horses regained their steady pace. Sir Godfrey, it seemed, was perfectly satisfied with the longer route.

Great Aunt Petunia's chamber was down a twisted passage with doors to the left and great halls and entrances to the right. The longer the route, the greater were Honor's misgivings, for it was only dusk but already hundreds of lit tapers heralded the way.

The floors were spotless but uncarpeted. Mahogany, Honor thought, but rather dark. Apart from a butler who had greeted them in the hallway in hushed undertones, there seemed to be not a maid or a footman in sight.

"Does your great aunt live alone?"

"Yes, ever since she was nineteen and the man of her dreams—an unsuitable fellow—did her the grave disservice of jilting her at the altar."

"You cannot be serious! I thought such melodrama was reserved for the pages of Gothic romance."

"Then think again, for Great Aunt Petunia is melodrama itself. But fear not, Honor, for I suspect she has recovered from her past disappointments."

"I should hope so, if she is now old enough to be your great aunt. Her disappointment must have been thirty years ago at least!"

"Quite. She is, however . . . eccentric."

"Nice eccentric or horrible eccentric?"

"Decide for yourself. We have come to her suite. Shall I knock?"

Honor had the impulse to say no, she would rather run away, but she remembered what my lord had said about dragons and smiled. Whatever he may think, she could handle any danger better than the one that he himself presented to her. Especially when he smiled like that, and leaned forward, a little closer, to reach the whimsical iron knocker above her head.

No, it was *not* to reach the knocker! It was to enfold her in his arms. Oh, but how heavenly! For an instant, Honor could hardly breathe, let alone move. Then her wild heart grew wilder yet as she realized with dawning wonder his intent.

Perhaps, at this stage, she should have moved, but she couldn't, so mesmerized was she by the strange beauty of his eyes. They were dark, and intense with little flecks of green. They were unutterably soft as they gazed upon her. Honor had never felt such a look, for though she had captured the force of many of his fleeting expressions—teasing, severe, quizzical, admiring, she had never seen or felt such a one as this. How could the very eyes caress? How could she melt under a mere gaze? How could she feel more precious than gold dust, more delicate than porcelain? How, oh how, could she suddenly feel as though he could see right through her gown, right through her petticoats, right down to those pearl-trimmed garters she had so teasingly mentioned?

A blush stole across her cheeks, for he was seeing more than that, or was it just her foolish, ridiculous, runaway imagination? She thought, at last, to move, but only entangled herself further in the well tailored lines of his waistcoat.

The pressure of his arms had increased fractionally, subtly, but oh, how subtly! Now she had to tilt her neck slightly to remonstrate with him and the expression had changed, again, in those fathomless eyes. They were not as intense as before; they were tinged, slightly, with arrogance and amusement and something else. . . . She was not perfectly certain.

She was not certain because her attention was wandering, slightly, to those scandalous shirt points that were still unadorned by a neckerchief. She could see the outline of his masculine throat and those treacherous silken hairs that had so riveted her attention earlier. Oh, surely it must be a crime to tease virtue in such a manner! It was hard, indeed, to be chaste when one felt so very wicked.

Gracious, he was going to kiss her! The kiss, the very kiss he had been idly threatening all morning! It did not occur to Honor to object, as Miss Bramble would have firmly instructed. She had done enough virtuous objecting for one day and now felt rebellious and delighted and utterly charmed. No, *charmed* is too mild a word to describe the feverish excitement of her eyes, or the soft parting of her lips as she breathed.

If he denied her now, it would have been a pain. She did not think she could stand such a pain. But no, he was hesitating only to push back a stray lock from her forehead and to place a light finger at the base of her throat in the very place where her traitorous pulse betrayed her. He held it there an instant, then smiled. It was a slow smile, a knowing smile that warmed her insensibly.

The candles flickered about them and shadows danced on the walls behind them. Dusk had deepened into the darker shades of evening light. My lord removed his finger from Honor's throat and placed both hands firmly on her cheekbones, holding her elfin countenance quite as still as one of Lord Elgin's marble statues.

Honor could not speak for the joy of it, for there was no

question of coyness or drawing back, or reputations or even of wickedness. It was more a matter of common honesty, of a deep, unspoken intimacy that tangled them together in a twine of invisible strength.

Honor felt the cords tightening about her, but they were silken, they allowed her to breathe, they permitted the whisper of a smile and the tenderest breath to escape conscious—very conscious—lips. He was so close she could feel the warmth of his chest emanating from that crisp lawn shirt that so nearly brushed against her bodice. Nearly, but not quite. The distance between them was infinitesimally small, yet Honor found it excruciating.

My lord, searching her features, probably sensed something of the kind, for he smiled. A charming smile, but heady and triumphant and distinctively masculine. At another time, Honor might have felt bound to protest. Now, however, she was too captivated by Merit's compelling enchantment to do anything more than moisten her lips in unconscious yearning.

My lord's intake of breath was sharp, but Honor hardly noticed. His hands on her face were firm, so firm, so warm, so enchantingly heady. He tilted her chin upward, slightly, subtly, so her eyes flickered to his. That was the very moment, of course, that he actually kissed her.

Honor forgot all her scruples as the caress proved every bit as delightful—and as shocking—as she had dreamed of. Slowly, she responded, for how could she not when he aroused every desire she had ever known? When his mouth commanded—no, *compelled*—a response, when to be passive would have been to negate the honesty of this intimacy?

When my lord finally desisted, she was shaking, her heart was beating faster than she had imagined possible, and she felt light, so light—if he had not supported her she might have bruised herself by swooning unsteadily onto those hard, mahogany floors.

Her legs no more seemed to support her than her lips seemed able to utter a single, solitary word.

My lord, rather enjoying the devastation he had wreaked, smiled and removed another tiny wisp of dark hair from her forehead.

"If I had any sense I would forget all about Great Aunt Petunia and ravish you here instead."

Honor searched about for a suitable response. She could hardly think of anything nicer, or more impossibly tempting. She nearly said as much, if only to see the gleam return to those green-dark, bewitching eyes. But she was a lady of sense as well as virtue, so she straightened her spine, ignored her shaking legs, and returned as dampening a rejoinder as she possibly could manage.

"Then I would kill you, my lord, and you cannot think that a happy outcome."

Lord Laxton's lips twitched. "Ah, recovering your wit, I see. I thought you dreamed of wickedness, Honor? Perhaps I should render you speechless again. So much more comfortable!"

His stare was mesmerizing but also so amused that Honor was torn between nodding and dreaming up a suitable set-down. She did neither, however, for the door opened suddenly and Merit pushed her to one side so that she gasped from the shock of it. Then, peering into the gloom, Miss Finchley realized she was face-to-face with Merit's dragon.

It was not a happy realization, especially since her appearance was now hopelessly disheveled and the dragon was staring at her rather as though she should be expunged. Honor quailed, but the dragon's glare passed beyond her to Lord Laxton, on the other side of the wide, arched door frame.

"Ha!" she said. "This is a fine thing, visiting me in my dotage and entertaining your little light o' loves in my very corridor! I've a good mind, Merit, to send you packing, only I have not a *damned* person who can play a decent hand of cards, hereabouts."

"Good evening to you, too, Great Aunt Petunia!"

"Humph!"

But the door was opened farther and the lady, dressed from head to toe in a type of flowing robe of scarlet and gold, stood aside to allow the pair to enter.

Honor's heart, already stressed from the intoxicating interlude a moment ago, now almost failed her. She quailed under the lady's stare as she softly entered the room, hardly daring to catch at Merit's sleeve for comfort. This was not a dragon, this was a gorgon!

Merit opened the heavy brocade curtains so that some of the half-light of the evening could seep into the complete darkness of the chamber.

A single wax taper burned, but given the splendid size of the room, it was hardly sufficient to meet the need.

The dragon drew them closed again.

"Meddlesome old so-and-so! I like the dark!"

"That may be so, but *we* do not!"

"And who is *we*, if I may so inquire?"

Merit opened the drapes again.

" 'We,' " he said, "is myself, Merit, Lord Laxton, fourth Marquis Laxton, Earl of Wright, Baron of Newhaven . . ."

"Go away, if you have merely come to bore my ears off! Who is the *girl*?"

"The girl, as you put it, is Miss Honoria Finchley."

"Do you have a second name, Miss Finchley?"

Merit turned to Honor as if such introductions were really rather commonplace.

Honor nodded, then blushed. "Chastity."

My lord's eyes gleamed for a moment and Honor really thought he might disgrace himself with a chuckle. He did not, but he was close, which caused a hint of laughter to appear on the dragon's face. It was only for a moment, however, and Honor thought she must have imagined it.

"Ah. Then I correct myself. This, Aunt, is Miss Honoria *Chastity* Finchley."

"Humph!" But the dragon was thoughtful.

"Any relation to Adelia Mallet? She married a Finchley, if I recall."

Honor curtseyed. She did not think to prevaricate, or to tell half truths or to be vague in any way. Something told her the dragon brooked nothing but plain dealing.

"Indeed, Madame. Adelia was my mother."

Great Aunt Petunia nodded. "Thought so. Queer in the attic, Adelia. Foisted a great many hideous names upon her children. I remember that."

Merit's eyes met Honor's. They twinkled, but she ignored him. She was beginning to rather like the dragon.

"Don't stand there gawking—sit down, sit down if you must."

So Lady Darfield—for such was her title, when she was not being called Great Aunt Petunia—heaved herself into a large, winged seat. It was carved from oak, inlaid with chestnut and adorned, on either side, by two large eagles. Honor thought they were rather like vultures, but nothing about Great Aunt Petunia now surprised her, so she forbore from comment.

Merit and Honor seated themselves modestly apart on two hard chairs on either side of an ornate occasional table. Way undersized for such a room, but Honor was not thinking of furnishings. She was watching, with fascination, as Lady Darfield took her snuff. She inhaled with vigor—and a rather indelicate sniff—then closed the box with a click.

"Shan't offer you, Merit—I know you are as lily-livered as a church mouse. I suppose you will be wanting dinner?"

"No . . ."

"Yes." Merit's voice was firm and overrode Honor's entirely.

Great Aunt Petunia rang a bell and almost instantly there was a knock on the adjoining door.

"Dinner, Robins. And something filling, mind—the girl looks half starved. She's as scrawny as a stick."

"She is not scrawny, Aunt, but slender."

"I'll be the judge of that! Some pigeon pies, Robins, and some of that goose and jelly wine sauce, though Cook was too heavy-handed with the ginger . . . never mind, it will do very nicely for a snack . . . some garden vegetables, lightly braised . . . what is that? Yes, yes, the forcemeat balls from the bacon and giblets."

Aunt Petunia stared about her thoughtfully. "What do we fancy for our second remove? Something light, I think—the child looks exhausted. I know! Manchester pudding with clotted cream, Hawthorne flower liqueur, and hothouse strawberries. Oh! Some ice cream from the ice house and two glasses of syllabub for the children. I shall have a decanter of that cognac we laid down . . . the good stuff, mind, not the rubbish we serve to visitors . . ."

But now she was interrupted by Lord Laxton. The gorgon glared. She did not tolerate interpolations lightly.

"*What*, Merit?" This, in tones of strict annoyance. Honor quailed.

"It might possibly have escaped your notice, but you spoke of children. I am no longer a child, Great Aunt!"

Great Aunt Petunia drew her lorgnette from her reticule and stared at him sternly.

"Yes, I noticed that. It is hard to overlook you are full grown when you persist in manhandling females outside my very door! Bad, Merit, bad. If you were any younger I would have you over my knee for such disgraceful conduct! It is one thing for an opera dancer, *quite* another for

Adelia Mallet's daughter, no matter how pea-brained she might have been."

Honor, hardly knowing where to look—certainly not at the dragon—sat straight-backed in her chair and tried to assume a sweet and maidenly posture. In truth, she was rather intrigued that Merit was getting a ticking off. She was very sure it did not happen often.

Her amusement faltered, however, when the lorgnette turned to her. As a matter of fact, she turned a bright beet-root and cast her eyes to the floor, wondering what horrible kind of verbal chastisement would be cast her way. Lady Darfield might be indulgent with her great nephew, but why should she be with her, a young lady who had obviously put herself beyond the pale?

She did not have time to take fright, for Merit shot her a look of sublime laughter. She nearly missed it, for her eyes were so cast down, but happily, she did not.

Grinning! The wretch was actually grinning! He did not even have the good sense to look chastened. He merely announced that since his aunt was so observant of his masculine attributes, she might desist from treating him like a scrubster and order up two glasses of the cognac instead.

"Nonsense! Syllabub is very good for you, Merit, and will serve nicely as a punishment. Two syllabubs, Robins, and hurry, if you please!" Lady Darfield glared one last time at Honor, then set down her lorgnette.

Robins curtseyed and disappeared into the adjacent room from whence she had appeared. Her expression showed nothing of the interest she must have felt at the preceding conversation.

CHAPTER 14

The dragon, it seemed, fostered the appearance of living in solitude though there had to be a hundred staff at least about her. Robins had not so much as blinked at the extensive order placed by her mistress. The kitchens had to be filled with all manner of scullery maids, footmen, butlers, housekeepers, and cooks to accommodate such a varied menu at such short notice. The castle, from all Honor could see, was also scrupulously clean—dozens of housemaids at least. Gardeners, too, most like, though she had not yet seen any of the extensive grounds.

"Humph! So now we make ourselves comfortable. Merit, get out the card table, will you—you shall oblige me with a game of cards. The chit can watch."

"Certainly not! The chit, as you put it, shall play. By the by, she is staying with you tonight and for the foreseeable future."

Lady Darfield, not up until this moment fazed in the least by Merit's arrival, now looked speechless.

"Over my dead body, she will not! Gracious, Merit, you know what I think of society! I am not going to . . . to . . . be forced to socialize with a schoolroom chit in my own home! Take her away, do you hear?"

"Aunt, you are being excessively uncivil!"

"Uncivil be damned! I am not having it, Merit, and so I tell you."

Honor, quiet up until now, stood up.

"Lord Laxton," she said quietly—and with a good deal of dignity, considering her chagrin and fury—"it is clear I am unwelcome. Please take me home."

"You have no home, Honor."

"Then take me away from here. I don't care!"

"Your reputation won't stand for it. Aunt Petunia is not the hostess I could wish for you, but she is all the option we have."

"*What?*" Aunt Petunia boomed. "What in the dickens do you mean, I am not the hostess you could wish for her? What, pray, is wrong with me?"

"You are a bully, Aunt, and a hermit! Not, perhaps, the best choice for Miss Finchley, who is a lady born."

There was silence as Lady Darfield looked in danger of exploding with anger. Just when Honor thought she might just do something horrendous like grabbing for her cane and positively beating Merit, she glared at him horribly, then started to laugh.

"You have always been an impudent rascal, Lord Laxton! I only hope the child does not lead you a song and dance. She is pretty, but not up to your usual standard."

"Aunt!" For the first time, Merit looked genuinely annoyed. Or was it embarrassed? His eyes glanced at Honor and they looked anguished.

She took pity on him.

"Oh, come, Merit, she may have deplorable manners but she is perfectly right, you know. I am passing pleasing but no great diamond, as I am sure you will know firsthand."

"Ho ho ho! So the lady has a tongue, has she? And plain speaking, too! Perhaps I have misjudged her. Come here, child."

"She is going nowhere till you've agreed to sponsor her."

"Sponsor her? Your scheme gets more and more farfetched, Merit!"

"Not so farfetched as you think. How is this? We will play a game of piquet. If Honor wins, she stays and you do everything you can to stop any talk that might arise. If she loses, she goes. If *I* win I will marry her out of hand."

There was a shocked silence.

"Done!" Lady Darfield suddenly boomed, her eyes gleaming more acutely than Honor would have dreamed possible. She raised her brow challengingly at Honor. "And you, gel? What say you to this preposterous scheme?"

"Done!" Honor said promptly, though not without a certain quizzical stare of her own.

She turned to Lord Laxton, on her right. He was examining a speck of dust upon his shirt cuffs and seemed not to notice the air of tension he was generating.

"Merit," she whispered, still feeling deliciously wicked at calling him by his first name. "Merit, is it fair to take advantage of an old lady in this way? I cannot entirely like it. You know she cannot win."

"Ha!" Aunt Petunia's hearing was quite as quick as her temper and she caught every whispered syllable of Honor's question.

"Ha!" she said, her eyes flashing brighter than fiery coals. "You think I am in my dotage, do you? Think I am easy game, do you? Well, let us see, little Miss Impertinence! And none of your airy fairy games of chance, mind—I want a regular game of skill, if you please!"

Lord Laxton finished with his impeccable cuffs and looked up. "One game, Aunt. We have not got all night to decide Miss Finchley's fate."

"Don't gammon me, Merit, my lord marquis and whatever your damned titles might be! I can see which way the wind lies and you'll be sorry, mind! Marriage out of hand, indeed. I have not heard such romantic rubbish this age and if you think to cozen me, you shan't!"

She smiled sunnily at her prey—Honor—and asked her to draw closer.

"No watering pots, mind! If I win, he leaves my house without you. In the morning, I shall hire a chaise, furnish you with a sovereign—though I don't see why I should—and send you packing to the nearest posting house in Bath. Are you agreed?" Lady Darfield's fingernails were sharp and rather too close for Honor's comfort.

"No, Madame, I am *not* agreed. I hesitate to call you a manipulative old harridan on such short acquaintance, but so, I fear, it seems to me!"

There was a gasp as two of the stealthy maidservants behind them dropped a series of silver salvers. They dropped the goose, the forcemeat balls, and two of the pigeon pies. The salvers descended to the hard floor with a clash rather like the sound of cymbals. They were ignored. Two pairs of eyes—one wry, one rather shocked, were fixed on Great Aunt Petunia. Lady Darfield's own eyes were growing rather round. Her face, in the half-light, seemed to be turning a strange kind of purple. She was holding her breath, Honor thought.

Just as Lord Laxton took a stride toward her, she exhaled. Miraculously, she also laughed. It was a merry laugh for one of her enormous proportions, and really rather pleasant.

"Spunk, hey? I begin to like this child, Merit."

"You shall like her more when you see her play."

"Ah, we shall see about that, we shall see about that!"

But Aunt Petunia seemed almost cheerful as she ordered the marquis to set up the card table and draw the chairs closer to her own carved seat. The vultures seemed formidable but Honor thought they faded into insignificance next to the dragon herself. She beckoned to Honor as Merit, deceptively meek, did as he was bid. As he passed, Honor could have sworn that she caught a conspiratorial wink.

Great Aunt Petunia regarded Honor closely.

"You must be passing good if he dared bring you here."

Honor never liked admitting to any skill before a game. She therefore smiled modestly and commented that no doubt her skill could not be compared to her ladyship's.

A good answer, for Aunt Petunia, never doubting that her reputation preceded her, nodded.

"Yes, I give your Merit a good run for his money. Impertinent young jackanapes but at least he has card sense. He can play like the very devil."

Oh, he can, can he? thought Honor in surprise. She was more determined than ever to beat him. And yes, Aunt Petunia, too. She had a feeling that the old woman would quite enjoy a thorough thrashing for a change.

The sandwiches—hastily made up as a replacement for the goose—were waived away when they arrived. The silver platters, the soup, the banquet laid out quietly behind them were all ignored. Merit dealt cards under Aunt Petunia's beady eye. Honor did not bother watching. She felt she knew enough of Merit's character not to have to bother that he, like Chittlingdon before him, would cheat.

No one noticed the silent attendants light more tapers as the dark dusk deepened into definite night. Then two footmen appeared with floating gas lamps flickering yellow behind tall, glass chimneys. They closed the drapes again and the smell of gas vaguely filled the room just as the luminescent light softly filtered into their consciousness. The players, however, were more concerned with the cards than the silent activity around them.

If one had been a witness to this game, one would have heard a pin drop, so silent was the play but for the occasional cough of Lady Darfield. It would be hard for any watcher who observed to determine which player was the more skillful or which face the more sober and determined. Hand after hand was played, sometimes Honor winning, sometimes Aunt Petunia, and sometimes, of course, the silent Lord

Laxton. They were not playing for money but for purple hairpins adorned each with loops of silver and tiny jewels, each a different color—here a sapphire, here a marquisette, here a diamond. It mattered not, for Lady Darfield's supply was plentiful—hard to imagine her shortish hair ever requiring so many pins—and each pin was worth a single point in play.

Merit's pile was growing, Lady Darfield's receding. Honor, playing steadily, showed neither joy nor dismay but quietly called and either lost a pin, gained a pin, or shared her hand without an alteration of expression. As time drew on, Great Aunt Petunia cursed most unsuitably, muttered under her breath, and fidgeted with her lessening pile of hair accessories.

Presently, however, a new expression entered her eyes. It was one of calculated respect. She regarded Honor anew. She no longer seemed such an unwelcome prospect in her household. Not unwelcome at all, if the girl could play as fine a game as this. It would not, she supposed, be too bad sponsoring a child who knew a thing or two about piquet. Merit visited too seldom to be any use at all. She threw her cards on the table with a bang.

"All right, damn you, you win! I shall take the girl!"

But Merit, curse him, did not look relieved. He merely said that she must hush, she was interrupting his play.

"Did you not hear me? I said I would take her!"

"Excellent, Aunt, but now I play her alone."

Honor's hands trembled, for she knew he was staring at her and that his eyes were blazing and that frankly she did not know how to meet them at all. Her hands were so traitorous that the cards almost slipped onto the table of their own accord.

She steadied herself, set down a card, then bit her tongue so hard that it hurt. Too late she realized that Merit held a winning hand. If he played the ace—and he undoubtedly had it—she would be lost.

For a long moment, almost a minute, he stared at her. She thought she read many emotions in that strong, masculine countenance, but she was in such a strange flutter of feeling herself, she could not be sure. Aunt Petunia was regarding them with a certain wicked and unfeigned interest, but they hardly cared. It was as if Merit bored into her very thoughts, reading whatever he could there, sighing a little, smoldering a little, impassioned a little . . . Honor held her breath as the candle burned into its socket. He played the four.

Aunt Petunia guffawed, then held her hand over her mouth. Honor just stared.

"You have won, I think, Miss Finchley."

Merit's tone was quiet, but wry.

Honor wanted to shout that he was lying, that she knew very well that he had deliberately lost, that he was unfair, wretched, an impossible imposter, but she was silent. Her heart felt far too heavy for a winner. She felt a tear brush her cheeks and pushed it away roughly and angrily. She ignored the burning lump in her throat. The jelly, just caught in her view, looked wobbly. She almost laughed.

How absurd to think such thoughts when she felt so leaden. Merit had feigned a loss. There could be only one reason. He did not want to marry her out of hand. His stupid threats were just that: stupid threats only. She could not, for the life of her, understand why she felt so bleak.

"Down, Rascal, down!" Rascal had forgotten Freddy's ankles as he caught sight of Sir Godfrey. Now he was growling and showed signs of chasing back up the hill.

"Come here, you stupid mutt!"

Faith clambered down from the chaise, her hems ripping a little as she did so.

"Rascal! Come here at once!" It was in the most commanding voice she knew, rather like Honor at her most severe.

The dog allowed himself one last growl and returned unwillingly to Faith's side, as if doing her some huge and magnanimous favor. The chaise above them wheeled off with a merry crack of the whip and Freddy was left staring at the wrong side of a pitchfork.

"Hoy there, laddie! Ruinin' me paddocks ye are an' don't give me no toffee-nosed excuses 'bout races an' all—already 'ad one last week, I did, and 'anded 'im over to the magistrate roit an' toit, I did."

Frederick, who knew the magistrate, one Sir Kenwick Hawkins, was just about to make some lordly comment to this effect—though in truth he did not feel lordly, only slightly abashed—when Faith stepped forward and curtseyed.

"Oh, we beg your pardon, sir! What a stupid mistake we made and that is certain! The dog distracted us and before we knew it we were tearing down the hill, heading straight for your lovely corn. Can you forgive us, do you think?"

She offered a delicate hand and hoped that the rosy flush on her cheeks caused by telling such barefaced lies would not be noticed. It *was* noticed, of course, but the farmer thought it charming, and rather modest. He permitted himself another glare at the curly-haired lad before him—shocking what gentlemen were permitted to wear in town these days—and bowed rather clumsily to Faith.

The pitchfork nearly tore her overskirt, but she had the quick wits to step back just as the farmer remembered it was in his hand.

Freddy, not a slow-top when given a hint, dropped his belligerent manner, forbore to mention Sir Kenwick's name, and set his not inconsiderable charm to disarming the annoyed farmer.

"I am sorry, sir. I will naturally reimburse you all your costs."

"Hmph! Well, that's more'n I can say about the sorry lot 'as was 'ere last week an' that I can tell ya! Is it an axle you 'ave broke, or what?"

"An axle and a wheel, I think. Must have jolted hard over some rock."

"Aye. It is rocky hereabout but nobbut can see it for the crops."

"Do you . . . do you . . ." Faith hesitated. "Do you possibly, dear sir, have a spare wheel?"

"So you can hare off an' break your necks?"

"No, so that I may return Miss Faith to her home before it is dusk. You must see the awkwardness of my position, sir."

The farmer laughed.

"Aye, that I do. Ye'll be marryin' 'er next, I daresay, an' a reg'lar treat that should be, 'er with that pretty face an' all. No, I 'ave nobbut you can use but there is a barn a little way yonder. Wait there while I call a wheelwright in from town. If yer blunt can stand it?"

The farmer eyed Freddy's triple-caped greatcoat, his stylish hessians, his gold fobs, his jeweled seals, and smiled grimly.

"Oh, yes, certainly, certainly . . ." Freddy pulled out a bag of coins and rewarded the farmer amply for his hospitality and the ruin of his fields and also, if truth be told, for not clobbering him to death with the lethal pitchfork that now lay harmlessly in some straw.

"Is there anywhere we can water the team?"

The farmer nodded silently. "Stream is thataway. I'll take them 'orses down an' tether 'em, shall I?"

Frederick nodded. "Thank you, sir."

The farmer nodded gruffly.

He did not hold with town bucks but this one seemed polite enough and the lady was a treat.

"How long before a wheelwright gets here?"

"Nobbut sure. Could be today, could be tomorrer . . ."

Faith looked shocked.

"Sir!"

Freddy patted her arm. "Hush! Miss Finchley, let us not worry about what we cannot help. Do you need a hand?"

Faith shook her head stoically. She was ruined! To think she was ruined before she had had her first ball! She tried not to dwell on her disappointment, for she was not, whatever Honor might say, a watering pot. Besides, Lord Manning looked worried and she wouldn't, for all the world, cause him any further distress. She followed him as the farmer led the horses in the opposite direction. Lord Laxton's cheerful carriage now looked forlorn indeed. Faith thought she knew exactly how it felt.

The owner of the chaise, Lord Laxton himself, was feeling just as bleak. Some miles away, at Darfield House, he was regarding the tassels of his top boots with a fierce frown. It was not carriages he was thinking about so fiercely, but Honor. She was regarding him without a trace of a smile and he knew with a certainty beyond all certainties that he had just hurt her deeply. Himself, too. He had just gambled away his chance of having her.

He could have married this mad girl out of hand, could have carried her away to his castle—not this one, but a magnificent one, covered in magnolia with gardens designed by Nash himself . . . but no! He must needs be chivalrous and cause those tears to glisten upon her cheeks. Even now, they were poised to run down that piquant face and wet her pretty, travel-stained gown. He did not think he could maintain his resolution if they did.

He knew now, as he had not when he surprised himself by proposing, that he would stop at nothing to have her. Something incalculable had changed in that short time between the carriage ride and now. But not this way, not by a mere game of hazard! Neither by force would he have her, nor by bullying, nor even by gentle coercion.

He remembered vividly the time he had set his doves free. He had wept such tears—mortifying for a dapper youth such as he had been—but had known that unless they came back to him freely, they were never his at all.

Honor must win her fortune, there was no question of it. Not in dribs and drabs, one old pensioner after another, one wealthy nabob here, one spoilt ladyship there; she must win her fortune at once, and a lot of it. She must be independent enough to deny him and in love enough not to be able to. That, he promised, must be her fate and he would do it, by heavens, or his name was not, confoundedly, Merit. Merit, Merit, Merit! Sometimes he wished he could just be willfully wicked and have done with it.

Honor, watching him, could not read his thoughts. She only saw the sudden straightening of his shoulders and the firming of his chin as he nodded at her, regained his composure, and finally, almost antithetically, winked. He shuffled his cards carelessly into the deck. The ace of spades eased itself in with several sixes, a ten of hearts, and a miserable pair of clubs. Not for him the mistake of Chittlingdon, who'd had no time to cover his tracks!

"You have won, my little butterfly. Stay here with the dragon and slay her with your bounteous sword."

It was the dragon, not Honor, who replied. Honor did not think she could talk at that moment. The dragon cast a beady eye on the girl and if she could have breathed fire, she would have. Merit would have been scorched hotly, for in truth the dragon was now rather fond of her chick and annoyed with Lord Laxton for trifling with her.

"She has slain me once, Merit, is that not enough? Now do go away and only come back when I have clothed the child decently. Not a beauty, to be sure, but passable, quite passable. What say you, Honor, to hunting down the brocades and rich silks I have kept in the attics this long age? If the Lady Darfield is to return to society, she is damned jolly well going to do so in style. Now run along, you foolish boy—this is woman's work and you are already underfoot."

"I want a word with Miss Finchley, Aunt."

"You want more than a word with her, Merit, and I tell you, so long as she is under my protection, you shall not have it! Now do go away and stop being so tiresome. I trust the child has not put herself entirely beyond the pale?"

"It is hopeless, Madame, I have!"

"What, a miserable kiss here and there? Or has the rascal ruined you?"

"I have ruined myself!"

"Nonsense, one does not ruin oneself! Merit, is the child chaste or is she damaged goods?"

Honor, indignant at such intimate questioning, nevertheless blushed as Lord Merit remarked coolly that he was not in the habit of deflowering innocent maidens and that his aunt should find herself a footman who would wash her mouth out with soap.

"Oh, don't get on your high ropes with me! So the gel is an innocent. I could have told you that the moment I saw her!"

"I want a word with her, Aunt."

"You are a damned persistent young jackanapes, but at least you have some masculine blood in your veins! Very well, five minutes and the door shall be open, so don't think you can try anything havey-cavey for I won't have it!"

"Yes, Aunt." Merit was looking at Honor now, and her heart seemed to have stopped. He was going to be very kind and say good-bye and explain that he was doing everything for her own good and that one day she would see he was right and that she would marry someone suitable. . . . Honor was perfectly certain she would scratch his eyes out if he said any such thing.

But he didn't. He stood, for a long moment, just looking at her.

Lady Darfield had risen from her seat and exited into the labyrinth outside long before he touched that single strand of hers. Her forehead felt flushed.

"I am going to make you win your fortune."

The comment was so unexpected, Honor forgot all her miserable intentions.

"How?"

"Give me your note of hand for the two thousand pounds you have laid by. I will advance you the money and take the further sum you won last night."

"To what end will you thus beggar me?"

"I will wager it a hundredfold that a woman could not enter the hallowed portals of Brooke's and beat any man present."

Honor gasped. "You cannot be serious! Ladies are not permitted up St. James Street, never mind into Brooke's itself!"

"That will make the wager all the more novel. You shall be anonymous. It will add to the mystery and increase the stakes."

"You must be mad. What if I lose?"

"It is a calculated risk. Honor, you can do it. I have watched you."

"Lord Laxton, for all your cheating ways, I *lost* against you tonight. You know I did."

"Only because I was mesmerizing you with my devastating good looks!"

"Coxcomb! How can I be certain I won't be mesmerized by any *other* young gentleman?'

"I shall kill him if I see any signs of it. You will win, Honor. With our talents combined, you shall win."

"How do we combine these talents, pray?"

"I am going to teach you things."

"*What* things?"

"Where to sit, whom to flatter, whom to defeat, whom to decline a game, whom to challenge, how to cope with trickery, how to see through a mesh veil . . ."

"How to what?"

"You will wear a mesh veil, my love, to protect your identity. You would not wish to be the talk of the *Tatler!* Let the papers rather say such things as 'mysterious lady vanishes with nabob's fortune.' You shall win it fairly, then disappear forever into the mysterious annals of history."

"You actually seem to believe this is possible!"

"I shall *make* it possible."

"How, precisely?"

But my lord only smiled and placed a single gloved finger on Honor's tempting red lips. He was aware of the clock ticking the minutes by and could think of no better way to silence her objections. Yes, he felt it, the warm, answering response, the slight closing of her delectable eyes . . . His own breathing grew unsteady and he carelessly dropped his hand.

Now was not the time to antagonize Great Aunt Petunia, whose affections were as unpredictable as they were strong. So he increased the distance between them and answered the questioning look in Honor's eyes.

CHAPTER 15

"If I kiss you, the dragon will very likely flay me alive, so I am going to resist that delightful temptation and ask you, Honor, to have faith."

"Faith?" Honor wondered at the coincidence of the term, but my lord seemed in earnest.

"My name is not inconsiderable about town. You tease me about being a coxcomb and very likely I am, but my word has weight. My friends, my acquaintances, and my mortal enemies have longed—positively longed—to have me scribble down some careless wager in their endless betting book. Thus far I have declined, for they have all been too ridiculous for my attention. The last one, if I recall, was a cross-country from Tilling when the veriest fool knows the terrain is treacherous for carriages." The marquis looked suddenly sober.

"No, Honor, this wager is not the most foolish I have come across, nor the most daring. It is, however, intriguing and that intrigue must work to our advantage."

"Why should you do this for me?"

Lord Laxton cast her an unfathomable expression. It looked like he meant to say something, but he held his peace. Instead, he said, "That is my concern. *Your* concern is honing up your skills with Great Aunt Petunia, who is as good an opponent as one could wish for. Be meek, Honor, but not so meek that you allow her to clothe you in gold-tasseled sarcanet!"

Honor laughed. How surprising was that sound in the midst of her despair! It seemed to bubble up from nowhere and made her forget that if she succeeded in winning a fortune, she would not likewise be winning the heart of the gentleman. She was now very sure she'd fallen far too in love with Merit for her own good.

It was nothing, she was afterward to scold herself, that he called her "my love." It was a mere trick of phrase, probably scattered about liberally with every female with whom he conversed. But a little, tiny, hopeful part of her refused—simply refused—to listen.

"All right, all right, time's up!"

The dragon reappeared but with so much noise that even if Honor and Merit had been clinging to each other in lascivious ecstasy, they would have had time to disentangle themselves.

Merit, decorously languishing near a Grecian pillar, made a polite bow.

"I shall be back, Aunt, at a more reasonable hour. Miss Finchley and I have work to do. You will oblige me by playing with her night and day and making sure she is passable in all manner of games."

"What scheme are you up to, Merit?"

"I don't indulge in schemes, Aunt."

"Ha!"

"So rude! Very well, I indulge in *plots*. Miss Finchley shall accord you the details. I trust it is wicked enough for your approval."

Then, with a rakish bow—for Merit had recovered his spirits—he kissed first one gnarled hand, then another, perfectly smooth but trembling—and took his leave.

* * *

It was now very dark and the roads were quiet. Not so much as a farm gig shared the cobbled paths that Merit traversed. He settled into his thoughts as Tom the coachman drove slowly across the wooded glades and out onto the crested ridge of North Tilling.

Presently, the gas lamp at the head of the carriage seemed to light another chaise. There was the flicker of a glow as if a lantern had been set down on the ground a little way off from the road and the cattle were being unhitched.

Merit called to Tom to stop, for it was not his custom to pass by trouble without lending a hand. His carriage, already moving slowly, ground to a halt slightly beyond the horseless cart. No, it was more than a cart, it was a chaise. Crested, too, though Merit did not rightly recognize the heraldry. The occupant, however, was releasing a few lively oaths. Merit descended his own chaise and strode toward the occupant. He smiled in rueful understanding.

"Good evening to you!"

"What the devil are *you* doing here? I thought Lord Manning came alone."

This unwelcoming phrase meant nothing to Merit, who was rather too caught up in his own tumultuous day to remember anything at all about Lord Manning. With two swift glances, however, Merit revised his sympathetic view of the hell-raiser before him. (Yes, he realized that the chestnuts were spent and one of the pair appeared to have lost a shoe.) Racing, most like, and on such unsuitable terrain!

His answer, therefore, was even but cold. "I have nothing to do with Lord Manning. I merely came to inquire whether you needed assistance."

"That is certainly a laugh, Lord Laxton! What do you take me for? A greenhorn?"

At this mysterious comment, the marquis who was not, up until now, paying overly much attention, suddenly focused his eyes on the sweating team. Good God! What was this about Freddy? He suddenly remembered the Tilling to somewhere or other cross-country and realized that they were now suspiciously near Tilling.

"Who are you?"

"You know me! We conversed at the Anderton Ball. I am Sir Godfrey Islington, sir, and by jolly, when I finish this race you'll be hearing from me!"

"And why, pray, is that?"

"Because Lord Manning is racing on your behalf and has crashed your chaise into a hay field. I will have attended to my needs and finished this scurvy race long before he has extricated himself."

Merit's lip curled. He found he did not like this bounder overmuch, nor did he any longer wish to dally assisting him.

"Do not be overconfident. Your own plight is not enviable and Lord Manning is more resourceful than you think." Merit's tone was sharp.

"Perhaps if he had not a lady by him, nor she a dog."

Lord Laxton gasped but did not expel the question that rose to his lips. The man was baiting him, for certain, and he would not give him the satisfaction of seeing he'd been caught.

"Good evening to you."

Sir Godfrey raised his hat. He was in the devil of a pickle but he was not going to show as much to the marquis. The next team that came by, he would either hire or purchase. His own team could be abandoned and if he offered enough, someone would be bound to help. He would do anything, in fact, just to win the confounded race.

Freddy, alone in the hay shed with Faith, was torn between despair and the overwhelming desire to feel the softness of her silken tresses. They were greatly enhanced, in his opinion, by the loss of her bonnet. He had never before seen hair with such rich luster or length. He longed to bury his head in it and luxuriate in her clean, fresh, apple blossom scent.

Darkness had fallen—there was simply no denying this truth and Faith, fatigued and shivery, looked rather forlorn under the light of the gentle moon. Freddy forgot, for a moment, Merit's wrath and the loss of the race. As a matter of fact, it was more than just a moment, for his eyes caught Faith's and her little gasp was perfectly irresistible.

"I am sorry, Miss Finchley."

"It is not your fault."

"It shows the tenderest heart that you can say such a whopper. It *is* my fault."

"Only because that beast Sir Godfrey cheats!"

"He did not cheat. I took you up willingly."

"You are very kind."

"I am not kind, Faith. I do believe if I were not hopelessly in love with you I would have left you to your fate!"

"What, with Sir Godfrey?"

"Never that. With my friends Peter and Bertram, though. I fear I might have abandoned you."

"But you didn't!"

"No."

"And you took up Rascal."

"Yes, confoundedly silly."

"Confoundedly nice, since he nearly chewed your ankles!"

"He did chew my ankles. I deserve it, Miss Finchley, for getting you in this mess."

Faith swallowed. She was so trying to be brave and good, but how dismal it felt to be ruined! Her only satisfaction was that she had had this time alone with Lord Manning and he was every bit as nice as she had expected. Rascal stretched out in the long grass and placed two golden paws in front of his face.

"Is your father really a duke?"

"Beg pardon? Oh yes, yes, he really is. I'm not the heir, you know."

Freddy suddenly felt a little anxious, as if this should matter.

"Yes." Faith smiled. "I am glad you are not. I am sure an heir to a dukedom must be rather too grand for me!"

"Do you think so? Well, I always did think my brother a pompous ass . . . oh, pardon my language Miss Finchley, I didn't mean . . ."

"No, no, it is quite all right."

There was a silence.

"I am not really the granddaughter of a duke."

"Well, of course you are not! How could you be when I have been forced to dance with every confounded one of them? Let me tell you, some are the worst wallflowers you have ever seen and some are simply shrewish."

"But I lied to you!"

"It doesn't count because I never believed you in the first place. Miss Finchley . . ."

"Yes, Lord Manning?"

"Oh, call me Freddy . . . all my friends do."

"But I am not your friend!"

"Miss Finchley, you have tolerated me racing you, jolting you, causing your hems to split, and your pretty half-boots to be muddied. No, wait! Don't interrupt. You have been ditched in a field, you saved me from a pitchfork, and you defended me against Sir Godfrey's taunts. I think I might safely say you are my friend."

This was the longest speech Freddy had ever made and whilst it may not have been the most poetic, or romantically phrased, Faith thought it the most wonderful thing she had ever heard. It grew more wonderful yet when

Freddy, forgetting, for once, that his coat—skillfully designed by Weston—should not be creased, drew her into his arms and kissed her.

It was not the sort of experienced, amused, heart-stopping caress that Merit was capable of, but Faith, in a perfect cloud of happiness, could find no fault with it. Indeed, when she had forgotten her initial shyness (excruciating), she even went so far as to stand on tiptoes and brush a kiss of her own across Freddy's masculine, rather delighted lips.

This happy state might have lasted longer than it ought to have, for Lord Manning, confronted with more strands of those perfect, silken tresses than he had ever dreamed of, took immediate advantage. Freddy might have been a beginner at such things, but he learnt quickly! Very soon his interest became engaged in the soft curves modestly hidden beneath Miss Finchley's fashionable riding dress.

Faith, her heart beating every bit as much as Honor's had, could barely move as she divined Freddy's intent. Her eyelashes fluttered. The moon seemed brighter, just then, and the murmured conversation between them seemed impossibly intimate.

The thought of being ruined, whilst terrible, was somehow more bearable as Lord Manning drew her closer again. But he did not take advantage of her interesting curves. He merely whispered that she was not to worry her head off.

"I will worry tomorrow, Lord Manning."

"Freddy."

"Freddy." Faith was shy. "Tonight is so . . . so . . ."

"Enchanting?"

"Precisely. How did you know?"

"It is what I feel. Faith, I know I am only a third son and not nearly so handsome as my brothers . . ."

"What? No one could be handsomer than you, Freddy!"

"But my hair curls and is red . . ."

"Nonsense, it is amber gold with reddish lights that gleam in the moonlight."

"Are you a poet, Faith?"

"Of course not!" Faith blushed, for she could not for the life of her see how she can have been so bold, only Freddy had seemed so forlorn . . .

"I have freckles."

"So do I, across the bridge of my nose, see? I use rose water essence and all kinds of possets so you can hardly see them. Honor says I am vain."

"My brothers say the same, but I *do* like looking up to snuff!"

"Me, too." Adoringly, Faith regarded Freddy for a moment. He was so handsome and strong, and she had been trying all evening not to look at his shapely thighs, though it was very difficult with such close-fitting doeskins. . . .

"Do you think . . . Faith, do you think . . . could you bear to marry me?"

Miss Finchley could hardly believe she had heard aright.

"Marry . . . gracious, you cannot be serious!"

"I am, never more so. Oh, say you will, Faith. You are as pretty as a picture and you do not forever nag at me and, oh Faith, you are such a dear, dear creature!" This said with so much unexpected feeling that he squeezed her hand for emphasis.

Rascal, who had had a bad day, had not caught a single rabbit (though not for want of trying), had not been given dinner, and had not been patted as he ought to be, now forgot his angelic poise, growled crossly, and jumped between them.

"Down, Rascal, down!"

But Rascal would not be fobbed off so lightly, so Faith had to pat him and Freddy had to withdraw his hand and cast the occasional darkling glance at the hound.

"We might as well have a chaperone!"

Faith giggled. "Bad boy, Rascal! Lord Frederick had something very particular to say." She felt in a positive mist of happiness and really no longer cared that she was ruined and cold. Only, of course, she was not ruined. Freddy was going to marry her!

"Freddy?"

"Yes, Faith?"

"I know I am meant to have two thousand pounds but I don't, really."

"Another tarradiddle, Faith?" But Lord Frederick looked charmingly unconcerned.

"Not a tarradiddle precisely, for Honor—my sister, you know—says she has almost won that sum, but I feel wretched taking it from her when she can quite easily use it for her gaming house."

"For her what?"

For the first time, Freddy was startled out of his sunny composure. So Faith explained.

"Good gracious! I am not perfectly certain, but I am sure it would be better if I settled a sum upon her. A large sum, mind, so she does not have to go to such lengths. The duke, you see, has some horrid notions regarding propriety."

Faith quite saw, and thought the matter most satisfactorily dealt with. Only she thought it right to mention that her sister might possibly have notions of her own.

"That might be all right, but Honor is extremely headstrong."

"So is my father! Do not worry, Faith, I am sure it can be settled." So Faith stopped worrying. That was what she liked about Freddy—he was so commanding! Freddy, never called *commanding* in his life, basked in the novel experience and stroked her hair reassuringly.

He was no longer panicked that help had not arrived as the farmer had promised. He hardly even minded losing to that miserable scrap of humanity, Sir Godfrey Islington.

The only thing he minded was Merit's reaction when he heard of this latest escapade. Still, there was no point fretting when Faith smelt so heavenly and fresh and clean, just as if she had bathed in lavender or roses or essence of snowdrops.

"So you will marry me?"

"Oh, Freddy, of course I will! Rascal can stay with us, then!"

Faith felt she would burst for joy. There was no one at all nicer, sweeter, or more handsome than Freddy. She did not at all mind missing her season as an unmatched debutante, for who could possibly be more debonair than Lord Manning, or more comfortable to be around?

Faith felt her bliss marred only by her anxiety for Lady Elizabeth. She only hoped that her ladyship had noticed her absence, assumed she had the toothache, and retired early.

Naturally, this was not the case, for Lady Elizabeth was currently suffering from paroxysms of anxiety—especially as she knew it was her own son who had been entrusted with Faith's care and no one had heard hide nor hair of him since morning. It was very fortunate indeed that Faith knew nothing of her concerns, or it would have spoilt a little of the happiness that was creeping every moment through her very being.

Every time Lord Frederick moved toward her, her heart gave a little skip of rapture. Unfortunately, Rascal seemed to sense this and disapprove, for he growled annoyingly, until Frederick ventured to say that when they married he should be tied up.

At this, Rascal nipped more than just his ankles, causing Freddy to curse—though mildly, for he was never more aware of a lady's presence—and announce that he should dashed well be given away immediately.

But Faith, loyal to the last, reminded him that but for

Rascal they would never have become acquainted. Freddy, seeing the justice of this, muttered that he would have to be placed in the country, then, and Rascal seemed to approve, for he wagged his tail and let go of my lord's ill-used tassels. So the hound was reprieved. He sniffed the evening air and behaved himself just so long as his master and mistress did, too.

The road narrowed slightly to the left, then revealed, in the shadows, a wide plain and a steep drop just below it. Merit, now rather concerned (though he would not for the world have said as much, even to Tom coachman), looked about him for the wheat fields Islington had spoken of. They were still near Tilling, so Freddy could not be far if Sir Godfrey had already passed him before his own misfortunes had occurred.

Merit alternated between grinding his teeth, threatening to thrash what was left of Freddy to a pulp, wondering who in heaven's name the unlawful passengers were, and fearing the worst.

What if Lord Manning had been injured? He doubted whether Sir Godfrey would have stopped to either know or care. Not for the first time, he wished he was mounted rather than riding sedately in his chaise.

"Hurry, Tom, can you?"

"Aye, sir, the moon is full so I can see clearly now." They drove on, Merit all the time looking for any wheat fields that might have been planted. At length, he found what he was looking for and the telltale trail left by his own chaise. Worse, he could see the abandoned carriage, looking rather mournful in the lonely moonlight. No sign of Freddy, though. Or a dog. Or a lady.

Perhaps Sir Godfrey had been dreaming.

CHAPTER 16

Lady Darfield did not lose time once she had made up her mind. All her ailments—real and imagined—seemed to disappear when she had something more important at hand.

Honor was startled to note that the air of gloom she had so carefully fostered was now stripped away. She rang bells, ordered up servants, forced some eel stew (the only warm thing left in the kitchens since the banquet had been allowed to go cold) down Honor's throat and generally called out so many conflicting orders one could have mistaken her for a general in His Majesty's army.

Just as hundreds of tapers had lit the corridors, Great Aunt Petunia now announced that hundreds must be lit in her chamber, for she was "blessed to know how she was meant to see for all the shadows."

Despite the ungodly hour, the upper chambermaids were sent to the attics to look for silks and pattern cards—very out of date but Honor had not the heart to say so—and in the meanwhile, Lady Darfield took Merit at his word.

"He said I must play cards with you as much as I can, my dear—teach you a little something, you know." She patted Honor's hand mildly. A very large sapphire glistened darkly upon her finger.

"At this hour, my lady? Perhaps he meant in the morning."

"Nonsense, he meant at all hours! Surely you are not such a namby-pamby miss that you keep early hours?"

Honor was stung, but also rather amused. "Certainly not! I was thinking of you, Madame!"

"Ha, a likely story! Sit down and we will see if I am in my dotage, hey?"

So Honor sat and played until the new wax candles were burning rather low. Even then, she shuffled calmly and showed no sign of fatigue until the dragon herself pushed the cards away.

"Oh, stop with the tiresome things. Tell me about yourself, miss. I wager your tale is more exciting than that damned impertinent novel I read the other day. What was it called? *Joseph Andrews* or something like that. Don't laugh, missie! I hope you have not read it, for it is perfectly disreputable and I shall write to the circulating library to tell them so!"

Honor murmured that it was not her custom to read Fielding, but the dragon eyed her quizzically nonetheless and demanded that she not turn the subject.

"How came you to meet my hapless great nephew? And no tarradiddles, mind, for I vow it was not at one of those dreary tonnish balls!"

"It wasn't, though I am not certain I really want to divulge the circumstances. . . ."

Great Aunt Petunia laughed. "Good! Something scandalous—I could tell the moment I set eyes on you! Tell me at once—I can keep a secret, you know."

Honor knew nothing of the sort, but she was wise enough to know there was no resisting Great Aunt Petunia. She was like an immovable object and it was pointless trying to be an unstoppable force—it simply couldn't be done. So she told Aunt Petunia, plainly and rather undramatically, all of the events that led to her acquaintance with Merit. All, that was, that related to Chittlingdon and the masquerade and the great chase of the mail coach. Certain more interesting bits she abridged and hoped, rather nervously, that they would not be missed.

When she had done, Great Aunt Petunia was smiling. She stretched out her arms, overset the dragon-footed occasional table brought in by Robins, threw her arms about Honor, and embraced her so warmly Miss Finchley was in severe danger of suffocation.

"My child," she said, "you are a chick after my own heart. If I were half my age I would have done the same myself."

Honor neglected to say Great Aunt Petunia would have to have been a third or a quarter of her age, for the words were meant very kindly indeed. The dragon seemed rather tame for someone who had been breathing fire but a few hours before. Honor smiled. She understood, now, why Merit had brought her here.

Lady Darfield was masquerading. She was not a dragon, but a great big puppy in disguise. As if to discredit this thought, Lady Darfield scowled fiercely once more and wagged her finger in Honor's face.

"And don't think, young lady, that I don't realize you have left a lot out in the retelling! Merit may be a lot of abominable things, but I don't think you can bamboozle me into believing he has milk and water in his veins! Good, you are blushing. Serves you right!"

So saying, her ladyship set her lorgnette to the pattern cards she had taken up, waived away several bolts of silk, and announced that they had never been more in need of a trip to Harding and Howell's in all of their lives.

"Drapers, you know," she said, with an expansive sweep of her hand.

The Marquis of Laxton was not thinking of drapers. He was peering into the darkness, looking about him for tracks. He had thought, at first, that there was no evidence of man or beast but now saw that he was mistaken. As his eyes adjusted to the moonlight, he could see a definite trail from the chaise. Two trails, in fact. He leapt down from his conveyance and asked Tom to remain above.

Then, heedless of his polished boots, he ran down the hillside, every so often missing his footing as he hit against rock rather than the softer earth. The marquis was as agile as a cat, so he stumbled rather than fell and was down at his canary-colored coach—the sign of the Four Horse Club— in half the time the farmer had been. He did not need to inspect the chaise. It was as plain as a pikestaff what was wrong with it, and very sorry it looked, too.

He wondered what had become of Dapple and Dimple and trusted that Freddy had attended to them. Now came two trails in opposing directions. He was just deciding to head for the stream he could hear trickling to the left— more than likely the watering place of his priceless matched grays—when he heard low voices coming from the opposite direction. He stood still a moment, listening, then heard an unmistakable growl. Sir Godfrey had muttered something incomprehensible about a dog. He walked swiftly now, in the path of the second trail.

What he saw as he rounded the slight bend to arrive at his destination stopped him utterly in his tracks.

Lord Manning—dear Freddy Manning, whom he had known as a boy and who he knew with perfect certainty loathed all specimens of the female sex—was now engaged in low, intimate discussion with a delicate-featured maiden. The maiden seemed to think the very world of him, for her eyes glowed with love, and her neck tilted upward toward him as if he were a font of wisdom.

This might have been startling enough if one discounted the dog, who was growling between his teeth such that Freddy was forced to remove his arms from about the lady's waist and declare with laughing exasperation that the hound was a menace.

"He thinks he is protecting me." The voice was soft, well modulated and rather musical. Merit moved closer, for it was apparently meant to be a night of shocks. No, he was not wrong, or permitting his passions to overshadow reality.

He drew a deep and level breath to still his heart and looked closer. The girl was, in essence, an exact replica of Honor. Well, not exact, precisely, for her eyes were merrier and they did not have the same degree of intensity or intelligence. Well, not to him, anyway.

Her mouth was very much like Honor's, only pinker, or perhaps that was just the shadows? He could not be very sure, but he could have sworn Honor's lips were a redder shade though both were shaped into that beautiful, almost perfect bow. The hair . . . yes, the chiefest difference was here—this lady's was lustrously long but sported none of the elder Miss Finchley's natural style.

He rather *liked* Honor's crisp, Grecian cut, and the tiny curls that just softened the effect. There were no curls now in evidence. This hair—the same silky dark shade as Honor's—hung luxuriously down the length of the stranger's back, giving the impression more of a dreamy goddess than a mere mortal.

He stepped forward. The pair became aware of the crunch of boots upon the earth and looked in Merit's direction.

"Do you think it could be the wheelwright?" Again that soft, gentle voice, half timid, half tremulous.

"Not at this hour. It will be morning before he shows his face, I shouldn't wonder. Perhaps the farmer has brought us some dinner." Murmured whispers as Freddy peered cautiously into the dark. Lord Manning did not like to mention he was afraid of footpads, for he saw no need for scaring Faith without reason. But his voice was bold as he called out in ringing tones:

"Who goes there?"

"It is I," replied Merit, appearing as if from nowhere. His voice was not grim, precisely, but Freddy looked as if he would rather have confronted a footpad any day.

"Oh, don't look so stricken, Freddy—you should know I would never beat you to a pulp in the presence of a lady."

At which caustic comment Freddy breathed an inward sigh, for he knew Merit well enough to know when he was teasing.

"I am so sorry, Merit. I really am. You can have no notion of how perfectly miserable I feel. . . ."

"Yes, I noticed that as I strolled down here on this rather . . . shall we say *romantic* . . . moonlit night?"

Faith felt herself blush to the very tips of her boots but she felt it only fair to speak up for Freddy.

"Oh, *pray* don't be cross. It was not his fault, you know!"

Merit smiled. It was a genuine smile and more amused than reproving.

"Yes. I do understand. Such beauty as yours must serve as a powerful excuse for distraction."

"Oh! I did not mean . . . oh, sir, you are teasing me!"

Which Lord Merit was, for he was interested to see her downcast eyes and the blush of confusion that reached her cheeks. Interesting, but he preferred the more direct approach of the sister. For sister Honor must surely be—the likeness declared itself in volumes.

"Merit, may I present to you to . . ."

"Stop! Let me guess a moment. Felicity? Favor? No? But how disappointing. Folly?"

Faith chuckled. It was a delightful sound.

"That serves me right, I suppose! Folly! Now there's a rare joke and quite deserved if you observe my predicament! I don't know how it is possible, sir, but I suspect you to be acquainted with my sister."

"I believe so, though she scrupulously neglected to mention a sibling."

"Why do you guess the initial 'F' then?"

"Something she once let slip. I might have misheard her. Could it have been an 'S' possibly? Salvation? Simplicity?"

"Gracious, not as bad as that! I am Faith, sir."

"Ah, Faith and Honor. I should have guessed."

"What in the blazes are you talking about?"

"Did you not know that Miss . . . er . . . Finchley . . . ?"

Faith nodded. "Did you not know that Miss Finchley has a sister?"

"You are to wish me happy, Merit."

"Indeed, after I have thrashed you thoroughly, I shall. A good choice, Freddy, though I fear your bride might be dowerless."

"She is not dowerless! She has two thousand pounds."

"For which I carry a note of hand. Does that matter, do you think?"

"You talk in riddles but of course it does not. Faith, Faith, what is it?"

For Faith looked suddenly very pale indeed.

"Sir, have you won two thousand pounds from my sister? She must be heartbroken. Where is she? Oh, take me to her at once!"

"She is perfectly happy, my dear. She has not lost the money to me, only delivered it into my hands for . . . eh . . . for investment."

Faith caught the amused hesitation in Lord Laxton's voice. She forgot her shyness in her alarm.

"You mean for the purposes of some totty-headed scheme!"

Lord Laxton's eyes twinkled. "Precisely. She can be quite tiresome, your sister, can she not?"

The color had returned to Faith's cheeks. She found she

liked the unknown gentleman, despite his threats and slightly arrogant manner.

"Not tiresome, precisely, but strong-willed. I love her dearly."

Merit wanted to say that he did, too, but he refrained from this startling announcement and mentioned that Sir Godfrey was stranded but two miles from the start post at Tilling.

Faith and Freddy stared.

"Are you funning us?"

"I have never been in more earnest. I do not like losing races that are driven in my name. There is still time to overtake the rogue and finish at . . . where was it?"

"Strathmore. But it is impossible, Merit! There is no sign of the wheelwright and I have twisted your axle and damaged a wheel. . . ."

"You are very bad, Freddy. I should strangle you, but there is no time if we are to win that race."

"How? How are we to win it?"

"What are the rules?"

"There are no rules save that it is a cross-county and that I arrive at the appointed finish before Godfrey."

"*You* arrive or may I?"

There was a sudden lightening of Freddy's features. "By gum . . ." Then his face fell again.

"No, it is no good, Merit. It has to be me. I remember now."

"Can you switch carriages?"

"I don't think so. Sir Godfrey would cry foul."

Merit sighed. "Very well, then, we shall have to swap carriage *wheels*. The axle is easily fixed if we put our heads together . . . there are tools in the paneled compartment at the rear. I don't suppose you knew of them?"

Freddy shook his head. "Not much I could have done anyway, without tools."

"Well, now you have one. Get cracking, will you? Miss Finchley, would you mind very much if you let Lord Manning complete the race without you?"

"No, of course not! Only, what shall I do? Wait here?" The wheat fields seemed rather lonely all of a sudden. Faith shivered but held to her purpose. She would not be any further hindrance to Lord Manning, she simply wouldn't!

Merit smiled at her foolishness but liked her the better for it.

"No. By good fortune my aunt resides hereabouts. I propose to take you there on horseback, for my own chaise will now be rendered useless."

"But . . ."

"No buts, Frederick. If we are going to save Miss Finchley's reputation—and we are—it has to be put about that she was residing with Lady Darfield, my aunt."

"But what will your aunt say to her arrival at this hour?"

"Leave the details to me. Miss Finchley must be in want of a good bath and some decent food in her stomach."

Miss Finchley, brave up until this point, now felt annoying tears well up at the thought of such a delightful prospect. Oh, for a hot bath and something good to eat! She had not liked to mention it, for it was a very unromantic thing to do, complaining of hunger when in the midst of an adventure with the gentleman of one's dreams—but she was famished and had been so since afternoon.

"Thank you, sir," she said shyly. Merit nodded briefly and smiled.

"The hound shall have to remain here with Tom coachman until morning. We can tether him near the horses and feed him from the picnic basket in my chaise."

Rascal, who had been about to bark in indignation, now cocked his ear to one side and subsided. Perhaps it was the picnic basket that had appeased him. Either way, he licked Merit—an honor that Freddy had not yet achieved—and behaved suspiciously amiably as he was gingerly patted by Lord Manning.

"Sit by that tree stump, Miss Finchley. I am sure our work will not take above an hour."

"Can I not help?"

"It is tough work . . ."

"I am less frail than I look. Oh, please, please let me help—it will make things much easier!"

"Very well, if you are certain . . ." Faith nodded determinedly. She won Merit's respect by not complaining once, even when the wheel proved very heavy indeed and the axle a nightmare to hold steady as it was mended. Tom coachman helped with the fittings and Freddy lay beneath the chaise to help with the wheel change and axle adjustments. Finally, it was all done. If Freddy set the spanking pace he had started with, the makeshift repairs would break in half a length. If he took things slowly and cautiously, he should make it to Strathmore without much incident.

"Be warned, Frederick! If you ruin this one I shall never forgive you! I would rather lose the race than have you break your neck."

Lord Manning nodded. He was very abashed at the silliness of what he had done. Sir Peter and the Honorable Bertram must still be waiting at Strathmore unless they had given up the ghost.

"You'll take care of Faith?"

"But naturally, you cawkbrained ninnyhammer! I am not going to ravish her along the way!"

"No, but I worry . . ."

"Leave all your worries with Uncle Merit. Go and win the damn race, for I misliked the look of that pompous, addlepated jackanapes. Tom, give the veal pies to the hound and help yourself to whatever you want from the basket. There is a decent loaf of bread and a smoked trout in there, if I recall. Oh! Also help yourself to the wine. Not the best vintage, but adequate for a moonlight wait, I suspect. Come, Miss Finchley, I think it best if we ride *pied à terre*. Will you manage?"

Faith nodded uncertainly. Lord Laxton's horses looked very large in the moonlight and she had never been so good a rider as Honor. She watched as the marquis chose Lightning to saddle and tried to look as cool and collected as Miss Bramble was forever insisting on she was meant to be.

"Hold on to me—no, forget your modesty, I am not going to eat you! Help her up, Frederick, will you?"

This was a job Lord Manning was eager to perform. Before she knew it, Faith was up behind Lord Laxton, her dainty feet delicately peeping from her skirts. Lord Manning averted his gaze, for naturally she was not wearing the longer, more suitable riding gown.

"Ready?"

Faith nodded. She cast one brilliant, pleading, hopeful, encouraging glance at Freddy and smiled.

"Ready," she said.

Lady Darfield's butler could hardly believe his ears when there came a rapping on the knocker door not only past the fashionable hour, but at the unsociable hour of midnight. He was already in his nightcap when informed of the commotion and though he found it irregular in the extreme, he was paid very well and precisely, he supposed, for this sort of occasion.

He took up a cudgel, for there had been speak, lately, of highwaymen roundabouts (though what they should want with the retiring Lady Darfield he could not fathom). He indicated to the two assembled footmen to stand aside, but within hearing. He was fortunate that he passed a looking glass as he did so, for in his haste he had entirely forgotten he had his nightcap on.

This he handed with what dignity he could muster to the more junior of the two night footmen and padded up to the door.

What happened after was food for much gossip in the kitchens, for it was the marquis returned, and with a lady, too. What a commotion! Two ladies—both passing fair— upon her ladyship's threshold in less than a few hours! What was more, her ladyship gave neither their marching papers, nor threw any prized Wedgwood vases at them, nor howled for the watch, but rather ordered up a hot bath and dinner in both instances.

Cook, got out of bed, grumbled, but it was such a vast change from the usual and so gratifying to see my lady pulled out of the doldrums and calling for her silverware, not to mention crystal decanters and goblets all of the finest golden plate, that her complaints were not too severe nor heeded overmuch.

Only Robins, worked off her feet, seemed slightly exasperated. Miss Finchley, it appeared, had doubled. Anyone disbelieving her could go and see for themselves. And Lord Laxton, all arrogant and thoroughly enjoying her discomfiture, she might add!

Another person enjoying herself for the first time in years was Lady Darfield herself, who refused—positively refused—to go to bed. Lord Merit, told in caustic terms that he should "go away now and never dare return with yet another Miss Finchley," bowed rather smartly and did precisely that, but not before his eyes had burned into Honor's, or his amused glance had noted that she was already directly under Lady Darfield's thumb. She was reeking of heady perfume and had, about her shoulders, an enormous—and perfectly hideous—peacock-colored shawl.

CHAPTER 17

Freddy took a great deal more time than he wished climbing the steep embankment just above the wheat fields. The carriage wheels creaked precariously and he was more anxious than usual about keeping a steady hand for the cattle. It was one thing driving a well sprung chaise, quite another leading a team of horses when at any moment one's repairs might break.

He took it slowly, though, despite the temptation to race, and was rewarded, at last, with a clear sight of the crest of the hill. From there, the country was slightly flat but naturally the route a trifle longer, the very thing he had been at such pains to avoid.

Still, the worst, he mused, was over. Miss Finchley was safe, Lord Laxton had been apprised of his crime, and he, Freddy, was not yet dead. A miracle! Lord Laxton's temper was notorious when aroused.

Freddy had to give him credit: Merit had seemed amiable enough under the appalling circumstances and had actually been rather encouraging. Freddy grinned. He should never have doubted the marquis—he was a great good gun despite his depressing name.

The horses were on a decently straight path now, if a little pebbly at times. The moonlight helped rather more than the gas lamp, which was flickering in its prison of tinted glass. Freddy had a nasty suspicion that Godfrey might have found the help he required, for he seemed to be stranded nowhere on the route. Fortunately for Lord Manning, this was a case of his simply being impatient, or else of Merit miscalculating the distance somewhat, for presently he came to that very welcome sight, a wreckage just some yards from the road.

"Hoy, you! A guinea for your team of horses!"

There was desperation in Sir Godfrey's tone and also a marked increase in the price he was offering. Earlier, it had been no more than a half crown, though naturally Freddy knew nothing of this.

Now, he tooled his horses skillfully out of the way of the wreck and its attendant cattle. Then, just as he passed, he doffed his beaver—retrieved, a little crunched, from the wheat fields—and declined the offer with a chuckle.

Maddened, Sir Godfrey could only spend the next half-hour wondering how on earth a blockhead like Frederick could have repaired his chaise. He then spent the next few minutes feeling sick to the stomach, and the few after that determinedly examining his horses himself, to see if he could not drive without a shoe. Of course he could not! The horse was already lame in the left leg and pulling. He had—he simply had—to find a new team.

Freddy's spirits rose considerably after passing Sir Godfrey. The night seemed blessed with a thousand stars and though his carriage was slow and his horses tired, he was nonetheless driving the smartest carriage in all of England. Oh, the mark of the Four Horse Club!

How perfectly heavenly to drive such a chaise and this time *with* permission. How perfectly heavenly, too, that Faith—dear, delicious Faith—was going to marry him. He must lose no time in speaking of the matter to Lord Islington, who he understood was her godfather. Awkward, of course, that he would have just thrashed his son in a race, but such things were not unheard of and he felt certain he could find some code of etiquette to cover the awkwardness.

He drove on, whistling, unaware that five miles or so behind him, Sir Godfrey had found his team. Unmatched they were, and lent out for a positively exorbitant price, but a team nonetheless, shod and able to ride despite the strange hour of travel.

Sir Godfrey was not so feeling toward his cattle as Freddy might have been. He left his own with the owner of the current pair and whipped these on, willing them to race though they were stubborn old cart horses and unused to such mad games as these.

Still, they felt the hand of authority—for Sir Godfrey was a good driver despite his weak character—and they responded, albeit grudgingly.

Frederick was hampered by his necessity to go slower than he wished but he kept his head and determinedly headed for Strathmore, remembering every obstacle looming ahead and taking good care to avoid overturning the chaise. This was easier said than done, for the countryside had become rather bushy and narrow in places. At one time, Freddy had to almost slow to a stop as he encountered rabbit holes—treacherous to his team. He knew perfectly well that one stumble could mean the end of the race, for he would not push the horses if they sprained a hock.

Sir Godfrey was making rather better time, especially as he kept to the tracks Frederick had beaten for him with his carriage wheels. It struck him, though, that while this gave him the advantage of being able to catch up, it did not give him the more crucial advantage of advancing forward to a win.

He was just coming to the point where the invisible rabbit holes were situated (for they are, even on a starlit night, practically invisible when you are perched up high and concentrating on a team) when the idea struck him that if he veered off a little, and took the road, he could get ahead of Lord Manning. Once ahead, he could veer back onto the earthen track and none would be any the wiser save himself. He, of course, would be a great deal richer and spared the pain of another lecture from his father, Lord Islington. Better yet, he would have taught that dandified Lord Frederick a thing or two without having to open his own purse strings for once.

Sir Godfrey was not entirely a villain so he only *thought* all this as he negotiated the rabbit holes and the bushes and the narrow verges. But the more he thought of the idea, the more it kept popping into his head, especially when he practically had to stop because the right colt had its hoof deep in a rut. He climbed down to coax it out and to soothe the team, for they were useless if they chose to revolt, and looked far into the black distance. If only he could see the light of Freddy's lantern! Then he would know how far forward he was and could take some action. But there was no sign of Freddy, only the tracks of his damn fine carriage wheels.

Sir Godfrey was disheartened. He did not fancy an evening's drive in these conditions only to lose every penny he possessed. The more he thought about it, the more he felt he deserved to cheat. Besides, it was not a cheat, precisely, for no one had said they were not permitted to take the road. Indeed, he specifically remembered stating that there *were* no rules. He was on shaky ground, here, for the very terms of the race was "cross-country," but he was now so set on this alternative that he found it perfectly possible to overlook this minuscule detail.

Besides, the chance of anyone realizing his deception was slim. If he veered back off the track way ahead of Lord Manning, none could possibly be any the wiser. Sir Peter Worthington and the Honorable Bertram Snell must have long given up waiting. If not, they would be at the finish and they were all so damned honorable he doubted whether it would cross anyone's mind to question his route.

Convinced, at last, of the correctness of his position, he headed his chaise toward the easy road and for the first time since meeting up with Lord Manning, he smiled.

Faith and Honor were tucked up in two enormous beds that were nevertheless dwarfed again by the cavernous room. Between them, they had convinced Lady Darfield to retire at last. Gentle pleading had not done any good, so Honor had bearded the dragon in her lair and become so fierce that my lady nearly beat her with her walking stick. Honor had not flinched, though inwardly she trembled at her own temerity.

My lady had then laughed, patted her with her gnarled hands, and told her she was a bully but a child after her own heart. After that it had been a hop and skip away from meekly ringing the bell for Robins and announcing that her nightclothes must be set out.

Relieved, the sisters had been escorted to their own hall—for it could hardly be called a chamber—and permitted their ablutions in privacy. A hot brick was already tucked into their beds and they noted that while the room looked unused, their sheets were of the finest linen and very well aired. When chocolate was brought in, their contentment was perfectly complete, though Faith still had nasty qualms about Lady Elizabeth.

In the event, they need not have worried, for Lady Elizabeth was long abed and by the time she woke up, Lady Darfield's card was awaiting her attention. This had been delivered by Merit's groom very early the next morning, for Lord Laxton was meticulous in all small details and had considered this a necessary contrivance.

In the meanwhile, however, the girls had time to exchange stories, though Honor was rather more reticent than

Faith, who, indeed, did most of the talking. She was trying her very hardest to cajole Honor into returning with her to St. Martin's Square.

"Lady Elizabeth begged me write to you at once! She would naturally have included you in the first invitation had she known you were without sponsor. She is a darling, Honor. Do, do say you will come."

Honor, cozily tucked in bed, thought what an easy solution this would be. Faith was dying for her to take up the offer, and really, she did not think her scruples were any longer founded. So why did she suddenly have a horrible hole at the pit of her stomach? Why did her delicious milk and nutmeg posset suddenly taste rather bitter?

The answer, she knew, lay in her own wild self. She wanted to be foolishly wicked and utterly beyond the pale! Here, she had the opportunity to be perfectly respectable and it paled in comparison with the danger being offered her by Merit.

It was not just the danger of becoming penniless rather than genteelly poor. It was not just the danger of being exposed inside Brooke's and stripped of her right to be called "lady." It was more, much more than that.

She wanted to be with Merit; she longed for those lessons he spoke of, wherever they might lead. She knew the danger—the greater danger—of his considerable attractions, yet she was drawn to those dangers as a helpless moth to the flame. Not helpless—that was deceiving. Willful. That was what she was, a willful butterfly dancing toward a tantalizing flame. The chances of being burned were incalculably high, yet she cared not. How much better to live passionately, if only for a moment, than to live properly all of one's life!

"No, Faith," she said. "I am sorry, but I shall—I must—forge my own path. "

"You don't understand! Lord Manning knows about the

dowry! He simply does not want it. You don't have to do this for me any longer, Honor."

"I am glad, Faith, truly I am. But you shall have your two thousand pounds—you deserve it. No, stop. Let me finish! It is not entirely for you I am doing this. To be honest, it is no longer for you at all. It is for me, Faith. I can't explain myself but I am doing this for me."

Faith lay back on her pillows. She was quiet a long time; then she slipped out of bed and kissed her sister gently on the cheeks.

"Knock them dead, Honor, " she whispered in the most unladylike term Miss Faith Finchley had ever uttered.

The race was all but over. Sir Peter Worthington, haggard from the lack of a shave and worry for his friend, waited at the requisite marble colonnades signifying Strathmore Park. He was taking it in turns with Bertram, who was more cheerful about the affair and said that he had expected it all along: foolishness to think the race would take only a couple of hours.

"Why, Pete," he had said, "it would take us longer by road! We got the calculation wrong, that is all. They can't *both* have been overturned! No, depend upon it—they will arrive, all right and tight, you see if they don't!"

But he had been saying this for hours now and even his own confidence seemed to be waning. It had just been agreed between them—by dint of a toss of coin—that he would be the first to test the delights of the Cobb and Partridge, a short distance from the finish point. No point in them *both* standing there like silly fools! He would hurry, quaff his thirst with the inn's finest, and change the guard as soon as he was able.

* * *

Sir Godfrey's pace quickened considerably on the firm, beaten track that was the confirmed route of the stagecoach from Banbury to South Haven to Tilling and then on to Strathmore and beyond. The road, as a consequence, was a Telford road, based on a trench laid with a small foundation of heavy rock. The top layer of the road consisted of six inches of compacted stone broken very small, so that it was an easy ride—a very easy one—for Sir Godfrey, who could now forget the annoyances of sand, grass, bush, holes, and other country hazards that made the ride inhomogeneous, varied, and slow. His pace quickened considerably as a result and though he still could not see Frederick, he knew he must be catching up fast. Just as he felt he must be close to driving six miles an hour at least, he noticed an oncoming farm gig in the opposing direction. He felt sure it would move aside for him, but it did not, causing him to have to bring his own cattle to a screeching halt and even some of his bits and pieces—nothing very important, only a small picnic hamper and maybe a sack of sweetmeats, or so—to tumble from his perch.

"Hoy! Can you not look where you are going, you stupid clothead?" The farmer, recognizing quality—but sour at being spoken to like this—muttered something about needing to fetch a doctor.

Sir Godfrey nodded curtly, for there was no point in dallying with the idiotish buffoon who'd caused him such inconvenience. He therefore did not ask the man if he needed any help or who might be sick, he simply adjured him to be more careful in the future.

Sir Godfrey did not wait for the indignant retort that followed, nor to pick up the remains of his lunch. He allowed the cart to pass (for it was completely in his way), then continued, trying, with ill humor, to attain his former speed. In this he was successful and he felt greatly cheered when he finally saw, by dint of a great deal of squinting, the light of Freddy's lantern not three yards in front of him, but a good deal more to his right.

If Lord Manning did not look back—and there was no reason for him to do so—he would not notice the chaise creeping up on him from the road. Quickly, Sir Godfrey dimmed his own lantern, so that he was now driving wholly to moonlight and what little light could be gleaned from the stars above. If anything, he was spurred to increase his pace, so the trot-trot of his horses' hooves became a more urgent trot-trot, trot-trot kind of sound, and the crunch of his carriage wheels seemed a little louder.

At length, he had overtaken Frederick and the temptation to follow him down off the road was great. But Sir Godfrey kept his head, fearing Freddy's own ability to increase pace, and stuck to the Telford road. After what seemed an age, he veered the carriage off the verge—to the annoyance of his team, who did not seem as inclined to travel cross-country as *he* now was—and resumed the race from the front. By his reckoning, Strathmore could not be far off. Indeed, he began to see the odd cottage, though the candles had all burnt to their sockets and there was no light in any of the windows. Still, he thought, here and there he could see the welcome drift of chimney smoke.

Freddy, behind him, was seeing the same delightful visions. He had no notion he had been passed by Godfrey and was thus feeling rather cheerful as he thought of a win for Merit and a well earned rest for himself. He wondered whether either of his friends would be there to witness the end and decided that one, at least, would. Someone needed to verify the winner and he was certain Bertie or Pete would not fail him in something so maddeningly important as this.

Imagine his shock as he rounded the bend and saw Sir Godfrey ahead of him, just negotiating a small embankment. His team looked rather the worse for wear, one a chestnut, the other—well, he was not sure what the other was, really. The point was, it was winning.

Frederick, who had been disinclined to speed due to the precariousness of his carriage, now let caution fly to the winds and increased his pace. The grays responded at once, for they were game creatures and unused to such moderate racing. The axle creaked and Freddy thought, with a groan, that they were lost at the very finishing posts.

But Merit's repairs did not fail him and the race, such as it was, was on. The Honorable Bertram, returning from the Cobb and Partridge, could only stare as the race drew to a close. He noted, with a pang, that the darling, canary yellow chaise was muddy, broken, and trailing in a poor second place. It was with a heavy heart that he reached the colonnades and Sir Peter. Both witnesses watched the subsequent proceedings with gloom.

CHAPTER 18

Merit, returning to Tom coachman and the hound, decided that they could fend for themselves for the night. It was more important, he felt, to relieve his two friends at the finishing post. True, they deserved the inconvenience that they must have suffered for encouraging Freddy in this nonsense, but his lordship considered they had been punished enough.

He was not sleepy at all, despite the hour, for the day had been one of many excitements and Lord Laxton felt in passing need of a good, bruising ride. If he had taken a chaise he would not by any means have made Strathmore in time, but the combination of the good Telford road, his exceptional beast, and his own desire for speed clinched the matter. With luck, skill, and clever timing, he would be in Strathmore long before Lord Manning.

It was not long after that that he realized Sir Godfrey was back in the race. There was no sign of his chaise or horses, save for some fresh tracks leading back toward Tilling, so Merit surmised he must either have given up or had achieved his unlikely objective of finding a fresh pair. He ruled out giving up when he saw ruts from carriage wheels in the direction of Strathmore. They were hard to see at first, in the dark, but Merit's eyes were quick, and he'd lit a lantern as he chambered down from Lightning.

He frowned a little, but still considered it unlikely that Sir Godfrey would catch up. Freddy had a good start, now, and was no longer overloaded weight-wise. He extinguished the little lantern and murmured soothingly to Lightning as he remounted. Lightning, a gem of an animal, responded instantly. He thundered on faster than ever, and only slowed when he felt Merit's light handling at the reins. This was because his lordship had noticed a gig facing him slightly ahead. The road was probably wide enough to allow both to pass, but Merit did not take chances.

As they drew closer, the occupant of the farm gig signaled him to stop; he did, though he rather wished the need was not that urgent. The man was panting.

"Sir, I need a doctor. The local man is out of town an' me wife is with child. They say it will be hours yet, but the sooner I 'ave a doctor by 'er bed, the 'appier I will be."

Merit smiled. "Her first? "

"No sir, but the first one died afore 'e was born, like. Right anxious I be for this one. It is early yet an' she feels the pains . . ."

"Have you a midwife?"

"Aye, sir, an' she says send for a doctor, just caution, like, there be nobbut tellin' what may 'appen."

"Very well then, do you want me to return to Tilling?"

"No, for I reckon Strathmore be closer an' yer be headed that way more'n like."

"Indeed. I shall be faster on this horse than you on this gig. I shall go at once. Where shall I direct the doctor?"

"To the manor house. Me wife is a cook in the kitchens. It can't be missed, like, the only large 'ouse 'ereabouts save for the squire's an' I reckon the doctor will know it. I will send a lad about to watch for 'im."

"Very well, I shall leave at once, for at all events I am in a hurry to reach Strathmore."

"You are very kind to stop then, sir, not like *some* wot I seen this night!" The man muttered darkly.

Something made Merit pause as he shifted lightly in his saddle.

"Meaning?"

"Meanin', me lor', that I passed a gentry cove a mile up yonder an' 'e was 'eaded for the village, like, but would 'e stop? Not a bit of it, though 'e knew it was a sawbones I was after. Nearly pushed me off the road, 'e did. After, when I seed 'e lost his picnic basket an' all, I called for 'im to stop, it bein' fancylike and monogrammed an' such, but 'e carried on down the road like the very devil was after 'im."

"Driving a chaise?"

"Aye, sir, top o' the trees one it was but with a pair o' cattle that would fair make yer weep, it would, so high in the instep was one an' so downright spotty the other! If I weren't so caught up in me own troubles I would 'ave chuckled, I would, for a sorrier-looking pair I've not seen, though I seen a lot, bein' second groomsmen to Squire Liversedge wot resides over these parts, beggin' yer pardon."

Merit nodded, an intriguing thought engaging his attention.

"Was the gentleman old or young?"

"Oh, passing young though I didn't stop to consider, only cursed 'im for a 'ard-'earted old . . . lor' luv me, I nearly disgraced meself wiv unsuitable language for a gentry mort!"

But Merit was not worried about cant, however descriptive. Certainly, if the man was Sir Godfrey, he could apply several epithets himself, but he resisted.

"He was on the road, not the turf alongside it?"

"Bless yer, 'e was on the road, all right! Nearly collided into me gig, 'e did, an' not a sorry to spare neither!"

"Thank you. I shall ride as fast as I can. Good luck to you and your wife!"

"Thank you, me lor'. Loik as not she'll have the wee one roit an' toit but I'm not the one to be takin' any chances."

The man bowed, cracked his whip, and nodded thankfully to Merit, who quickened his own pace, partially out of urgency for the man's sake, partially out of curiosity.

It seemed very likely indeed that it was Sir Godfrey who had been in such a hurry. If so, Sir Godfrey was nowhere near where he should have been, for cross-country to Strathmore was a very different thing from taking the road.

It was a fool's cheat, for the chances of being caught out were high. Still, a great deal of money was at stake and it was likely that Sir Godfrey might try to even up the odds.

He drove Lightning to a canter and scanned the horizons before him. He saw nothing, only the twinkling of stars and the bright, cheerful moon. It was hard to see if there had been any traveler before him, for darkness obscured the more usual indications. Somehow, though, the more Merit thought of it, the more convinced he became that Sir Godfrey was cheating. He wanted to get to Strathmore before either Islington or Freddy finished the race, but time was running out. In frustration, he rode poor Lightning harder, but the horse did not falter. As a matter of fact, it was magnificent. It rose to the occasion and literally flew over the beaten track, so Merit was certain he would achieve his objective.

Very soon he reached the village of Strathmore. It was dark, save for a few public houses with flickering tapers lit and the odd ostler's stable, hung with gas lanterns. He passed the colonnades of Strathmore Park—it looked deserted— and headed straight on for the nearest posting inn, which happened to be the very place that Bertie had disappeared into some hour before.

The innkeeper at the Cobb and Partridge directed him at once to the doctor, who lived very close by and was already awake despite the lateness of the hour. It was a simple matter of a very quick explanation and a gleaming coin exchanging hands and Merit's object was achieved.

By the time he returned to Strathmore Park, however, the race was at an end.

Freddy, dejected, was descending from his chaise. Merit noted with approval that it had sustained only very minor damage since its repairs and that Freddy must have driven skillfully indeed for this to be the case.

Lord Manning looked white, and Bertie and Peter—both back on duty—looked fairly miserable as they strode past the winning chaise to help Freddy descend. Sir Godfrey needed no such help. He carelessly threw his whip down on his perch and descended with a light leap that did nothing to harm the modish attire in which he was outfitted.

Merit, a dark figure silhouetted slightly in the moonlight, pulled up his reins and waited. He had approached from the Strathmore side rather than the Tilling side so his arrival, as yet, was unnoticed.

Freddy approached Sir Godfrey as Bertram looked to Lord Laxton's precious horses.

"I don't know how you did it, sir, but though I regard you as a blackguard and a villain, you won fair and square. You are therefore to be congratulated. You shall hear from my banker in the morning."

Sir Godfrey, who had always thought that sticks and stones could break his bones but never words, ignored the comment about villainy and bowed rather pleasantly.

"Thank you, my dear sir. Though I don't doubt your integrity for a moment—no, not a moment—I would prefer, if you please, a note of hand. Always tidier in such affairs as these, don't you think?"

The smugness of his tone was such that Sir Peter stepped forward to pummel the living daylights out of him, but it was Lord Manning, the loser, who divined his intentions and stopped him.

"Don't, Pete! He is not worth risking the watch. I shall write him the damned note of hand."

He turned to Godfrey. "You shall have my note, sir, but if ever you speak a word of this evening or so much as men-

tion a certain lady's hand in this, you shall have me to answer
to and that I warn you!"

Sir Godfrey bowed. "Why in the world I should give
that silly little widgeon a passing thought is beyond my
comprehension. You have my word, Lord Manning, just as
soon as I have your purse."

"You shall never have it."

This was the moment that Merit made his appearance
known. Dressed in black, he was still seated on Lightning
and presented a rather unexpected element to the assembled
party.

"Merit! I . . ."

"Don't say anything, Frederick. I know it all."

Sir Godfrey, at these cryptic words, experienced a curious
churning in his stomach. He told himself he was being fanciful, that Merit was not a mind reader, that no one could
possibly know of his cheat, but the more he regarded the
marquis's immovable features, the less he believed his own
platitudes.

He thought of bolting, then told himself not to be a
complete jackass. It was impossible for Lord Laxton to do
anything more than suspect, and suspicions were worth
less than a ha'penny eel pie. He must brave it out.

"Islington, I suspect you have something to confess.
Confess it now and the matter shall go no further."

Merit's words were ominously firm and confirmed Sir
Godfrey's worst fears. The marquis knew! Against all
odds, he somehow knew of the cheat! But how could he?
He had been nowhere in sight when he had taken up the
road, he was positive of it.

How then? How? Sir Godfrey decided Merit must be in-
dulging in a little calculated guesswork. Well, guesswork
he could deal with. It was all a matter of maintaining a
simple poker face. How many times had he managed in the
past when his father had suspected him of mischief and

threatened him with a beating? He had wriggled out of many a punishment with that simple poker face. He must do so now, for the stakes were higher than a childhood whipping. He needed Freddy's purse to survive till the next quarter, and Freddy's purse he would have.

"I have no notion of what you are referring to, my lord. Lord Manning has conceded the race and the affair is now entirely between the two of us."

"Not so. The race was undertaken in my name, on my behalf. I do not like losing, Sir Godfrey. It is not my custom." Merit flicked a speck of dust off his immaculate greatcoat. "Further, I don't like cheats."

"Cheats!" There was an audible gasp as all the players in this little interlude gasped, save Merit himself.

Sir Godfrey ignored the accusing eyes upon him. He ignored, too, his own desire to slap Lord Laxton's face. He was clever enough to realize that offering such an insult to the most notable swordsman in London was rather foolish. With a gulp he also remembered Merit had something of a reputation at Manton's. He played the innocent.

"I have no notion what you mean, Lord Laxton."

"Have you not? You should have fetched a doctor, Sir Godfrey. Wiser, far wiser. If you had been so obliging, I should never have met up with a certain farm gig on the main Telford road to Strathmore. I should never have had any interesting discourse with the driver of that gig and your cheat might never have been discovered. As it is, well, you were not so obliging and all the rest, therefore, has come to pass. Very interesting I find the matter, too, as I am sure Lord Manning here will agree."

"No!"

"No what?"

"You can prove nothing!"

But even as he said it, Sir Godfrey feared the ghost was up. He could see it in the confident manner in which Lord

Laxton laughed and in the dismissive, curt glance he cast over his person.

Godfrey, dressed to the nines, a veritable fashion plate of gentlemen's fashions, now felt small and rather grubby. It was a nasty sensation and one that made him panic, slightly, as though he had no air. He adjusted his cravat nervously.

"I fear you are wrong, Sir Godfrey. I can prove your cheat very easily, thanks to the obliging young man you abandoned on the carriage route to Strathmore. He holds, among other things, a monogrammed basket of yours that you might like to collect from him. Quite costly, by all accounts. I am certain you should like it back."

But Godfrey did not want anything of the sort. He should have liked to run, but his legs were shaky and the horses were restive behind him.

The Honorable Bertram had now passed from dire gloom to extreme triumph. The same sensation was just passing over Sir Peter, though Freddy still looked too stunned to believe his own good luck.

Merit winked. "Might I congratulate you, Lord Manning? Not quite in my own inimitable style, perhaps, but a tolerable ride. Yes, a ride for which you must, I suppose, be congratulated."

Freddy, at last seeing the truth, grinned.

"By jingo, Merit, I always said you were a trump!"

"Indeed. Now if you will be so kind as to take Sir Godfrey's note of hand, we might all retire for a cozy drink. I don't like to complain, but I find I am parched and I smelt an inviting cellar at the Cobb and Partridge."

Freddy stepped forward. "Well, Sir Godfrey? The tables have turned, indeed. If you require a quill, I believe there is one in my chaise."

Grandly put, and Merit's lips twitched, for strictly speaking it was *his* chaise, but he felt no need for corrections.

Sir Godfrey, seeing the game was up, now looked

younger than his three-and-twenty years. There were four experienced gentlemen of the world glaring at him—two peers of the realm—and he really had nothing to say. Worse, his pockets were to let—which was why he had challenged this race to start with—and his note of hand would not stand up to a banker's sneeze. He could write a promissory note, but he would be a laughingstock—not to mention a social pariah—when he was found to have no substance backing the promise.

He took up the quill and scribbled something fiercely.

Merit languidly perused the document as Freddy watched with interest. "This is satisfactory, young man. I hope you have the funds to cover it, for if you do not, you shall be hearing from me."

Godfrey reddened. He tried not to, but he did and even in the strange moonlight the reaction was visible to all but Bertie, who was still tending the handsome team of horses.

"Ah. I see we understand each other." Merit flicked the note contemptuously. "Tut tut! A grievous waste of ink and parchment, I fear. We shall, however, keep it, Sir Godfrey. It is your lucky night. We shall not bank this document, but hold it as collateral for your good behavior, so to speak."

"My good behavior?"

"Correct, if such a thing is possible. If it comes to my ears you have bandied Miss Finchley's name about, whispered a word of this evening's events, touched a hair on her head, approached her with any manner other than scrupulous respect, this chit shall be banked and the story of your cheat will be as common as ditch water. Do you hear and understand me?"

Merit's voice was low but it cut like a whip. Godfrey nodded, not knowing whether to be relieved at his reprieve, or angered by Lord Laxton's withering tone. In the event, he was both, but since he could do nothing about the tone without suffering a beating or a duel for his pains, he cravenly nodded and gruffly promised to accord Miss Finchley her due measure of respect.

"Not a hair on her head, you understand, nor a whisper to your cronies on pain of correction. We understand each other properly?"

Godfrey nodded. He understood, he thought bitterly, only too perfectly.

CHAPTER 19

Lady Darfield's antiquated carriage seated Miss Faith Finchley, a maid, a dresser, and a liveried footman. Lady Darfield never did anything by halves and if she was set on returning Faith to St. Martin's Square in style, nothing would do for her but a suitable retinue of staff and a letter to Lady Elizabeth in her ancient seal.

She might be a recluse, but she was a noble recluse—very rich, very eccentric, and very high-ranking. Consequently, it did Faith's reputation no harm to be seen traveling down Mayfair under Lady Darfield's banner—not ducal, precisely, for that was her brother's prerogative—but ancient and noble nonetheless.

Lady Elizabeth, so relieved that no harm had come to her and warned of her advent by Merit's letter, did no more than scold mildly and bid her rest.

Faith did not feel like resting, but she meekly curtseyed and did as she was told. She considered lying down when she was all aflutter and full of emotions, a small penalty for the exciting events of the evening before. As a matter of fact, resting upon her pretty bed and dreaming of Freddy was really not so very bad a punishment, so that by the time the evening came she actually felt rather cheerful and the luckiest lady alive.

If anything spoilt her composure, it was the thought that she still did not know the outcome of the race. She also worried that she might have to dance with Sir Godfrey. If she did, she would stand on his toes.

Miss Honoria Finchley was far too vigorous to spend the day in bed, even if Lady Darfield had wanted her to, which she did not. As a matter of fact, the dragon was so much in her element that Honor's day could not have been fuller, what with fittings and fussings (Honor's worst), but Lady Darfield was firm, hinting slyly that Lord Laxton was a man of discernment and taste and that his eye would not fall on anything that was drab, slovenly, or not in the very highest of good taste.

If Honor had stopped to think for a moment she would have laughed, for Lady Darfield's notion of high good taste was very far from her own and, she was perfectly certain, Merit's. By now, however, she was very fond of the old lady, so she allowed herself to be draped in a crescendo of diamonds and cabochon rubies such as would make even the hardiest of princes blink.

Then, of course, there was little time to do anything more than grab a handful of Valencia oranges and a few hurried slices of Stilton cheese, for my lady wanted to make every bit of use of Honor's talents. It was not often she had a creditable player in her house (or, strictly speaking, castle) and she dashed well intended to get her games in!

The day was spent amiably shuffling, dealing, muttering oaths here and there, examining the indices of certain cards with a lorgnette, peering here and there for the odd refined cheat (Honor held her cards too close, damn her!), and so on. My lady was never more mortified when she was beaten, nor more satisfied.

"Well, my dear," she said, "if anyone can bring Boodles to their knees it is you! I wish I were half my age—I'd do it myself. Wish I had thought of it, but there, there, you can't cry over spilt milk."

Honor smiled. "It is Brooke's, I think, ma'am."

"Oh, Boodles, Brooke's, they are all the same, these gentlemen's clubs. Need taking down a peg or two, I shouldn't wonder, and you are just the one to do it! Now, have you tried rose water essence for those freckles?"

"My sister has, Madame."

"Very sensible, too! Now, no argumentation, Honoria, we are going to apply some this very evening."

"Why? I am perfectly accustomed to my freckles."

"Blemishes. Blemishes, Honoria. We must deal with them."

"Why? I am to wear a veil!"

"It is hardly likely Lord Laxton is going to require you to wear a veil when you are married!"

"We are not getting married."

"Tshaw!"

"Beg pardon?"

"I said tshaw! And don't think to cozen me, young lady— I was not born yesterday, and if Merit does not intend to marry you I shall have him over my knee in a twinkling."

Honor laughed. "He is too old to go over your knee, Madame!"

Lady Darfield ignored the interruption. "You too, young lady, after all that canoodling I saw going on! You shall marry him or have me to answer to!"

Honor stopped laughing. "Oh, pray do not say anything of the kind to him, ma'am!"

"Why not? He is used to plain talking."

"He has already asked me. I have already refused."

"What has that to say to anything? He will ask again."

"Then I shall refuse again."

"Stubborn girl! Do you want to be cast beyond the pale?"

"It is rather fun."

"You are very wicked, very delightful, and a terrible, terrible liar. It is not fun at all and your voice is trembling."

"Only because I am overset."

"You are not overset when you lose a king, you are not overset when I win a round, you are not overset when your reputation is all but destroyed, but you *are* overset thinking of my rascally great nephew! What am I to make of that, I wonder?"

"Whatever you like, only don't pester him!"

Lady Darfield smiled. "Only if you use the rose water."

Honor sighed. It was not good throwing a pillow at her hostess—she was so fat it would bounce off unnoticed. There was only one thing, she supposed, she could do. She strode across the room and drew down the blue glass bottle Lady Darfield had ordered up earlier. Essence of rose water. She applied it under Lady Darfield's approving eye and wondered how she had been so foolishly snared by the dragon itself.

It was almost dusk when Merit, Lord Laxton, was announced at Darfield House. Honor—still draped in gems— had her back at the dragon by insisting that all the drapes be opened and the windows flung wide to allow in fresh, circulating air. Already, the place had a different feel about it and this was increased a thousandfold when Miss Finchley blackmailed my lady to leave her chamber and grace the opulent receiving rooms below-stairs.

The dragon had grumbled, had breathed fire, had coughed and complained, but Honor was adamant. Not a card more would she play in the bedchamber, not a roll of dice, not a simple trick, not a rubber, not a quick game of *vingt-et-un*. If my lady wanted to play, she must needs dress and make her way below-stairs.

Lady Darfield, used to bellowing, raging, and otherwise getting her own way, found this treatment diverting, if annoying, and finally succumbed to the greater benefit of all, for the castle had been more a mausoleum than a home and Honor firmly set her mind to changing matters.

His lordship was announced, therefore, by a more animated butler than usual and amid a bevy of housemaids who would normally have slunk quietly about their business, hardly daring to breathe, let alone make a tiny sound.

They now whispered a little, and even dared a giggle, for my lord was passing handsome whatever anyone might say, and though he wore hardly a jewel upon him, it was clear as a pikestaff that he was of the first stare. The butler took his silver-topped cane with a reverent bow and led my lord not up the stairs, as was his custom, but down the lower spiral to the receiving rooms.

Lady Darfield looked up from her cards when he entered. Honor startled, but remained similarly seated. She was suddenly shy, for he looked very dapper indeed in his evening clothes and though the missing cravat was now intricately tied between his shirt points, he looked no less seductive than she had been remembering.

As a matter of fact, he was possibly more so, for now he was elegance itself, and his dark hair seemed darker yet against the crisp white of his lawn shirt. His jacket, cut in the first style—had she but known it, by Weston—did nothing to hide the close-fitting nature of his doeskins. Not knee breeches, for he was not attending any formal functions that evening, but long, elegant pants, the line of which just covered his understated, polished shoes. They appeared to be two-toned, in black and white, but Honor could only really see the tips. Her glance took her upward again, so that she blushed and in her confusion discarded without thinking at all.

Lady Darfield, eagle-eyed, pounced on the talon and smiled triumphantly. "Ha! Two quints for thirty points. I do believe I have a repique! You should have declared your carte blanche, Honor."

But Honor was not thinking of carte blanches. Or not the card sort, anyway. She was staring at Lord Laxton, framed in the doorway. He raised his brows in that quizzical manner of his and entered.

Lady Darfield laid down the scorecard. "Ah, Merit!" she said. "Thought you'd show your face at last, hey?"

The dragon hardly looked up from her hand but her beady eyes noted with satisfaction that his lordship was looking as handsome as always and that he was bearing two posies of flowers.

"Thinking of turning us up sweet?"

"Well, of course, my dear aunt! These are for you, colorful and rather wicked with their exotic stems."

"Well! If I had my fan about me I would rap your knuckles for such impudence! Robins! Where is that woman? Oh, there you are. A vase, Robins—two, by the looks of things!"

Lord Laxton extended his arm to Honor. He did not need to say anything, for the flowers were the sweetest, most subtly scented Honor had ever smelled. They were also deeper than crimson, and softer, it seemed, than velvet.

"For you, my dear. You deserve them for surviving a day and a night in Great Aunt Petunia's company!"

Honor laughed but she felt a slight constraint between them, as if they were strangers wondering how to renew their acquaintance.

Then she was shy no longer, for my lord's eyes had just roved over her throat and across her neck and down, ever down, to her wrists and her fingers and fluttering, again, to that pulse at her throat half hidden for all the plethora of gems.

The amusement could not be ignored and Honor, in sudden sympathy, had a hard time stifling her own laughter.

"Good God!" was all he said, but Great Aunt Petunia, scrutinizing his stare with interest, nodded in a satisfied fashion. She leaned over to Honor and rather loudly whispered that diamonds could always be counted upon to arrest a gentleman's attention.

Whereupon Honor nearly chortled and my lord, not so circumspect, actually did.

"Leave us, Aunt. You have so stimulated my . . . my . . . masculine desires that I really feel I must be permitted to be alone with this young lady instantly."

To both Merit's and Honor's utter astonishment, the dragon rose at once from her chair and departed from the room, but not before spoiling the effect at the door by announcing that they could have ten minutes—no more, mind—and only because she was fetching out a book to peruse.

The pair nodded rather too innocently, so she pointed a gnarled finger in their direction and muttered that they could jolly well put all lascivious thoughts straight from their minds.

Once alone, both the marquis and Honor found this last request hard to do, for they had not seen each other for what seemed like an age and yet spent the whole day thinking, in fact, of little else. Small wonder Honor's heart was beating and my lord was tempted to push aside the gems merrily resting upon Honor's rather low-cut spencer. ("The very height of fashion," the dragon had stated firmly.)

"You look . . . beautiful."

"Like a gaudy parrot, you mean."

"Well, yes, that, too."

Honor laughed. "Wretch! But tell me, who won the race?"

"I am not wasting our precious ten minutes talking about Freddy's stupid scrapes!"

"What, then?"

"Come here and I will show you."

"Wickedness, Merit?"

"Miss Finchley, you do not know the meaning of the word. I would like to show you sometime."

"Sometime soon?"

"What a merry smile you have upon those intriguing lips! If you say things like that, it will be sooner than it ought to be and I shan't answer for the consequences!"

Honor felt very bold as she twinkled up at Merit, the diamonds reflecting the sudden light in her dark, intelligent eyes.

"I thought you would never come. The day seemed very long indeed."

"So I should think, closeted up with the dragon!"

"She is not a dragon, Merit, you lied to me!"

"I never lie. Ask anyone. Lady Darfield's reputation is renowned. People quiver and quake when she is about!"

"Not I, and I suspect you knew it would be so."

"Of course. You are a dragon slayer."

There was a moment's silence as the two smiled at each other. Then, ever so gently, Lord Laxton did what Honor had been dreaming about all day. He bent his head, tilted her chin ever so slightly, and kissed her. It was just the tiniest, sweetest, gentlest of kisses, but Honor felt it deeply. The warmth of it flooded through her very being and suffused her with the type of utter, innermost happiness that she would hardly have dreamed possible only a few days ago, when she had happily—but clinically—planned her gaming establishment.

Then she remembered that Merit had deliberately lost his game so that he need not marry her. The pain of it came flooding back worse than ever, worse because she had shown him that joy, there was no hiding it, nor her eagerness for whatever he had to offer. But no! She would not feel ashamed or embarrassed, only wary. She must learn to cover her heart a little, that she did not discomfit him. It was all Lady Darfield's talk of marriage that had muddled her.

She gently increased her distance and even removed the hand that had crept, unseen, about her waist. Merit, sensing the sudden constraint between them, was puzzled.

"I have offended?"

"Not at all. It is merely that I have been too forward."

"Impossible. That presupposes I do not want you to be."

"And you do?"

"Of course. You are a beautiful woman."

"Beautiful, but not beautiful enough."

"Now what does that mean, I wonder?"

But Honor was already wishing she could have stopped up her lips. She must love him but not with any lingering bitterness nor any false hope.

He had made his position very plain. He was kind and witty and perfectly miraculous, but he was not meant for her. She must enjoy him, but keep her distance. When she set up her gaming establishment it would be easier. She would have something to think about other than him.

Gracious, what had she thought about before she met him? Any number of worthy things, she was certain. How mortifying that she could think of nothing, now, save for his earthy presence and the burning need to make him smile at her in that special, secretive way.

She shook her head. "It is nothing—I am merely being fanciful."

"You are withdrawing from me."

"Am I?"

"You know you are. I want to know why."

"Why?" Honor suddenly longed to yell at him, to pummel at his damned muscular chest and shriek that *why* was because she could hardly bear contemplating the rest of her life without him and he had thrown her away on a cheating pack of cards. But she could not say as much; it would be churlish when he had been all that was handsome, all that was impossibly endearing. She knew for a certainty he would move heaven and earth to make her win this ridiculous wager. She turned the subject.

"Are you still so set on Brooke's?"

"Of course. I penciled the wager in this morning and by noon the page was full."

"Really?" Honor felt suddenly faint and rather afraid.

"Yes, and you need not look like that—you shall win every last penny!"

"I hope you are right, for I have staked everything I possess, including my good name."

"Then let us begin our lessons."

"Lessons?" Honor's heart fluttered uncontrollably.

His lordship smiled.

"Do you mean to tell me, Honor, that you have forgotten my promise?"

It was impossible to lie to him when her lips suddenly needed to be moistened and her hands trembled a little and the dragon sailed into the room with a great stamping of her stick and a quizzical eye cast in their direction.

Impossible, when his eyes never wavered from hers for a single second and not even Great Aunt Petunia's caustic comments—shockingly ribald—broke the intimacy of his stare.

"No, I have not forgotten." Honor almost whispered this, for the words were unwillingly spoken and her lips even drier than she could have wished. If she moistened them, my lord would think . . . oh, he would think . . . she glanced up at him and stared at him directly.

"Merit," she said, "you are perfectly abominable but you shall teach me all you know."

At which my lady chortled and muttered that it would be over her dead body until a special license was procured. Merit then muttered darkly that one of these days he would strangle his aunt with his own bare hands and

Honor simply blushed. It was a delightful blush and all the more effective for its rarity.

"I meant cards, Lord Laxton."

"How very disappointing but I trust I can sustain the shock."

And Lady Darfield? She just snorted and buried her head in a Minerva's Press novel—a great deal more unsuitable than Fielding's *Joseph Andrews*. Honor, if she had not been otherwise engrossed, would have laughed out loud.

CHAPTER 20

The lessons, when they happened, were the brightest part of Honor's existence. While Faith flirted at balls and shocked her sponsor by dancing with Lord Manning almost twice in a row, Honor was content to learn shuffles and guile and devious ways of reading not only cards but expressions. She had a natural aptitude for the rules of all the key games: when to declare, when not to, how to build on tricks, what to discard, and so on. This, combined with her memory, already made her a formidable player. What she did not know was some of the finer subtleties.

These Lord Laxton worked upon, showing her how to read tension—not in faces, but in the flutter of hands, the odd distracting comment, the play of pulse at the base of throats.

It transpired that Lord Laxton was an excellent mimic and when she was not concentrating fiercely, she was in fits of laughter, for his renditions of such personalities as Colonel Hoskins and Lord Mariner were so true to life that Honor could swear she knew them already. Occasionally, Lady Darfield, asleep in her great winged chair, would chortle gustily so Honor knew that her sleep was feigned.

Dear old woman, she was trying so hard to be subtle in her chaperonage! Sleeping, indeed! But it kept Merit and Honor on their toes so that not the slightest impropriety occurred between them though it seemed that the very air tingled, at times, with their restraint.

Occasionally Merit would stand behind Honor, to watch how she handled her cards, to show her how to cover them from sight, to fan them only slightly, to memorize only the index featured on each card rather than the card itself. He mimicked Lord Apperton signaling to the imaginary Lord Gladstone on the left, he showed her all kinds of cheats to be wary of, all manner of sleeving and rigging that shocked Honor, who was far more used to plain dealing.

"If you want to open a gaming establishment you must suspect every man to be a cheat. You dare trust no one, Honor, or you will be wickedly paupered."

"Even gentlemen of gentlemen's clubs?"

"Especially them!"

"What about the famous honor of gentlemen?"

Lady Darfield opened an eye and chortled. "Ha!"

Merit ignored her but with a creeping smile about his wide, sensuous lips.

"Good question. Most, like myself, are *utterly* trustworthy." Another "Ha!" in the background (again, ignored by Lord Laxton). "But some, like the baron you encountered, are less scrupulous. In their cups, gentlemen are not to be trusted at all."

"Even you?"

"I am never in my cups."

Now Lady Darfield forgot about feigning sleep and sat bolt upright in her enormous Chippendale wing seat.

"It is true, Honor, and how he does it is a puzzle. I swear he drank all of my finest Louis the Fourteenth brandy one night and he still had the confounded impudence to beat me at loo!"

Merit smiled and shook his head but his eyes twinkled delightfully with laughter. He showed Honor what to watch for—how it was possible to "peek" by a simple, almost indiscernible movement of the thumb. Not behavior he was suggesting for her, but behavior she needed to be on the lookout for in her opponents, especially dealers. Oh, so many tricks! Honor thought her head might spin, but always, when she seemed most confused she was steadied by a reassuring smile and perhaps a hand on her arm that made her think of rather more than her play.

Oh, how wicked she was! She forced herself to concentrate on trick after trick. It was a pity they could not play whist for want of a fourth player, but Lady Darfield was dragged in for lessons in loo requiring a third. For piquet, it was just Merit and Honor and finally some great, gusty snores from the winged chair.

Merit set down his cards and regarded Honoria with a wry smile. "I will play you for those gems."

"They are not mine!" Honor was shocked.

"I should have rephrased that. For the removal of your gems."

"Oh!" Honor blushed a faint pink but she could hardly see anything wrong with that, so she played and the strangest thing was, she kept losing. With every conceded trick, she removed a necklace or a bangle until the card table was heaped with a king's ransom and she had little more to provide save a sparkling ring embedded with what looked like a thousand dancing diamond lights.

Once, my lord lost and he inclined his head to one side and regarded her with a faint, speculative smile. Then, without saying a word he removed from his finger his single adornment—a heavy gold signet ring glowing dark with a color Honor could not quite fathom. He set it slowly upon the table, holding her eyes as he did so. For no particular reason, Honor felt herself very warm indeed. She reached out for Lady Darfield's heavy, ivory fan and fanned herself rather falteringly.

This did not help matters, for my lord's smile widened

slightly and he declared a quatorze, which forced her to concentrate once more on her hand. Sadly, the quatorze was her undoing, so she was relieved of her last trinket and wondered what Lady Darfield would think when she woke up and found her gems scattered all about the table.

It was strange, for she felt perfectly sinful though she had removed no more than Lady Darfield's gemstones. She had been wearing a lot less in breeches and greatcoat at the Greenstone Inn, but now, without the glittering jewels she felt naked to her skin, and her gown, cut far too low for comfort, was more revealing than she had realized.

Yes, she could just capture her image in the cheval glass situated behind my lord. She did not dwell on his back, dark in its stylish evening jacket—she had done that already—but rather, for a fleeting moment, on herself. Far too much creamy skin and rounded curves for comfort. Oh, how she wished she had thrown a cashmere shawl over her ensemble! But it would not have suited the diamonds and Lady Darfield had been adamant.

Lord Laxton, who did not need a glass to be aware of the curves that had been plaguing him all evening, now rose to pour a glass of something liquid from the decanter. He pressed it to Honor's mouth as she stood up. It was sweet, but burned of fire on her lips and as it trickled down her throat.

"Trying to make me drunk, my lord?"

"Do I need to?" The voice was very low and rather deeper than Honor was used to. He was still holding the glass, but she was far closer to him than the usual social distance. She did not know whether that was his fault or hers.

"You know you don't." Honor still found it hard to lie flirtatiously. She dealt in straight truths, but the truth was difficult when it extracted a response like Merit's. He drew closer, so she could almost feel his breath upon her upturned cheeks. If he kissed her again she would be lost.

"You stray from the lessons."

"Hardly. I was waiting for Great Aunt Petunia to snore before I began them. Come, Honor, let me hold you in my arms. It is a just reward for all the trouble I am going to."

Honor wanted to ask him why he wanted to. Why did he bother with her when he was so very eligible and so rakishly . . . free? She did not, however, have the courage. Neither did she have the resolution to resist him.

Lord Laxton, in his evening gear, with his eyes upon every golden button of her gown, was far too impossibly attractive. She was beyond the pale already—why should she not be deliciously more so? Testing out her theory, Honor proved so swift a learner that Merit groaned and put an abrupt end to this interesting tuition.

"But why?" Honor frowned, for she had very much liked the feel of her arms boldly about him and his hands, equally bold, exploring aspects of her gown she hardly knew existed. But, just when he had discovered various catches and clasps, he had stopped. He almost looked exasperated! What could this mean?

For an instant, Honor thought her fervor must have been greater than his. Perhaps she was not as attractive as his paramours? Perhaps, oh, perhaps he had expected her to rebuff him! To slap his face as Miss Bramble had been so scrupulously careful to teach! Perhaps he had been testing her, testing to see whether she really was an innocent, or utterly beyond redemption, as he suspected. If so, she had failed dismally.

Red stained Honor's cheeks and she turned her back so quickly that Lord Laxton's exasperated desire faded into sudden concern.

"Honor?"

"It is nothing. It is just, you see, I'm not used to such . . . such games."

Merit breathed a relieved sigh. As a matter of fact, he

laughed. It was a low laugh. A chuckle, really, and very reassuring. Honor felt herself able to face him again though
her eyes remained inquiring.

"I am glad you are not used to such games. As a matter
of fact, it is a supreme relief to me! I reserve the right, you
see, to be your sole tutor in such matters."

"Then why did you stop?"

"Only because Great Aunt Petunia is bound to wake up.
She is very annoying that way. No, no, don't look at me so.
I am not speaking from experience, precisely, only clever
guesswork. Also, my love, you have matters of your own
to resolve before I can . . . before I dare approach you in
this wild and wicked way again."

Honor did not know what he meant, only that the twinkle was gone from his eyes and he seemed suddenly very
tender and very serious. She wondered, again, why he
should go to so much trouble for her. If only life were like
the fairy tales! Merit would sweep her in his arms, carry
her out the door, marry her out of hand . . . Oh! She must
not think of it.

He had that option and he had ignored it. Worse, he had
cheated his way out of it. It was this that she could not
understand, that she found so bitterly hurtful. She must
hold on to her hurt. The sting of it would help her resist the
irresistible.

The irresistible, now, was gathering up his cards and
cane. The jewels still lay glimmering on the table. He
leaned toward them, hesitated, then softly called out
Honor's name. "These jewels are Lady Darfield's, else I
would take my winnings or one, at least, as a memento.
When you are rich you owe me a trinket."

Honor inclined her head in agreement, but qualified his
statement with a small smile. "*If* I am rich, my lord."

"The rate the wagers are being laid, you shall be. But

come! You must keep this, at least, for it is mine and you have won it fair and square."

Then my lord startled Honor by placing the gold signet ring in her hand and closing her fist over it gently. He placed his finger over her lips as she began to protest; then, with an odd smile upon his own lips, he closed the door and departed so swiftly that not even the butler—waiting up for some hours—had the chance to make his bow.

Sir Godfrey was skulking in the library, his temper very short after a singularly unpleasant interview with Lord Islington, who had refused to forward him another quarter's allowance. It did not seem to be a good time to mention the debt of honor hanging over his head, so Godfrey could only ruminate on a long stretch of incalculable boredom. Lady Islington had scolded him horribly when she had learned a shy, very condensed version of the affair.

It seemed very ungrateful indeed that she had put a lovely young woman in Godfrey's way and he had not only failed to take advantage of his opportunity, he had actually caused her to fly into the arms of Lord Manning. Now she was all but betrothed and Lady Elizabeth's fun was dimmed, for it was one thing escorting an unattached debutante, quite another chaperoning an engaged couple!

Still, little Faith was a darling and her brightness seemed to spill out from her, so it was not such a very dreadful thing, after all, only she was still as cross as crabs with Godfrey. Lord Islington said he should rusticate in the country for a while and Lady Elizabeth was mindful that this was not such a very bad idea. Godfrey, though she did not like to say it, was becoming a dandy with his padded shoulders and nipped-in waists. Goodness, the other day she thought she caught a hint of rouge on his cheeks! Something must be done about him, but she was not perfectly certain what. She took up her needlework and sighed.

Brooke's had never buzzed with such excitement in all of its long history as a gentleman's club. The bets laid in the betting book had held some extreme—and actually rather foolish—wagers, but Lord Laxton's was the one that seemed to capture the most interest.

This was possibly because my lord usually eschewed such enterprises and possibly because news of his win on the Tilling-to-Strathmore race was still circulating. My lord noticed with resigned amusement that it had not yet been displaced with other, more salacious news.

Of course, it was Freddy who had won, but strictly speaking, since the bet was laid in the marquis's name, it was he who was entitled to claim the credit. Not that he did, of course, but this still did not stop people congratulating him and pointing and tipping their hats to him in a manner which he might have found irritating but which he now cultivated. The marquis wanted as much money laid on his current wager as the bank at Brooke's could afford.

Unknown to Honor, he had upped the stakes considerably by backing the wager with a small fortune of his own. Two thousand pounds was a considerable sum but a paltry figure to wagering men like the Duke of Bannister and the Viscount Holbrooke, who needed something more stimulating to part with their not inconsiderable blunt. So my lord had sweetened the enterprise and to startling effect—gentlemen were literally crowding to set their names down in the book, all sublimely confident that they could beat any female at any game she chose.

Sir Godfrey, strolling into the bedlam, ignored the cut direct he received from Lord Manning—though he burned with anger inside—and gasped at the amounts being punted.

His pockets were to let, however, so he accepted a dish of tea—all he could afford—and glowered darkly into his cup.

The bets were closing, for in an hour Lord Laxton's chaise would depart for the much vaunted lady. Sub-bets had been laid as to who the female could be, for no one's recollection could stretch to anyone suitable of Lord Laxton's acquaintance.

"If it is that old harridan, Lady Darfield, then I will have my blunt back, thank you! Laxton stipulated *young* lady and not an old maid in her dotage." This, from a worried Sir William Dax, who had wagered rather more than he could afford on the affair.

"Hear, hear!" muttered Mr. Thomas Reeves, but the Honorable Reginald Hargreaves disagreed. "Merit is not such a fool as to say *young* when he meant otherwise. I say it will be a young lady and what is more, I'll stake my blunt on her winning."

There was a gasp all around, then a great shaking of heads at Reginald's foolishness.

Still, such asides added spice to the wager, so by the time the appointed hour of nine o'clock had arrived, the entire club was talking of little else, and one could almost hear a pin drop at the entrance, where the footman had been told that for this evening, at least, Brooke's claim to be exclusively a male preserve was shattered.

The footman, who had worked at the establishment all of twenty years, could hardly credit his ears, but it was not his business to question his superiors, so he bowed in the regal manner that was his custom and agreed to admit that dreaded of all creatures—the female—into the age-honored portals of Brooke's itself.

As the great grandfather clock struck nine—and as it was mirrored at Bow Street and Whitehall—my lord entered. He was dressed rather more formally than usual, in velvet knee breeches and silk clocked stockings. His evening frock coat was sumptuously covered over with spangles of spun gold, over which embroidery of silver and a rich, rose gold was intertwined. His waistcoat was dark, like the breeches, his buckles set around with cabochon-cut emeralds and the faint hint of diamonds.

This in itself was intriguing, for my lord did not aspire to the dandy set and was usually simplicity itself in garb. As a matter of fact, to the scrupulous eye his attire *was* simplicity itself. The lines were sharp, the shoulders unpadded, and the stitching so perfect it was nigh on invisible.

Still, the fabric was richer than my lord's custom, and the effect startling, for about his cravat he wore an emerald the size of a pigeon's egg. There were no seals or fobs hanging from his waistcoat, but the omission had the effect of drawing attention to that jeweled throat and the high starched shirt points. He looked magnificent, but though people stared, it was not so much at him as at the lady he had in tow.

The lady, heavily veiled, was a vision in the loveliest gown anyone had ever seen. It shimmered as she moved and was radiantly rich, in the selfsame spangles as my lord's evening coat. She carried herself with grace, and her hair, almost as dark as my lord's own, could just be detected beneath the shimmering veil. Her skin was as white alabaster and her gown deliciously low-cut, but not so low as proclaimed her a member of the demimonde. No, she was elegance itself, but high elegance, an elegance that most women aspired to but very few ever achieved.

In truth, she was a diamond, the veriest diamond of the first water and whilst most felt this assured them their stake (for how could such loveliness also be skilled?), most also felt an accompanying twinge of envy for Lord Laxton, who so carelessly held her upon his arm, as if it were his prerogative, and his only.

But wait! They were accompanied! Alas, yet another of

that forbidden species was now darkening the portals of the sublime establishment of Brooke's. What was the world coming to, one wondered, when females could come and go unchallenged? But the doorman was bowing low and the lady, though veiled, was unmistakably a member of the *haut ton*.

How could she not be when her gown was made of the purest silk and her turban created by Madame Lispine herself? Oh, how many plumes drifted over that crimson creation? Nobody dared count, for she was glaring through her veil and though her eyes were obscured, the indignant thrust of her shoulders was not. A formidable chaperone, and quite as intriguing as her charge.

"Gentlemen, may I introduce to you two ladies? Their names, for the present, shall be withheld, but I am certain you can have nothing to complain of in their play."

"Their? Their?" came the chorus. "You said nothing of two ladies, Merit, only one!"

"Did I not? How remiss of me. Very well, then, only one it shall be. Miss . . . will you step forward, please?"

Merit released Miss Finchley from his arm and propelled her gently forward. She felt bereft, for a moment, and speechless, as the gaze of Brooke's was upon her. Then she smiled, and in very musical tones, invited whosoever pleased to have a game of their choosing with her.

CHAPTER 21

The crowd had not been so entertained in months. They started with a simple game of loo and progressed to whist, *vingt-et-un,* and piquet very rapidly, the lady saying little, only smiling somewhat and inclining her head gravely when she won.

Most gentlemen lost with a great deal of humor and a vast quantity of renewed respect in their eyes, but some were crusty, or stricken (for many had betted on what they considered a certainty), and some were downright rude. Lord Chittlingdon was not present, but many like himself were.

Once, Honor caught a gentleman sleeving a card and though her tone was mild, she did not blink when she apologized politely and mentioned this to the culprit.

He blustered at first, making some deprecating remark about females and turning his head for some laughing encouragement from the crowd. He got none and was forced to resort to bluster and a stupid comment about only "funning" when he was obliged to retire from the group.

From then on, play became more serious. Merit did not himself play, but he stood close to Honor and had to literally hold his arms down when he saw her making a mistake, or declaring too early, or bidding too high. He was rewarded for this self-restraint by finding that though Honor might have lost a trick or two, when it mattered, she won. Her hand was steady and her voice was as firm and unwavering as any gamer could wish.

Lady Darfied—for naturally, it was she—found her fingers itching to play. When she had satisfied herself that her protégée was far too good to come to any harm, she snapped her fingers and ordered up the strongest drink in the club. This in itself raised eyebrows and some of the older set found their focus gravitating to her, rather than the ravishing chit at the tables.

Soon Lady Darfield had a court of her own and she found she rather enjoyed the attention after so many years as a recluse. Now and then her big, boomy voice pealed out in laughter and when she drank her drink in one gulp, better than any man present, she was accorded the high accolade of being a very fine and fetching lady indeed, not at all like "the flighty young things of today."

Several aging old noblemen forgot all about their countesses and duchesses at home and admired Lady Darfield's enormous and ample proportions. But the evening was drawing to a close and so, too, the conclusion of the bet. Just as Honor was being proclaimed winner, Sir Godfrey, who had been staring at her for some time (for nobody was paying him the attention he deserved), stepped forward rather maliciously.

"I know you, my lady luck," he said. "*You* are Miss Faith Finchley."

There was a murmur all about the room, for Faith was well known as the newest debutante, and being admitted to Brooke's for whatever reason must certainly mean her ruin.

The lady startled and spilled the ratafia she'd been offered. Her hand was clearly trembling.

"See! She trembles at her temerity!"

Sir Godfrey, enjoying the attention suddenly cast upon him, scrupulously avoided Lord Laxton's eye.

He would not like to see the flint in those dark, uncompromising features, nor the threat of his confounded note of hand. No, for tonight he would get his own back by ruining Faith's reputation. He had caught the silhouette of her features beneath her veil and though her long, lustrous hair was not visible, he was perfectly certain it must be pinned up somewhere.

No, by her height, her slenderness, her fashionable attire, her youth and her beauty, she must be Faith. Faith, stupid Faith, who had caused him to lose the Tilling-to-Strathmore race—Sir Godfrey had never yet learned to blame himself —and who had caused his own mama to turn against him. She deserved a lesson and a lesson she would get! He rather enjoyed exposing her. It was with a certain thrill of pleasure that he watched Lord Manning jump up in a sudden fidget.

"You are mistaken, you blackguard. The lady is not— could not be—Miss Faith Finchley. I demand you retract and apologize at once."

But Sir Godfrey had no intention of retracting. He was enjoying himself. To make Lord Manning further squirm, he answered, "I will retract when the lady unveils herself. If she is not Miss Faith Finchley, I will naturally apologize."

Lord Manning and Lord Laxton muttered in unison, though few were paying them any attention. All eyes were fixed on Honor. She looked once at Lord Laxton, as if for courage, then turned to face the onlookers. She would not have Faith put beyond the pale!

Oh, what had she done? There could be no turning back, but she must save Faith this disgrace. It was clear from the eyes of the crowd that those who had lost a fortune would not mind revenge in the least. Her reputation, for doing such an unthinkable thing as braving this masculine preserve, was lost. But it was *her* reputation, not Faith's, and she must bear this ignominy alone.

She stood up.

"Sirs," she said, "you are mistaken. I am not Miss Faith Finchley."

Something in her dignified tone made Sir Godfrey squirm. Could he have been mistaken? He would look such a fool if he had been! But that coloring, that bearing . . . he could not be in error, he simply could not!

"Prove it," he said loudly, spitefully, and yes, a little fearfully, for his own father was looking daggers at him. If he were wrong, he would be forced to rusticate in the country without so much as a brass farthing for his entertainment. Worse, Lord Laxton was now impossible to ignore, so hard and burning was his gaze. If Merit pressed for a duel, he would be lost.

Merit murmured something to Honor, but she was too enraged and embarrassed to hear. She stepped forward and before Lady Darfield, who had heaved herself up from her comfortable seat, could intervene, she removed her veil.

"What did I tell you! It *is* Miss Faith . . ."

"No, it isn't!" said Frederick, Lord Manning, furiously. "I believe I should know my own betrothed and this is not she!"

"Freddy, Freddy! What's all this! Are you betrothed?" Now, another little side stir as Lord Manning admitted he was and that the notice would tempt their gazes in both the *Tatler* and the *Gazette* the very next morning.

"And I can tell you," he said, "she is *not* my Faith!" With that, he turned around and looked very challenging indeed. There were soothing murmurs as gentlemen held up their monocles and inspected poor Honor as if she were a bolt of silk at a bazaar.

The marquis, beside her, was still but his hands, if anyone noticed, were clenched and his countenance unusually immobile.

"I trust you are satisfied, gentlemen? Though there is a

remarkable similarity between the two young ladies, Miss Faith Finchley, you will note, has abundantly long hair while this lady has a charming coiffure in the classical Greek style, I believe. Further, you might, if you had the felicity of being acquainted with both ladies, note that the freckles across the bridge of this paragon's nose are slightly more pronounced—though very fetching." This, with a twinkle, as Honor nearly protested. He could almost always make her laugh, even in a situation so dire as this!

My lord continued rather more seriously. "You will also note the rarity of her skill, which I fear is unequaled in Miss Faith Finchley, delightful though that lady might be." This qualification hastily interpolated as Freddy began to glare at him.

There were murmurs as Honor stood still as a statue, secure in the knowledge that she was rich; vastly rich; she had won a king's ransom that night. It should not matter to her that the crowd would soon turn from her, might mock, might laugh.

Very soon she would be bereft of her rightful status as a lady. It mattered not at all, for now she had the freedom to set up her gaming establishment, she had her independence, and most of all, she had Faith's dowry. Nothing else should matter at all. But it did. It did, horribly, and she really thought she might faint.

But ladies of character did not faint. They will themselves to have a straight back and a proud posture and a heart of steel. Which was what Honor did, to the growing admiration of most of the gentlemen present, even those who owed their evening's losses to her.

"Who the flaming hell *is* she, then?" one young buck called out. There were some repressive noises from some of the more sympathetic voices present, but the call continued.

Lord Laxton was just stepping forward to say something

when he was rudely shoved out of the way by the only other lady present. The dragon, it seemed, was breathing fire.

She threw back her veil and announced in ringing tones that if anyone wanted to brand ladies who entered Brooke's as unworthy, they'd better jolly well start with her.

There was a gasp as the gentlemen recognized Lady Darfield, who, though eccentric, was quite unquestionably quality. Apart from her nobility of rank, she was known to be scrupulous in her assessment of character. She might be a recluse, but she was an exceptionally well connected one. What was more, she was as rich as any person had a right to be—richer, actually—and in Boodles or Brooke's, it mattered not, that was all the qualification one needed.

She glared at the assembly. "Who dares denounce me?" Honor, watching her with admiration, suspected she might actually have caught a glimpse of fire from the dragon. Lord Darrow, catching her eye, must have thought so, too, for he muttered something deprecatingly and shook his head.

"What's that? What's that? Speak up—I'm a little deaf, you know." A lie, but used to great effect, for Lord Darrow had to positively bellow what he had only muttered before.

"No one can dispute you are a lady above reproach, Madame." He yelled.

At which Lady Darfield patted his head rather mildly and announced that he was not so much a curmudgeon as she had always been led to believe.

Which set Lord Darrow blushing, for he was generally rather timid and mild-hearted, and the rest of the gentlemen guffawing. Lady Darfield glared. They all quieted down.

"Now," she said, "who dares utter a single word against my legally declared heiress?"

No one, it seemed, dared.

Honor had hardly time to register her astonishment at

this announcement, which seemed to change matters dramatically. Gentlemen whistled and several young rakes started coolly assessing their chances with her.

Lady Darfield eyed every person at Brooke's as if they were mere scrubsters brought to her for the purpose of correction. At length, she nodded crisply.

"Very well, if we are all agreed the lady is not only above reproach, but also wealthy in her own right and well connected, I shall not beat your silly bottoms with my cane but take my leave. It has been a long and tiresome night and I have probably caught my death of cold.

"Miss Honor Finchley and I will be receiving morning callers tomorrow at five. You may all attend if you are sober and properly attired. Lord Laxton, you may escort the lady back to Darfield House. Her maid awaits her outside. Lord Darrow, you may escort *me* to my chaise."

Which Lord Darrow, still a little overawed (and a bachelor though he was near nigh five-and-seventy), most summarily did.

It was close on an hour later that Honor, now openly revealed as Faith's sister, left Brooke's on Lord Laxton's arm. In her reticule was a banker's note for her winnings. Upon her neck, hidden from all sight but her own, she wore a certain signet ring. It felt warm against her skin and she was never so aware of it as the marquis helped her into the waiting chaise.

"Evening, Tom!"

Tom grinned and doffed his cap.

"Evenin', me lord . . . evenin', miss . . ."

No sign of his previous impudence but a tolerant grin on his face nonetheless. The marquis smiled, shook his head, and helped Miss Finchley with her elaborate gown and spangled gauze-and-gossamer light cape that was very fetching but not at all suitable to the evening's drop in temperature.

Robins, Lady Darfield's personal maid, stepped out from

the shadows and aided Lord Laxton in his endeavors. Several gentlemen leaving the club noticed this and nodded their approval. Some looked downright sour, for despite the chaperone it seemed unfair to them that Lord Laxton should have the heiress all to himself. He was rich enough not to have to court Lady Darfield's stated heiress.

At Darfield House my lord did not leave, as Honor supposed he would. He dismissed Robins—who meekly curtseyed—and drew Honor into one of the smaller antechambers that lined the great passages of the castle.

There was no sign of Lady Darfield, though Honor could not imagine that after such a redoubtable performance the old lady could be sleepy. She had no time to wonder, for my lord had busied himself with a tinderbox and several candelabras already twinkled with light. Then, again without a word, he closed the door in what could only be described as a perfectly improper manner.

Honor felt suddenly shy. He was looking at her with such intentness that she was positive he was going to kiss her. But if he did, she would be undone, all her resolve would come crashing about her, she would never, never be able to feign an indifference to him. And she must. She truly must, for he desired her but did not love her, and she did not think she could live with that.

Merit must ever after be kept at arm's length that she might smile and laugh when he married, that she might never show him the grief she felt inside. She was not being dramatic, merely prosaic. When he pulled her to him, she turned away.

"Honor."

"Merit, do not do this."

"Whyever not, my heart?"

"Do not persist in calling me such things when they are not true!"

"But they are, my love, they are!"

Honor thought her heart might burst, for he looked so serious and tender and honest and earnest that it was hard to believe he was merely funning. Yet he had turned down the chance of marrying her. She knew it with all her intellect. He'd had the ace and he'd played the four. There would always be that between them.

"I do not mean enough to you. When I give my heart it will be forever."

"Good, for I shall tolerate no less."

"You speak as if I shall give it to *you*."

"Can you tell me you have not already?"

Damn Merit! He played on her honesty! He knew she could not lie. Not to him! He forced unwanted truths from her so she was vulnerable and horribly exposed and nothing like the glittering princess she looked in her gown of spangled gold.

"If I have, that is my own affair."

"I like to think it is mine, too."

"Why? What would you do with such an unwanted, unwelcome gift?"

"I should treasure it and prize it above life itself."

He was not smiling, and his eyes were dark and ablaze with something that made Honor tremble though the fire had not yet burned out in the grate and if anything, she felt warmer than the evening strictly merited.

"I . . . I would like to believe you."

"Why should you not? Do you need me to seize you and kiss you to be convinced? It is a task I shall perform most willingly, you understand."

"No! Your kisses muddle me. Why did you lose that game, Merit?"

"Ah, the game." He did not look discomforted, merely amused. "How that wretched game shall haunt me! You shall tease me with it when I am in my dotage, I am sure. Honor, can you not see? Think. If I had married you out of hand you would have been the Marchioness of Laxton but you would also have felt yourself my pensioner. You would have dreamed of your wretched gaming house and the damn independence you might have had. You would have been bereft of choices and though you might think it rather selfish of me, I would rather be a choice than a last resort."

There was a moment's silence as Honor watched his face. The fire, burning softly in the grate, threw shadows upon his dear, so familiar countenance. It was hard to believe they had been acquainted so short a time. Honor felt she had loved him forever.

"You would never be a last resort."

For the first time, Merit's wide smile touched his lips. "No? I should very much like you to prove that."

"Are you saying, my lord, that you actually *do* wish to marry me?"

"Good lord, Honor, for an intelligent, magnificent, passionate woman, you seem remarkably behindhand! Of course I do!"

But the moment was too much for Honor. It was too impossibly wonderful to be true. She would wake up soon, in a dream, at Miss Bramble's Seminary for Young Ladies and find that Merit was merely a figment of her tired, overworked imagination. Her head spun.

Lord Laxton moved forward and caught her lightly in his arms.

"Don't swoon, Honor—it is mortifying for any gentleman in the throes of a proposal."

But Honor only felt his strong arms about her and his lips, tantalizingly close to her own. His breath, light and sweet, was somewhat close to her ear. She settled nicely into a faint and closed her eyes.

My lord, rather than being flustered, kissed the tips of her eyelashes and warned sternly that there might be more if she did not wake up.

Which naturally meant that Honor opened her eyes to make a sharp retort and found Lord Laxton laughing. She pulled herself from him but trembled, still, for his very presence seemed to fill the room and she had never been so aware of anyone in her life.

"Honor, Honor! You hesitate, still!"

"I would like to believe you."

"Very well, I suppose I shall have to prove the matter to you, though the veriest fool I feel, reduced to poetry like any young lovelorn jackanapes!"

"What are you talking about?"

"I am talking, Honor, about this." My lord withdrew from the folds of his magnificent court dress a piece of parchment. It was inscribed, Honor could tell, in the most elegant of all handwritings. She wondered if it was his own.

"Yes, Honor, it is mine. I shall make a clean breast of it and admit from the outset that I am no better than a lovestruck greenhorn. I have been reduced to writing poetry, so ardent are my feelings, so damn ridiculous is the depth of my passion. I hope you feel proud of yourself, reducing me thus, for I swear I feel like the veriest fool!"

So saying, he thrust the page in her hand and stood back, watching her face.

Wondering, trembling, Honor read. The words were not sickly, like Byron's, but intimate and slightly self-mocking. They struck a chord in Honor that made her doubts fade as the moonlight did with morning.

> *You need not masquerade, my love*
> *Nor hide thine eyes for fear of mine*
> *Though scorched you are with bright intent*
> *I burn with praise, not sentiment.*
>
> *No idle words will I expound*
> *On pearl white teeth in pink surround*

Though white they are,
I'll not forget
that Honor's truth
Is whiter yet.

Fie, my dear, to think that I
Might dare to frown
Might, foolish, try
To stem your whims and 'rageous wiles
For fear of what?
Some idle smiles?

Oh, no, my love
You are to me
My sanctum and my synergy
Much more I say, for hear my oath:
I'll honor Honor as I plight this troth.
'Pon my word, what greater grace
Than Honor true and its sister, Faith?

"Come here, Lord Laxton."

"Why?"

"I wish to exercise my freedom of choice."

The anxiety faded from Merit's face as the humor reappeared.

"Indeed?"

"Indeed. Now stop talking, if you please, for I wish to be wonderfully wicked."

"You will have to wait, then, for the morning. I have a marriage license burning in my pocket and the wedding booked for nine, the earliest Lady Darfield vowed she could stomach it."

"Merit, you are funning!"

"I have never been more in earnest. I have done my utmost to win you a fortune that you might lose it again."

"In marriage to you? I will take my losses."

"How poor-spirited! I have ordered the lawyers up, too. They shall write a codicil reflecting that your fortune remains your own."

"You are really very managing! How many more poor persons are to be ordered up at your command?"

"Only Faith and, naturally, Freddy—and we cannot have a wedding without the dragon herself."

"No, indeed! Unthinkable! Do you not think we should possibly practice before the wedding?"

"Practice?"

"You know? Make sure we are ready for our vows? Possibly a kiss like this—or like this—"

Honor was growing rather bold for someone who only hours ago had forsworn all such delicious temptations. Merit groaned, for his planning had not included fighting off his heart's desire. He knew he ought to, really, but the irrepressible child was more tempting than she knew and really, a kiss here, a kiss there, could not be so very bad . . .

"Merit, Lord Laxton, you should be ashamed of yourself!"

The dragon almost roared as she pushed open the door with her gold-encrusted cane.

Honor, already flushed, flushed some more under dear Lady Darfield's penetrating stare.

Then she caught Merit's eye and had to stifle a giggle, for Lady Darfield in her nightcap was rather an amusing sight.

Lady Darfield stared at her sternly.

"Honoria Finchley, you are to be wed tomorrow. Do you wish to do so with bags under your eyes for lack of sleep? Go away, Merit—all that lust can wait a few hours. No, do not blush, Honoria—I am a plain speaker and a plain speaker I always shall be! Now do come, dear, for I have ordered up a wedding gown. It will suit you perfectly, for it has acres and acres of lace on orange velvet, you know, with peacock plumes and spangled trim in a delicious saffron color . . ."

My lord grinned. His bride, he was perfectly certain, would look simply hideous. He waited only to hear that there was going to be gold fringes and a row of frills at the hem before bowing himself out with a pained expression on his handsome countenance.

Honor laughed, and did not disappoint him by appearing ravishing the following morning. Nevertheless, as a concession to Lady Darfield, she did wear the fringes and the velvet, though the peacock feathers were rejected and the layers of lace lay sadly upon her mantel.

Still, my lord chuckled and teased about the saffron-spangled trim until Lady Darfield threatened to dismiss him from his own wedding and Honor bade him hush, else the service would never take place.

At last, the ceremony was behind them and the small wedding party feasted on sweetmeats and sugarplums and hot chocolate in steaming pots.

Presently, my lord leaned forward and whispered something to his bride. He was being extremely benevolent, for he offered, in the wickedest of tones, to remove Lady Darfield's hideous handiwork.

The Marchioness of Laxton grinned. "Yes," she said, "I should be most grateful. Rescue me at once from this ghastly gown."

And so, a very short time later, in the privacy of my lord's own residence at Mayfair, he very kindly obliged.

Embrace the Romance of
Shannon Drake

More Regency Romance
From Zebra